SUSAN RODGERS

the floating days

ACORNPRESS

Printed in Canada

Cover: Tracy Belsher
Designed by Rudi Tusek
Edited by Penelope Jackson

Library and Archives Canada Cataloguing in Publication

Title: The floating days / Susan Rodgers.
Names: Rodgers, Susan, 1966- author.
Identifiers: Canadiana (print) 20240354907 | Canadiana (ebook) 20240354915 | ISBN
9781773661551 (softcover) | ISBN 9781773661568 (EPUB)
Subjects: LCGFT: Novels.
Classification: LCC PS8635.O337 F56 2024 | DDC C813/.6—dc23

Canada Canada Council   Conseil des arts
for the Arts   du Canada

The publisher acknowledges the support of the Government
of Canada, the Canada Council for the Arts and the Province
of Prince Edward Island for our publishing program.

ACORNPRESS

P.O. Box 22024
Charlottetown, Prince Edward Island
C1A 9J2
acornpresscanada.com

[For Christopher and Steve]

chapter *One*

Catherine got a card in the mail. Express post. It wasn't your standard greeting card, with a sappy poem that didn't rhyme. It was a designer card, with cover art fashioned by some obscure watercolour artist.

She flipped it open. Inside, the card contained a salutation and three simple, shaky, handwritten lines. No substandard attempt at verse printed in large block letters. Like water-soaked sponges, the handwritten words expanded and filled Catherine's deepest recesses. Even the blank spaces in the card made their way inside her body, creating voids that nestled snugly in her belly, her arms, her legs, and in the anterior chambers of her ice-blue eyes.

Store-bought prose would have been extraneous. It might have caused her to burst.

The card was postmarked *Gozo*, the second largest of the Maltese Islands. When she first saw the name, Catherine's mind immediately flashed to the young Second World War fighter pilots whose lives she sometimes intensely pored over when she used to work at the museum. The boys fighting over Malta had gone through hell. She'd read about one hapless young sky-fighter who watched in terror from his Spitfire cockpit while his childhood schoolmate survived a fiery midair crash; watched his buddy dangle hopefully beneath a patched parachute on a final, fearful journey towards the Mediterranean Sea. Until a German pilot saw an opportunity for target practice and swung his plane around. The horrific tale ended with the enemy's squadron mates flying away. Catherine pictured them turning their greasy Messerschmitts towards home in disgust, ceasing fire on other easy kills as the doomed parachute floated its hopeless burden downwards. It made her sick to think of it. In her mind, she framed up the childhood friend who saw it all go down. In his trusty Spitfire's graceful bosom, she was certain he would have bowed his head to cry.

There was no rest if you were posted to the Maltese Islands during the war. The pretty little islands could be deadly, and generally offered no reprieve from the overhead whine of engines and the unremitting rat-a-tat-tat of the hunt. The dogfights. The kill. The kills.

But that was a long time ago.

Mrs. Catherine Kelly.

Catherine forgave the writer for that. Forty-four and long divorced, in a newish common-law relationship now, she usually used *Ms.*, but she often received mail marked *Mrs.* Her curiosity had kept her going past her name. Let the awful words in. After swiping a stray brown hair back with one long finger, her eyes had swept over the *Mrs.* with a sigh before she read on.

I don't know how else to tell you this. Ryan is lost. He is gone.

The card was not signed, but as long as Catherine stood there staring without comprehension at the words, the author was not in doubt. The hand, though shaky, was that of Kate, Catherine's twenty-one-year-old son's steady girlfriend. His main squeeze, his lover, his best friend, his confidante. A lifetime ago, it seemed, the two freedom seekers had left their homes in Prince Edward Island and gone travelling in Europe on an adventure-driven holiday, living a free life that didn't include the discipline of study, a steady paycheque, or the acquisition of material goods. They were rock climbers, heli skiers, skinny dippers, sunbathers, cyclists, hot-air-balloon riders, undersea-cave dwellers, swimmers, hitchhikers, free thinkers—*free spirits*.

Reality check. The unforgiving, horrendous words mocking Catherine from the stiff white card stock had taken hold in an instant. Catherine's brain filled to bursting and her heart cried out. A trembling hand dropped to her side, and the pretty designer card drifted to the new hardwood floor she had installed with her newish partner, Jack. They had been forced to wear earplugs to block out the piercing, splitting shriek of the pneumatic nailer. *Thwick! Thwick! Thwug!* They couldn't hear each other while they worked. Not that it mattered. Catherine and Jack didn't talk much anyway.

A scream built somewhere deep inside Catherine. Later she would ask all the important questions: *What do you mean, lost? How was he lost? When did this happen? Why? Why, why, why?* But in the moment, all she could do was allow the outcry to build and build and build like the pressure of the obnoxious air nailer, until someone could cue its release so she could be free.

JACK FOUND HER on their new floor, her eyes vacant and staring. Catherine was belly down in a leap-frog position, like in the silly game she'd played as a child. In a confused kind of yoga child's pose. Her arms and hands were tucked beneath her, and she was rocking back and forth. She'd been sick recently with a virus in her left eye she first contracted years ago, which caused the eye to get all painful and inflamed. The intraocular pressure built and built until she was so nauseous and miserable she got Jack to drive her to the hospital. That was the last time Catherine had got all locked up into herself this way. So much pain. She hadn't been able to escape it—twisting and turning brought no comfort or relief. At the hospital she'd wanted to moan aloud as she did at home, but she forced her pain inwards instead because others would have noticed her if she let out little mewling sounds. Besides, she was scared Jack would tell her, as he sometimes did, to stop whining. He'd accompany the directive with a frown and a sharp exhale and an annoyed "away look."

In the end during the awful eye thing, he offered her his lap, which Catherine gratefully accepted. She laid her cheek on his hard, gym-toned thigh. But lying down was no help. Nothing helped. So, she stirred and stirred and moaned inwardly in the eternal seating area on the fringes of Emerg, waiting for the nurse to call her name while Jack read the paper.

They took good care of her in the hospital that time. The doctor was steady, patient. Kind. Peering at him through her nausea and pain, Catherine sensed his concern when he read that her eye's pressure was forty-four. A pressure reading of fifty can cause permanent damage to the optic nerve. Sight can be lost. But Catherine wasn't worried. Her vision was impaired from the layers of infection—pus—in her eye. But she knew it would come back. She would see well again. Her pressure had been forty-eight the last time this virus flared up. She knew that with the right prodding, like coddling with drugs and drops, things would improve. She would get back down to a pressure of sixteen, or maybe even fourteen, and she would see again. Mostly.

But for now, on this weird day with the card from the mail, because of the eye virus her pupil was dilated and her vision was cloudy. She looked at things cross-eyed because her good right eye was always fighting with her left. Leap-frogged on the floor, Catherine mused vaguely through her shock and stupor that she would have to tell the doctors and nurses that her eye was meant to be that way, with its dopey dilated pupil that made her look and feel like a freak. She would tell them so they wouldn't worry when they assessed her. She knew there would have to be a trip to the hospital again today.

She had been in the hospital for a small procedure on her bladder a few years ago. When she woke up from the anesthesia four nurses were standing over her, calling her name, pulling her back from the nice place where she had lingered in her dreams. A good-looking male nurse asked a businesslike lady coworker about the eye. "Normal," Catherine heard the female nurse say. "Her eye was like that when she came in. The pupil is nothing to be concerned about."

She remembered wanting to stay asleep that time. Catherine never wanted to wake up from sleep. It was usually safe, sleep. That last time when the virus flared up, a friendly nurse had covered her with warm blankets. She remembered asking through the fog of pain and nausea if there was a blanket oven in some mysterious back room. She thought oddly what a great invention a blanket oven would be. Every household should have one. Truly.

On the new floor now, Catherine knew Jack would have to take her back to the place with the warm blankets. How safe she had felt, spending a night in the hospital. How nice it was that everyone seemed so concerned and took such good care of her. Of *her*. How nice the drops felt when they were forced into her swollen, piss-red eye. They burned, but Catherine knew from years of experience that they would work their way through the inflammation and release the unbearable, searing pressure. How nice the staff was, how dark and quiet the little curtained room. How blissfully serene and comforting, the warm blankets from the blanket oven thing, as the gentle nurse tucked them over and around Catherine's tense body.

She hadn't felt she deserved it at the time. The care, the attention, the warm blankets. Like a druggie from the streets, Catherine just wanted the drops. *Give them to me*, she remembered screaming inwardly. *I don't need to be triaged, I don't need to fill out forms, I don't want to be trying to sit all mature and grownup-like out here in this endless waiting room. I don't need my pressure checked, I don't need to make small talk with the nurse, I don't need to be here in pain! I just need the drops and a referral to my ophthalmologist. Give me what I need!* Initially Catherine would have gladly taken a few bottles of eye drops and gone back home. But oh, how nice it was when they actually kept her in for the night and took care of her instead. She tried to rationalize their attention. *The doc thinks I ought to be here, and he's the doc, right? So, I ought to stay, I guess. And let them cover me with their warmth.*

And I shall rest.

chapter *Two*

In their kitchen, Jack bent down and touched Catherine's head. He pulled back her hair so he could better see her eyes. She was near the new island they'd hired a local guy to build and install. She hadn't stopped rocking, and she didn't appear to notice him. She wasn't crying. He could see no tears. Panic seared Jack's gut, but he set his jaw and fought to rein it in. A harsh crackling raced over his nerves, starting with his toes and fingers. Breakneck speed. Headed towards his heart.

Jack was a specialist with anxious, nervous, unbroke, or simply panicked horses. They could buck and kick and cuss and swear all over him, but he had a knack for quelling their fears. Catherine called him an animal whisperer. Her kittens, Oscar and Oliver, and even Old Uncle DC, the resident striped fat cat, were always rubbing his legs or curled up on his lap. With one touch of a finger, Jack could put them in ecstasy.

Catherine had told him that was how she knew she could love him. When she saw how much her cats could, too.

"Catherine?"

No response. Not even a blink.

The card on the floor—Jack toed it. As if he were afraid it might bite. Somewhere in his subconscious he noted hazy cliffs and ocean. Ethereal watercolour art. Indigo blue. With a concerned glance at Catherine, he squatted down on his haunches underneath the island's laminate overhang. With his back to the beadboard pine base, Jack slowly opened the card and read Kate's lines. Took a deep yoga breath. Another, and another, only shorter than he was trained to do in class. He tried to catch his breath because he figured at least one of the two of them ought to be breathing in case help would need to be beckoned. As he did so, he took in the brevity of Kate's unstable script.

My god. My god. The stiff designer card was somewhat mishandled, its edges torn and its script smudged. *Smudged.*

My god, he thought again. *Kate.*

Jack thought he had the upper hand on life. Hell, he'd lived five decades of it, a whole decade more than Catherine. What more was there to derail him?

This. This derailed him.

Jack got up on his hands and knees. Stayed there a few seconds before stumbling to the landline he and Catherine kept but rarely used. A shaking finger poked out the numbers 9-1-1.

WHEN AN AMBULANCE pulled into the driveway and two EMTs rushed in, a guy and a girl, it took a lot of prodding and a nice injection of some mysterious calming substance to convince Catherine to at least get her knees out from under her and lie on her side. In her pseudo-detached state, she allowed herself to think ahead. She thought of the comforting warm blankets that surely awaited her. She spied the thin newspaper that Jack had brought into the house earlier. It was lying crooked on a nearby chair where he had hurriedly dropped it, one corner drooping down over the edge of the chair's baby-blue plaid cushion. Because of the newspaper's thinness, Catherine's brain clicked somewhere deep inside, telling her that it must be Monday.

Not much news, she caught herself thinking. *Not much news, and no bright, cheerful flyers hidden inside. Good,* she considered. *It won't take Jack long to get through that paper. Maybe then he can focus on me.*

On the way out in the stretcher, she reached for his hand. It jarred her to meet his worried eyes, to spy him looking anxiously down at her. She let her eyes flutter beyond him, where a gentle wind was trying to whisper secrets through stiff, frigid branches. A seemingly mistaken, wayward sun shone down on Catherine. She blinked, then let her eyes close; let them shutter out a world that should be grey and angry instead of sunny and bright.

"Bring it," she murmured to Jack with slurred speech and dopey eyes, meaning the newspaper, thinking oddly that he'd have a long wait at the hospital again.

Nodding grimly, Jack gripped the worn designer card; he'd grabbed it, not the paper. As if he could find clues by reading between the lines. As if it alone could provide answers to the unimaginable slew of questions whirling around his mind. He would have to make some calls, find Kate. *Is she okay?* Mentally, he made an account of his finances, which were in a rather grim and sorry state after his and Catherine's recent move and renovations. *Someone needs to go for Kate. Someone needs to find out what happened to Catherine's son.* Jack retched at the thought of it. Wildly, his mind leapt to a burial. A memorial service. *I wonder what it will cost to fly Ryan home? His...body?*

Jack wiped his palm over his forehead in exasperation. This was too much. Even for a Monday.

As the EMTs eased Catherine smoothly into the ambulance, she thought about what it was the addicted, the forlorn, the *druggies,* liked about their treats. It was the lovely slowness of the *stuff* easing through their veins, filling the emptiness, numbing the void. Drugs slowed racing minds. Inside Catherine's soul, Kate's damp, big black script was losing its unsteadiness, and was shrinking, just a little. The blank, white areas that consumed Catherine were turning grey, losing their sharpness. The pain wasn't going away. It was just withering, like that last low-hanging naked branch Catherine glimpsed before the closing of the ambulance door shut out the world. The overpowering scream threatening to make her head explode was growing distant; it was still building and building and building, as it would for a very long time now, but now Catherine could barely hear it. Could barely feel it.

Resting her head sideways against the fresh-scented, snow-white pillow and its fleeting offer of short-lived salvation, she let the voices around her fade. In the faraway present she could hear Jack talking to one of the emergency technicians.

"No, it's okay, her eye is just about always like that. Dilated. Over the years, steroid drops wore away the muscle that makes a pupil small again. It's a virus. A pressure thing. It's her normal."

A pressure thing, Catherine thought. *It's my normal.*

Oh, how she longed to be at the hospital where a nurse could bury her in warm blankets. She was desperate for this sudden unbearable ache to disappear inside a tomb of total warmth.

chapter *Three*

Ryan didn't really understand the whole post-dead thing. He had always thought his mom was a bit flaky when she talked about this stuff. Kate too. Not that he thought Kate was *deeply* flaky, in any way. No, she was beautiful and real and freckled and tanned and he liked her hair better when it was naturally curly and not straightened or tamed with the iron. He didn't give a hoot whether or not she ever shaved her legs. That was how he knew he loved her. That was how he rolled.

He knew Kate was in love with him too, because when they went off on their travels, she'd left her curling iron at home. The outside pocket of her knapsack, the small one at the top, was stuffed with a bunch of those fat elastic bands Kate called scrunchies. She used those for putting her hair up when the wind blew the loose ends all around and she couldn't see and it drove her crazy. She was never tidy about her ponytails, though. There were always odds and ends of hair sticking out this way and that. *Island hair*, Ryan called it. *Prince Edward Island hair. Windblown and wild, just like this free-spirited girl of mine.*

He smiled, remembering their discussions of what to pack and what not to pack. This kind of trip was the hippie kind. Ryan was insistent that they only take what they really needed. Kate had drawn the line at her hand-held razor. *I need it,* she had said when he jokingly told her to leave it behind. *Not every day. Just sometimes. Besides, it's only small. I can tuck it into a corner.* Kate's forehead had puckered up into little worry lines, the kind Ryan got a kick out of teasing her about. The kind that made him think of tempestuous rivers and the rush of adrenaline-fuelled kayaking.

Kate packed her razor, Ryan packed his, and off they went on their happy-go-lucky journey. Ryan was a little sorry about not continuing in university, he'd only gotten one year in, but he didn't want to waste money that he would only have to pay back in spades. He didn't know what he wanted to do with his life except be free. It didn't make sense to him to check in every day to a nine-to-five job or do shift work, even if there was supposedly "lots of money in the trades," as his west coast father hammered into him every chance he got.

Ryan figured he would find a way to survive life, maybe by living off the power grid in a solar-heated log cabin somewhere, making music with Kate if she chose to stick around. Ryan wanted wings. He craved the right to live as he chose, gliding over the earth like an eagle in flight. Or swimming underwater with his eyes wide open, bursting through the surface like a dolphin at play.

His parents, from their polarized homes across the country, asked him to consider his options. Begged him, really. He would ultimately have a family, and health care costs, and would need stuff like toothpaste.

"Everybody needs toothpaste," they said. "Without a job, how will you pay for these things?"

They told him he wasn't being realistic. "Besides," his mom once said, "in life, things sometimes have a way of coming up that you don't always count on."

Ryan figured she meant pregnancies. Like, well—him.

The thought jarred him back to the present. His head was woozy, like it was stuffed with cotton. Ryan gave his head a shake. Those insane discussions with his parents seemed so recent, so real, yet he knew they had happened ages ago. *Must have just had a crazy dream*, he thought. *Did I just wake up?* It felt like the time he'd had wrist surgery after crashing on a snowboard trick that was way out of his league, but he'd wanted to learn it anyway. Back then, when he woke up in the recovery room, he remembered everything being cloudy for a while afterwards. He was "with it," but not exactly on top of his game. He'd look in one direction but his eyes would take a while to catch up.

He tried that now, looking from side to side. True enough, the world was kinda slo-mo again. He half expected to see flattened animated rainbows trailing behind his vision, the thick ones his little cousin Grace sometimes drew with her fancy smelly markers. They would be shaky looking, of course, since Grace was just learning to draw. Which would totally fit the way Ryan was suddenly feeling.

Ryan half-laughed to himself when he finally clued in to why things seemed so off-kilter. He face-palmed his forehead the second he caught on to what felt like the weirdest, biggest joke ever. Sure, the whole dead thing was a serious life twist, yeah, but he thought it was freaking hilarious in a messed-up kind of way. Ever the adventurer, he didn't bother taking even a second to dwell on the far-reaching implications of his new reality. Worrying about what would happen five minutes into the future was as useless as worrying about whether his boyhood cats would choose to spread out on the couch or curl up on chairs.

"Okay," he chuckled with a lazy-assed grin. "I'm an adrenaline junkie. I guess this is the biggest thrill of my sort-of life. Death. Half death? No sign of St. Peter or the Pearly Gates!" The grin was really for his mom. "Catherine," he mused. "Mama Bear. Ever the believer in ghosts and afterlives and spirit guides and angels. Ya really got something going on. Who knew?"

Coming from matter-of-fact Ryan, that was a pretty big compliment.

Kicking back, Ryan decided to enjoy the trip. He allowed the truth to consume him, let it soak into his tissues and rocket through his veins. It was a total rush, similar to the huge highs he got from bungee jumping or from riding the rapids. Or like that time he sailed the thermals in an ultra-light, swooping down to earth in expansive, wide circles like an eagle. Or when he was sailing his friend's Laser and heeled over as far as he could, so far over the port side that he arched his back with his body stretched fully out and skimmed the tips of his fingers over the ocean to send refreshing spray up in towers of sparkling diamonds. What a perfect day that was! Sunny and hot, not a cloud to be seen, the sky so blue and unspoiled that it went on forever.

Like he thought he would.

Ryan considered all the old fun. *I packed a lot into a short time, didn't I?*

All those times when he grabbed life by the balls, Ryan was all in. Long ago, he'd learned to detach himself from fear. He guessed it started when he was not yet three and his mom told him they were gonna live away from Daddy. Self-preservation. He went outside himself, started to live for the moment, to let fear go. He was already so badly hurt; what could fear do but sink him further?

Ryan was never afraid to act like he felt. He hollered and whooped with sheer delight when the rush got too big to keep it all in. It was the best release, ever. Even better than sex with Kate, sometimes. Never afraid, that was Ryan, especially when it came to being real. Authentic. His hidden, deep-down soul came out on his adventures; his body was the tool he used to set it free. His vessel. His mask.

Vital, always challenging life. That was Ryan. Seemingly immortal. Always on the run to set himself free.

Opening his mouth, raising his chin in an I-dare-you stare, he tried the hollering part he remembered from all the earlier highs. It came out exactly the way he wanted it to—five parts glee and five parts gratitude. Loud. Boisterous. Using every bit of air he could force from his woozy, cloudy lungs. As always, his whoop didn't come out sounding even a little bit scared.

He was floating. Ryan had no idea where, and at first, he didn't give a sweet shit. He just soaked up the floatingness. Closing his eyes, he grinned and let loose a big *Heck yeah, baby* because he thought it was so cool that his mom was right after all. And because he felt so free. The most free of all.

While he floated and basked and thrilled to his new super-high-octane state, beneath him Ryan's colourful old world had suddenly turned grey. But since Ryan was Ryan, always holding the hard stuff at bay, it didn't cross his mind that others might feel pain because of him until he rolled over in his dreamlike state and saw Kate.

She was walking—well, almost stumbling, really—down the narrow main street of a little village called Munxar, on the Maltese island of Gozo, which was almost smack dab in the centre of the rolling Mediterranean Sea. *She is as tall, tanned, and beautiful as ever*, Ryan decided with a proud, knowing smile and a puffing out of his strong, youthful chest. But something seemed off with her. When Kate turned her head, Ryan was able to see beyond the dark sunglasses that hid the watery, doe-brown eyes he loved. Her face was red and puffy, the soulful eyes moist and hurt. Stealing a closer glance, Ryan was hit by a sudden, piercing pain. It doubled him over.

Startled by the intensity of the unexpected, lightning-fast emotion, Ryan stilled. Breathless, he watched Kate lift a weak hand to slide dark sunglasses off her pretty nose. Dropping the hand so the glasses dangled by a hip, she stopped and turned to look behind her. Scanning intently, breath held, she searched the village street.

From above, Ryan saw her mouth move. It was a bullet to the heart.

It looked to him like she'd said his name.

chapter *Four*

Jack once told Catherine he thought she was manic. They were in bed, exhausted, in need of sleep, but as usual he wanted to feel her up and "start something," as he put it, and she was okay with that, but she always wanted to feel close to him, first. *It's a girl thing*, she supposed. She got that sex helped guys feel loved, but for women like her—the uber-sensitive writer types—it was important to feel close before diving in.

For her, that closeness came through talking, usually about her day. And through trying to gently nudge Jack into sharing the ups and downs of his day. Sometimes, a lot more often than Catherine liked to admit to herself, those one-sided talks evolved into conflict. Jack would get tired of the talking, roll his eyes, let a few heavy sighs escape. Roll onto his side away from her. Maybe roll back once she got quiet. Gently start to caress her soft spots. Catherine would get frustrated at his seeming lack of interest and attention in *her*. At his refusal to open up about himself. She thought maybe his cheating ex-wife trained him that way. To close up like a clam.

It was a night like that when she heard him mutter *manic*. She called him on it. "What did you say?"

He played dead. Dead silent. Surprise, surprise.

Poking Jack would have been cause for him to use his strength to poke harder back, which always hurt. Stilling both arms at her sides, Catherine knuckled her fingers up into fists and stared straight up at the ceiling. "What did you call me?"

Jack quickly rolled onto his side away from her and mumbled into his pillow. This time, Catherine heard him loud and clear.

"Maniac." He laughed, the sardonic, wry kind of laugh that meant Catherine was on another planet. By not admitting he'd first called her *manic*, he was backpedalling, something he was exquisitely good at. Like Oscar-worthy good at. "You're a maniac."

Lying on her back in bed, covered by a floral cotton duvet awash with the mystical white light of soft moon rays, Catherine bit a lip. Jack. Why would he say such an awful thing? It stung. She was too hurt to delve any deeper than that into his psyche. Didn't matter anyway, because she knew her quiet man had shut down. He wouldn't be offering any more on the subject.

In the end she decided it wasn't what Jack thought about her that hurt. What derailed her entirely was knowing he was right.

When they'd first gotten to bed that night, Catherine had gone off on one of her bizarre tangents. This time it was about boxes. Boxes were on her mind. Jack, herself, and Ryan had just moved from the cute little one-and-a-half-story Victorian house she and Ryan had lived in for the past six years. The light brown cedar-shingled house was nestled in the welcoming heart of Bedeque, a rural village originally settled by long-ago Loyalists. Quaint and serene, it sat at the top of a gently sloping, barely there hill, leafy green in the summer and blanketed in sparkly crystal-snow in the winter. Catherine's cute century home sat proudly by a narrow country road across from a small, solemn church, the white clapboard type. The inviting rural church's austere steeple was designed by renowned nineteenth-century architect William Critchlow Harris. Or stolen, so the rumour went. From Harris's plans, that is.

In the old days, Catherine loved to sit in her bright sunporch on her favourite white wicker rocker, use a toe to propel the rocker back and forth and back and forth, and watch the sky turn endless shades of orange-pink over the Harris-lookalike steeple with its carvings and shadows and supposedly nefarious past. As the rocker creaked in contentment, she was always reminded that the church wasn't real, at least it wasn't a truly authentic Harris, not one part of it. Nor was it a fully restored heritage treasure in its own right. To a student of history like herself, the modern black-glassed door the parishioners had installed at the entrance below the French gothic steeple was jarring, enough so as to divert dreamers from visions of what life may have been like in the past. The door was incongruous, unsuited to the original period in which the church was built. Never mind the copied steeple.

Some days, then and now, Catherine wondered if anything was truly real. Whether she could get away with dreaming anymore, or whether she should even try to get away with it. All around her, on the good days and on the bad, life seemed to insist on forcing her into reality, a reality that called the shots, that was far too in control. Shortages of money, raising a wild kind of kid on her own, lack of passion, that kind of control. She craved an authentic life, instead of one at the mercy of bills and lack.

Mistakes. Bad choices. They got her to this place. She made her bed, she had to lie in it. Literally. Breathe in, breathe out. Get older, one breath at a time. Watch the years rush by in an instant.

Was Jack a bad choice? Had it been too easy hooking up with an older man, one with the financial stability Catherine longed for? Should Catherine have waited longer for some kind of soulmate?

When friends asked why she and Jack got together, Catherine turned her head to the side and whispered, "Sex."

Eleven years as a single parent...enough said. Like Dr. Phil said, take the 80/20 rule. If 80 percent of the guy is good, you can live with the 20 percent that's not perfect.

So where did Ryan get his adventurous spirit? Ha. Catherine admitted to being almost jealous of his ability to go for it, of his drive to live with passion. Hell. She WAS jealous. Why lie? He was young. He'd settle down eventually, especially if he stayed with the fun-loving but more practical Kate.

If Kate could hang on to him, somehow keep him on the ground.

Catherine missed her heritage house and the quiet life she had lived there. She longed for the days when Ryan was younger and he would sit in the curve of her knees, cuddled up with her while they watched a rented movie from the cute little country village store. They usually had a pizza, or donairs, or maybe subs that they'd grabbed before they motored out of Summerside, the small nearby town where Catherine worked and where Ryan went to school. They had their best chats in the car. The twenty minute drive home did more for their relationship than any forced chat over dinner could ever hope to do. The day she gave in to Jack and let a realtor list the house, she made it known. She told the realtor to tell people the short drive to Bedeque was an opportunity, not a bother.

She doubted it would be a selling point, but Catherine felt it should have been.

Jack didn't believe in eating out. He didn't believe in ordering donairs or subs or pizza. He knew Catherine would miss her little house, but it was just too small for all of them. If they had a bigger house, his two half-grown boys might come over to visit. Might spend some time near their dad. They would have private spaces where they could sleep.

So far, they hadn't been over much, Jack's boys. But the little glued-up family had only been living in town for a short while. The boys might come over.

Someday.

So that's why Catherine was thinking about boxes that night—because of the recent move. She had done some marathon unpacking, but things were still pretty chaotic in some of the rooms. There were still boxes in the garage, a lot of them. Unopened. Mysteries. Jack's things. Bicycles, Jack's kayak, the hand-pushed gas lawnmower, and an old rickety hockey net of Ryan's were still stored in the rustic little barn in Bedeque. They would move those when the weather improved, or when the house sold, whichever came first.

Boxes. The night Jack called Catherine manic she had been going on about boxes. In the nighttime when things were black and lonely, it kinda seemed like he wouldn't hear her anyway. After all, she couldn't see his eyes. Couldn't see the usual glazed-over look that was her daytime, plain-view cue to stop going on about stupid things, about things that didn't matter—to him. Catherine compared it to rattling off an email to someone about stuff she would never say if they were right there, if their souls were looking at her for reals.

Things were different in the daytime.

Lying on her back next to Jack that night, Catherine was embarrassed. Too embarrassed to even move, to mumble a hushed apology or to roll over onto her side away from him. Of course her man thought she was manic. Why wouldn't he?

The boxes. A big one—it surrounded her. She could see its outline—a three-fold, three-dimensional solid black line. She was inside it, in its middle, floating, floating. Safe. No one could touch her there. That was why she liked to work from home to try to make a living as a writer. Crafting endless magazine articles, or grant-writing for not-for-profits. Hardly paid the bills, but at least she was at home, in her box. She could see out and people could see in, but they couldn't touch her.

That was what she had told him. Jack. That night. The manic night. She supposed she was testing him. Wanted him to try to touch her, *really* touch her.

He couldn't. Nor did he want to, after she went on about boxes.

He was right. Manic. She supposed his backpedalling *maniac* worked too. Finally, Catherine had turned onto her side away from him, and closed her eyes.

Jack eased back over and spooned her. His warm toes curled around hers. After an eternity and a few wet tears, Catherine stopped staring out the window at the moon. She closed her eyes, let out the breath she was holding, and slept.

chapter *Five*

*W*ow. *If he thought I was crazy then, what must he be thinking now?*

Catherine was in the living room, wrapped in an ancient afghan and snuggled into the broken white wicker rocking chair her ex-husband gave her for Christmas when Ryan was two. The rocker was the same one she used to sit in for hours in cozy Bedeque.

A special aunt—the one Catherine was named for—crocheted the afghan when Catherine was in high school, which made it extra comforting. When the aunt was little, she suffered seizures that left her with deficits. Somehow the challenges she faced her entire life made the afghan that much more special, as if it were imbued with the strength the aunt needed to carry her through life, when she was teased at school or when people looked at her funny. It was crocheted in a Jacob's Ladder of colours one would never see today. A too-bright blue and a candy-floss pink, mostly; popular colours of the day, touched up with a little creamy beige. The creamy beige saved it. Otherwise, it would have been doomed. Bad colours, tempered by good. Just enough good to make it salvageable, colour-wise.

The afghan was heavy. It staved off the cold. Radio announcers were warning folks to be careful today. Stepping outdoors would mean exposing one's body to a wind chill of minus thirty.

Jack was trying to save on the oil bill. "Every time you turn up that knob, it costs money."

Most times when he told Catherine that, he was smiling. Well, half-smiling. In a Jack kind of way, the kind of smile that didn't really light up his eyes, at least not fully, because his serious intent soaked up some of the light. Trying to be amenable, Catherine always just set a firm line to her lips and put on sweaters and wrapped herself in afghans or throws. But sometimes when she knew her fella would be away for the day, she got cocky and turned up the heat a notch or two. *Rebel*, she scolded herself. *I've always been a rebel at heart.* Sitting on the freezing toilet was the worst. Even walking through the frigid air to get to it was excruciating. Catherine avoided peeing so often that when she poured her coffee in the mornings she cringed in anticipation.

Today Catherine didn't care about the cold outside or the usual lack of heat inside. She thought it had been about three days since the horrendous card from Kate landed in her mailbox, but she wasn't really sure. She was still drugged up pretty good. Ativan was her new best friend.

Cricking her head to the side, she listened to the rhythmic rocker on the hardwood floor. *Creak, creak, creak.* Eventually Oscar, the black-and-white kitten, murmured hopefully and jumped into her lap. She petted him absently. He deserved the love, if only because he was usually passed over in favour of the softer, stripy Oliver with the cute, innocent face and delicate paws.

Ryan adored—had adored—the kittens. He'd played favourites with the two, but Catherine hoped the kittens had never figured that out. Oliver's downy fur and distinct markings simply endeared him to people; his colour, by nature of birth, awarded him a mysterious, aristocratic bearing. Tawny black stripes even encircled his pale eyes, so that when he fixed his gaze on a person and accompanied it with a pitiful, wounded mewl, that person would have to be an ogre of the third degree not to soften. For all intents and purposes, Oliver was an innocent child-cat, pure as the fresh powdered snow on which he feared putting his tiny padded paws.

Oscar, on the other hand, had an eye that always ran. A forever cold, maybe, or just a broken tear duct. A broken eye. Like Catherine's. Sort of. Thinking of that and how it was a thing that set her and the kitten in her lap apart from others, Catherine petted Oscar earnestly. She let her fingers drift to the soft sweet spots behind his ears. Her grandmother once told her to scratch kittens there, behind the ears; she'd said they liked it, that it was extra-special loving for them. While Catherine scratched and Oscar purred, Catherine frowned down at the cat's angular white-and-black head. A skeletal, bare-bones bloom of kinship tugged at her forever-damaged heart.

Ryan had had a unique way of entertaining the kittens. And himself. He did it with a foot. He'd put the foot under a furry belly—didn't matter which kitten, they each got a turn, although, remembering, Catherine thought he usually got a foot under Oliver first, most times. He'd tease the kittens, call them "little motors," then raise them up and fly them easily through the air. They always landed on their feet. When Catherine chastised him, Ryan would say that he wanted to see if they could fly.

"Relax, would you? Hey?"

"They're not birds, Ryan. Do you see feathers?"

Ryan never called Catherine *Mom*. It was always *Hey*. Even from a young age he had an outside-the-box way of doing things *in the name of freedom*, she supposed. She always figured if he called her Mom, it would mean he needed her in some way. And that meant chains. Bonds. A neediness Ryan would never acknowledge, could never admit to. Fought hard against.

"Hey. They always land on their own four feet."

Not *They always land on their feet*. No, it was *their own four feet*. There was something magical about the way he said it; an essential element of childhood had survived in Ryan over the years. It was evident in the way he—Catherine's tough, sprouting teenager—spoke those simple words. She would smile every time, even if she was annoyed with him for the mess of his room or for coming home late. It made him three or four again, a gangly arrangement of elbows and knees and scrapes and hugs.

That adorable child would be with his mom forever. Right?

On Oscar's furry head, Catherine's fingers stilled. Dipping her chin, she exhaled slowly.

She shivered, and Jack came to mind. Jack played more with Oscar than Ryan did. His thing was to wrap his large hand around the kitten's tiny head so that Oscar's soft, dewy ears peeled back and his jaw stuck out. Then Jack would bob the kitten's head up and down.

"Bobble-headed kitty," he would say with a grin, looking up at Catherine for approval. Or "Alien kitty. Alien kitty!"

Ryan's half-grown peach-fuzzed hardcore teenage friends would dissolve into hysterics. Normally Jack left Oliver alone. He "attentioned," as he put it, the kitten that had to fight harder to be loved. But that was his way. He had a soft spot for the underdog. Even the manic kind.

A heavy pull on a motor—outside, something big was cruising around the street corner. Tilting her head to listen, Catherine's pulse quickened when she realized it was the school bus. It must be around three-thirty. She was half out of the chair to check that the door to the house was un-locked before she remembered it didn't need to be. Oscar voiced his annoyance with a low murmur that could only be interpreted as a cat's version of *pfffft*. Bracing his fragile paws against her body, Catherine settled back down, calm-ing herself with the reminder that she used to do this before Ryan...

She couldn't say it, and she couldn't allow herself to think it, either. Any kind of voice, either a scream into the wind or the silent whisper of a mouse, would give credence to a truth Catherine fought with every ounce of her soul, with every strained, unfocused breath. A racing started in her heart. It had momentum, a weight and power that built and built until her fingers and toes started to tingle in warn-ing, until her teeth clenched and her jaw ached, until walls formed in her throat. Until her voice, if she chose to speak, would come out high-pitched and speedy, more of a panicked, terrified wail than individual words with any kind of distinct intent.

Poor Oscar was suddenly the recipient of a claw-like squeeze, which elicited a vociferous, mewling protest followed by a hasty leap to the floor in search of a less bothersome place to doze. He padded over to a sunny patch that filtered onto the floor through the curled brown leaves of a neglected house plant, and flopped down for a more restful nap. Catherine talked herself out of panic mode by repeating again and again that everything was okay, that Ryan was freewheeling around Europe—perhaps Spain. Kate liked Hemingway; there was talk before the trip about scheduling time to search out some of the famed writer's old haunts. Maybe at this very moment Ryan was thinking about home. Maybe he was missing the kittens.

Oliver, at least.

Letting her eyes drift shut, Catherine compelled her body to slow down, her breathing to even out. The gift of imagination came in handy sometimes, especially now, when she brought up images of her only son in Spain, a country whose leafy groves and narrow rural lanes she could pull up in her mind because of movies she'd watched or books she'd read.

When Jack peeked in on her later, she was sound asleep, her head resting on her right elbow on the broken arm of the white wicker rocker. Strangely, a slight smile gave ease to her taut, pale face. Both kittens were curled up in the late afternoon's wintry sun nearby. No way was Jack going to wake Catherine and rouse her to the oppressive misery of their new existence, so he scratched out a note, left it on the kitchen island, and emerged into the biting chill for a midwinter walk.

chapter *Six*

Once, Ryan had bounded home from school all geeky and excited about wallpaper, and about gravity. He was in grade eleven, had just turned seventeen, had won the school's winter carnival talent show that day by playing a Celtic medley on drums alongside a bagpipe-playing friend, and could hardly wait to explain his "revelations." Catherine, remembering, cozied deeper into her ancient afghan and let the memory sweep her up. She even let the corners of her lips turn up; a flicker of life danced across her eyes before it sank below the glistening surface and disappeared. Ryan's excitement that day was contagious.

Ah, memories. Such sweet bliss.

He'd started talking about "cross-hatched" wallpaper, he called it.

"You stare at it long enough and after a while some of the lines jump out at you, appearing like they are just a few inches from your face. So, it's like you're looking at an invisible wall of lines, or at new wallpaper just in front of you. You can wave your hand through it, so you know it's not really there, although your brain interprets it as real. How cool is that?"

Ryan had gone on to say that in physics class that day the teacher had asked the class to explain gravity. At the time Ryan was messing around with his calculator, dropping it from one hand and letting it land on the other, over and over again, without thinking about what he was doing. The teacher explained that gravity is a force—like a pull—towards the earth. A bond. You let go of something, the earth pulls it back.

Ryan was wired that day—he had said excitedly, his hazel eyes bouncing and flashing, that when you let go of something, it doesn't fall. It is pulled.

"This stuff has changed my entire way of thinking! I left class feeling like I only ever understood a seed."

Catherine wondered what he understood now, whether all the secrets of the universe had been revealed to him. She, a woman of great faith, a believer in earthbound spirits, heaven, God, psychics, angels, and past lives lived, wondered whether her good and only son still existed.

If only you could be pulled back down to earth, Ryan. If only gravity could bring you back to me now.

THERE ARE OH-SO-MANY ways to feel free. Ryan laughed giddily, remembering the lunchtime talent show at school. He and his piper buddy, Jeremy, had kicked *ass*. Three teachers sat as judges, and all three made the Celtic rock duo the winners.

It was epic, wailing away on drums, either on Ryan's marbleized, oyster-finished Pearl set, or on the stand-alone snare drum with the Celtic College's pipe band drum corps. What a feeling—rocking free with arms and legs flailing, adrenaline coursing through his veins, or playing flams and double paradiddles in the drumline, trying to stay in perfect sync.

Ouch. Remembering *hurt*.

That piercing pain—Ryan's mother, with all her supernatural beliefs in the existence of the afterworld, hadn't so much as hinted about this kind of emotional pain after dying. *Must be the memories catching up to me. Taking me by surprise, catching me off guard.*

Ryan was awash with a magnificent, lighter-than-air freedom that hadn't tickled his soul in years. *I can check in on my mom in Prince Edward Island or on Kate in Gozo with just the merest, simplest suggestion of thought. So dope! But I truly love—loved—being a drummer. It's who I am. Uh—was.*

He took a look around. No hides to beat. No drums in sight. With a sigh, Ryan closed his eyes and pictured his beloved Pearl drum set, snug but lonely in the basement of the new house in Prince Edward Island.

Suddenly he was there, on the little round black stool behind the drum set. Thrilled, he grinned and used a toe to happily swing himself around. The sticks were lying on the floor where he left them months ago, but bending down seemed like too much work. Focusing so hard on them that his eyes narrowed and his lips curled down in a tiny frown, Ryan imagined picking up the dusty wooden sticks. He didn't see them move, yet they landed in his hands as familiar and comforting as trusted friends. His admiring gaze followed a finger he ran lightly over a stick's soft, pale wood.

His left foot tingled with urgency. Almost of its own free will it landed on the high-hat kicker, just about the same time his right foot found its usual spot on the kicker that gave the bass drum life.

Bah-doom. Bah-doom, bah-doom, bah-doom.

Oh, God.

Shoving the heels of his hands over his eyes so that the sticks stuck out at odd angles, Ryan tried to push away the pain. The Friday nights and the Sunday afternoons when his friends gathered to jam were sacred, the best times ever. The new house had this neat designated "teen room," his mother called it, perfect for Ryan and his pals, who set up their amps and guitars and just played. There was even room for girls; sure, they had to sit on the hard, carpeted benches that lined one wall, but nobody ever complained, even when the music got loud enough to send the cat-kens into hiding. Those days rocked.

Literally.

Ryan's mom always fed the teens, she made them chili or some kind of invented homemade soup, *hippie soup*, she called it, because she threw in whatever she had on hand in a casual, free kind of way. And the homemade biscuits, fresh out of the oven—well, they never lasted long. They melted in Ryan's mouth. He always soaked them with butter, which melted instantly to form trickling yellow rivers that, more often than not, dripped down over the sides.

Ryan instinctively licked his lips. He opened his eyes. The drumsticks slipped out of his grasp and fell to the floor, bouncing before settling near the bass drum. They wouldn't budge when he tried to thought-pick them up, and he didn't have the energy to reach for them. He mimicked playing, and stayed for hours, banging away free-form, yet never making a sound.

Upstairs, Catherine's damaged rocking chair went *crick, crick, crick,* but in her head, she heard *bah-doom, bah-doom, bah-doom. Boom chicka crash boom rocka chicka boom.*

Bah...doom.

And then—silence.

A CROOKED TRAIL snaked quietly through a park in the woods behind the new house. The city had tried to care for it the best they could with limited financial and human resources, but somewhere along the line they'd either run out of both or forgotten about the park. Signage along the trail was disfigured and outdated. Any paint that remained was peeling off in cracked strips or covered with scrawled graffiti tags that only held meaning for wry, ornery kids with spray cans clutched in cocky fingers. Still, the blue jays and chickadees who gave life to the park always seemed to be clustered around seeds left for them in homemade wooden feeders. Jack saw the feeders here and there throughout his solitary walks. Folks young and old sauntered along the trails, sometimes stopping to feed the small critters. Occasionally Jack had to halt his lumbering gait and wait in silence, mid-trail, for someone with an outstretched, sunflower-seed filled hand to attract a diminutive, charming chickadee. Almost always a small grey bird would come swooping in to gobble up the seeds and go zipping off through the trees with its easily gotten loot. Only then would Jack continue down the trail, sometimes with a bob of his head or a dip of his chin to the person or people clustered around a chickadee mecca.

The squirrels, too, seemed accustomed to regular treats. As Jack's big boots crackled their way over the crisp snow, the furry little fellas Jack considered bushy-tailed rats often stopped chewing momentarily so they could stare at him and size him up. Their little cheeks would start bulging again once the tall man in the funny green toque and old grey parka passed by. Jack laughed out loud when he pictured taking their little heads in his hands and going "bobble-headed squirrel." His even pace almost slowed as he seriously considered trying it. But he didn't figure the squirrels were really all that comfortable with humans, even though their winter foraging had been made so much simpler thanks to humankind, and even though they were known to sometimes leap on a pants-covered leg in their greedy pursuits of "more."

Today Jack chose the path marked *Heritage Trail*—or, more aptly, *Her ag ail. That's original*, he thought, running his mind over the name. *The sign suits, with the paint all peeled off and wood cracking like that. It looks tired. Done in.*

As he trudged along flanked by elegant, snowy evergreens, a great aching sadness filled his heart. He liked Ryan, although sometimes the kid was a spoiled one-er, meaning he had no siblings, which occasionally showed. He could be lazy. Self-centred. All about himself and the immediate world that revolved around him.

Jack caught himself. *It's not good to think ill of the dead*, he chastised, grinding his teeth in consternation as he eyed the well-trod snow on the popular trail ahead that he had yet to further tamp down with his own ancient, worn boots. At a rustle in a tree overhead, he looked up, then laughed disparagingly at himself. *What, did I think Ryan was floating above me, chiding me for my thoughts?* He struggled to clear his mind, to wipe any untoward black marks off of the confused whiteboard in his head, the one he used to organize the detailed particulars of each and every day.

The thoughts circled him back to Catherine. Jack wouldn't be gone long on this walk. The idea of leaving his gal alone with her thoughts—thoughts that surely wounded her further—was disconcerting. Jack just needed a few moments to let the biting cold wind swirl around his face, to breathe in the pure, windswept air that was sweeping in off the frozen gulf. He didn't mind the blistering cold temperature the radio announcers were having a field day with; minus thirty just helped Jack feel alive. Before leaving the house, he'd pulled on fleece-lined jeans—thick pants that Catherine bought him for Christmas a few happier short years ago. They were warm and insulated on his weather-aged skin, and offered comfort.

Yeah, it was damn cold outside. But cold was something Jack could easily escape.

chapter *Seven*

It wasn't that she'd been a total bitch when Ryan and Kate first announced their plans to go travelling in Europe. Instead, Catherine felt she'd been a good mother. She felt she'd handled it well. She didn't immediately freak out—that came later. Initially, as her blood pressure started to rise, she put the questions to the youngsters. Where were they planning to go? For how long? Were they going alone or were some of their friends going to go travelling with them? Had they drawn up a budget? Were they planning to stay in hostels? What about Kate's school? Ryan's future?

The usual helicopter parent stuff.

The announcement had come just like that—an announcement. Ryan and Kate had already made up their minds. There was no room for discussion. When Catherine tried to talk to Jack about it, he just shrugged and said, "Good for them." Then he flipped to the next page of his newspaper. Catherine had always believed in *carpe diem, seize the day*, ever since she had seen that old movie *Dead Poets Society* with the incredible Robin Williams, bless his soul. She just didn't always act on it. It was a sorrowful moment to sit down one day, look deeply within, and discover that she thought she believed in a lot of things that sounded good in theory but were harder to pull off when push came to shove.

Like, a few years after she watched *Dead Poets Society* on some streamer, life took a twist, and she left the guy she married. Single parenting. Wahoo. (*Not!*) There were perks to that—she and Ryan had become so close, with no one else in their household. But life as a single mom was like rolling uphill in a snowstorm. Babysitters? Seriously? She couldn't afford to pay some teenager to sit and watch TV while her kid slept. At the time, Catherine was moving from city to city, where she knew nobody she would trust to watch her child so she could go out for an evening anyway. In the early days of singlehood, she went back to school and started working as a curator in small community museums, taking short-term contracts wherever there was work. But by the time she ended up back in the Maritimes—the east coast of Canada known as the "poor cousins"—most museum work or, for that matter, any work in a non-profit arts or independent cultural organization, paid *shit*.

They barely got by.

Like any mother, Catherine dreamed of more for her son. Year after year, families flocked to the Dominican Republic or Cuba for winter holidays. Some even went on sailing excursions to the British Virgin Islands or Guatemala. Others boarded cruise ships. Year after year, Catherine sat back and watched them go. Ryan was great, rarely complained, but on occasion he would demand more—lunch money she didn't have, or trip money for that excursion to New York his high school band was taking. The one true grace was the Celtic College. When they'd finally moved back to Catherine's hometown of Summerside, it wasn't long before Ryan discovered he could take drumming for free at the college. A benefactor had left the college enough money to ensure any child on the Island between the ages of eight and eighteen could study piping or drumming. Ryan didn't hesitate, and Catherine was grateful her son had found an interest that she could support. Eventually it cost money for private lessons, uniform accoutrements, and trips around the Maritimes to compete (over fifty dollars just to get off the Confederation Bridge to the mainland! But no charge to come back—phew). But by then Catherine was making some money as a freelance writer, and she'd found Jack, so finances were easing up.

Who wouldn't want more for their child? Ryan had chosen to leave post-secondary education while his friends pursued goals of higher education and careers that would pay well. Her son wasn't lazy, he just didn't want to go to school at this point. He told her of his idea to pursue an adventure-oriented business. His dreams would put him maybe in the Rockies, or perhaps on the west coast where he could join the Simon Fraser University Pipe Band, one of the best in the world. Ryan had *dreams*. His mom just had *worries*.

Catherine tolerated the idea of Ryan owning his own business, but in her heart, she didn't believe her son had it in him. Ryan was too carefree, too happy-go-lucky to keep a set of books. And he wasn't interested in learning about marketing or accounting. She trusted he would learn the ins and outs of white-water rafting or heli-skiing or whatever other sports his fictional adventure business would offer.

But the rest? It was hard for Catherine, a single mom who thought she knew her only son from the inside out, to imagine.

So, there were sparks, big sparks, the kind that could easily ignite into a raging inferno. And when the inferno was imminent, Ryan and Kate quietly bought tickets and arranged their trip and packed. They packed cameras, jeans, lightweight layers for adventuring, pocket snacks.

They didn't pack for death.

The night before, they said goodbye to Jack. They asked him to care for Catherine. They didn't really know how fragile his relationship with Catherine was at that time. They were wide-eyed, innocent kids in love who believed all their dreams would come true; how dare they not?

Kate was a little more jaded than Ryan. But at that time, she was still oh so *full* of hope.

The night before they left, Kate had said a simple good night to Catherine and Jack, who were watching *The Horse Whisperer* for about the hundredth time. Catherine was already choked up from watching her favourite movie waltz scene EVER, so Kate did not give in to her instincts, which were to come clean about their plans. Quiet Jack was not noticeably edgy unless Kate looked real close and realized he was still awake. *The Horse Whisperer* (and Catherine's cooking shows) always put Jack to sleep. Despite the deception filling the recesses of the dusky corners, this was in fact one of the family's better evenings together, period. Dinner was great—scalloped potatoes with lots of butter—and the conversation flowed easily, and now Catherine was snuggling against Jack on the couch, arms around her knees. Jack merely sat with one arm draped around Catherine's shoulders, a cat on his lap, and warily watched Kate ascend the stairs to her bedroom.

Ryan had given his mother a hug and whispered, "Goodnight," and, "I love you." He delivered this sentiment in his usual casual, upbeat way so as not to disturb his mother. But it had been hard for him to truly say goodbye. He knew in his heart that what he and Kate were doing wasn't nice, but what he hadn't realized was that it was rather cruel. Was he punishing his mother for not believing in him? In his dreams? Or was it just that he did not want her negativity infringing on his right for happiness? He had read that you ought to avoid negative people if you want to live a happy, fulfilling life.

No, all would be well. Ryan would send his mother a postcard from everywhere he and Kate landed, and especially from Malta. She would like that. Maybe Ryan would find an aviation museum somewhere in the area and send her a picture of a Spitfire pilot. His mother was always musing about those Spitfire pilots. Heck, right now she was gasping back tears just watching Robert Redford heal a badly injured horse, while a twelve-year-old Scarlett Johansson gulped out *Whosever gonna want me now?*

So, Ryan had walked up the stairs from the rec room into the kitchen. Catherine looked up and watched him go, and he smiled a little sadly at her before he turned the corner and went up to the bedrooms. And then his excitement got the best of him, and when his mother was out of sight, he ran the rest of the way and jumped on Kate's bed for one last hug before sleep.

Catherine had nuzzled in closer to Jack and turned back to the movie. "I know where he goes," she mumbled, after Redford's character told her a story of a paralyzed boy who just let the world go and went somewhere else in his head. Catherine imagined if she ever had to face that kind of pain someday, she would go there too.

When she got up in the morning, Catherine found a note from Ryan and Kate in the kitchen. She screamed once and then balled it up and threw it on the floor, where the cat-kens attacked it with gusto and glee. Jack knew he'd be in shit when she found out he already knew. But he was prepared to keep his distance for a day or two. That night, when Catherine pulled away from his arms, she said she'd just wanted a chance to say goodbye.

It wasn't fair that she never got to say goodbye.

She should have gotten to know Kate better. If Catherine wasn't so shy, afraid of talking about anything "real" when Kate moved in with them after university, after her father's passing, Kate might have opened up and spilled the beans instead of tiptoeing sadly around the house these last few months.

Too late now.

Jack had a response. A good night of loving would fix everything. He liked this new turn of events—now that he and Catherine had the house to themselves there were, after all, certain perks. He wasn't unfeeling; this was simply his solution to their immediate problem. In his brain, sex was the answer to everything.

Catherine had left their bed that night and spent the night on the couch with Old Uncle DC and the cat-kens.

She had never felt so unbelievably, utterly misunderstood and alone in her entire adult life. She drew her imaginary box around herself (with super thick lines), curled up into a ball, and lay awake the whole night long.

Outside, the stars twinkled with godly grace, and Catherine, in her abandonment, imagined an airplane flying high amongst them, ducking in, out, and between each silver light, the plane's pilot playing flying games that her laughing child and his one true love would surely adore.

chapter *Eight*

It took Catherine a good few weeks after Ryan and Kate's rather ungracious exit from her household to process the fact that the two young lovers had left. She was emotional—angry, and then despondent in turn. She went through phases of hardly speaking to the opposite extreme of ranting and raving. Jack was a good sport; he went for lots of walks in the woods nearby and told the squirrels in no uncertain terms to keep their distance from his house if they knew what was good for them (this had nothing to do with the three cats currently prowling the yard seeking playmates to torture).

Calming down, Catherine began to remember things. She was a worrywart by nature. Jack said she worried and fretted about everything. The things that she recalled about her only son before he died were different than the things she remembered after the accident. Since she worried about his safety right after he left, sporadic memories popped up that reflected what he knew and perhaps didn't know about survival, from *will he remember to look both ways when he crosses the road* to *will he remember to drink lots of water so he stays hydrated.*

There was this one day a few years back when they had all gone swimming ...

Abby, Catherine's sister, had called—she was a teacher, and it was March Break, so she was taking her fourteen-month-old daughter, Grace, to the pool. Ryan had a friend overnight, and both were keen to go for a swim, so Catherine loaded the big boys into the small Sunfire she'd nick-named Spunky, and off they went. Ryan drove, since he had his beginner's license and needed all the practice he could get. Catherine sat shotgun, her right hand knuckled around the door's safety hold, her knees tense and her legs poised in pre-crash position. The hardest part was convincing her son that it wasn't necessary to listen to loud rock music while he drove. She was afraid he wouldn't hear her yell out a warn-ing if need be. Truly a happy-go-lucky kid, Ryan flicked the volume back up every time his mother turned it down. He had a big grin on his face; how could Catherine possibly get mad at him?

The drive was uneventful until they got to the parking lot of Summerside's new wellness complex. Catherine had forgotten to warn Ryan that parking lots breed fender bend-ers. Ryan immediately cruised down the centre of a lane be-tween parked vehicles. Since he was learning to drive on a stick-shift, he was going faster than he should have been. Rounding a corner, they came face to face with a red van full of sticky-faced little kids with a harried mom at the wheel who was probably wishing March Break didn't exist. There was some quick finagling with brakes and steering wheels, and somehow, they avoided a collision.

By the time they got parked, Catherine was wonder-ing how she would survive watching her son grow up. This driving thing was a thousand times more stressful than giving the kid his first bicycle. Sure, a kid can get hit by a car for careless bike riding, but the parent can generally watch and monitor her child and therefore remove the bike when things get out of hand. With a car—well, Catherine had already replaced her front bumper twice, but she wasn't so much concerned about scratches and dents on the car as she was about her son ending up scratched and dented. How could she remove the car from Ryan if she couldn't see what he was doing with it? Would his friends yell out a warning if they saw a van full of rowdy kids coming at them?

Catherine doubted it. Teenagers would be far too busy listening to loud rock music. Ryan would be drumming on the steering wheel.

Trust. Catherine would have to learn to trust her only child as he took the wheel of his own life. He would do the best he could in his happy Ryan way, and she would have to give her fears up to God.

That long-ago day, Catherine played with Abby and little Grace in the kids' pool. She watched Ryan and his friend Daniel flirt with girls as they horsed around in the deeper pool. After a while, she decided to get some exercise, so she jumped into a designated area for swimming lengths. As she passed the boys nearby, Ryan called out to her. She looked over and saw him treading water, again with his characteristic big grin. Daniel was hanging on to the side of the pool, watching him.

"I'm seeing how long I can tread water for," Ryan announced. He was huffing a little. "You never know when you're going to need to tread water."

Stopping across from him, treading water herself, Catherine frowned. "How long are you planning to go at this little test of yours?" she asked.

"Eight minutes," he replied with a slight gasp, while Daniel laughed from the sidelines.

"How long have you been treading water so far?"

"Three minutes." *Gasp.*

Catherine swam nearer. She wasn't worried at that point because Ryan was very close to the side of the pool and there were lifeguards everywhere since it was, after all, March Break, and the van full of sticky-faced kids were only a small minority amongst the rest of the school-aged kids at the pool that day.

"You need to learn drownproofing," Catherine told him.

"Drown what?"

"Drownproofing. We learned it when I was a kid, at swimming lessons. Like this."

Catherine took a deep breath, then tilted forward on her belly and floated that way for a bit, relaxing her arms and legs to conserve strength before pushing up to take a breath and then floating just below the surface again. When she looked up, Ryan was trying it. When he came up for air, she told him that it was a good way to save his energy if he got in trouble in the water.

Ryan didn't make his goal of eight minutes that day. Daniel started teasing him by swimming underwater and grabbing his feet, and both boys erupted in a frenzied splashing and chasing sequence that caught the attention of the lifeguard nearby. Since he was a friend, the lifeguard took the opportunity to chat with the boys until his supervisor caught on. Ryan and Daniel headed for the waterslide before they got kicked out, while Catherine swam a few lengths and pondered how tired it made her. Swimming was harder than it looked.

Even *before* Malta, she'd had midnight dreams about losing Ryan in a swimming pool. She'd be on the deck of the pool watching him sink to the bottom, frantically waving her arms around in the murky water, desperately feeling for him, clutching at nothing, unable to touch him or grasp him or pull him up by a clump of hair. She wondered if her guardian angel had been trying to tell her something.

Occasionally when Catherine felt strong enough, she let herself ponder Ryan's last moments, always wondering if he had at least *tried* drownproofing like she'd taught him. Anger would take root and seed into a tree, and if Catherine was alone (or sometimes walking the aisles at the grocery store) she would scream inwardly, "Sometimes you needed to listen to your mother! Sometimes I was right about things!"

There were so many things Catherine tried to teach her son that he ignored.

chapter *Nine*

One time in the summer when Ryan was working as a tour guide and performer at the Celtic College during the day, Jack and Catherine went on a day trip. They were still living in Bedeque at the time, and there was a sweet warm little beach called Chelton "less than one song on the radio away." It was THEIR beach (every Islander calls their fave beach THEIR beach), but on this particular day they wanted to change things up and go for a nice drive through lush patchwork farmlands and colourful fishing villages, so they packed some water, barbecue chips (as much a must as sunscreen), a novel for Catherine and an outdoorsy magazine for Jack, towels, and a change of clothes, and headed across the Island towards Cabot Beach on the north shore. The ocean would be cooler than on the south side, but it was a blistering hot summer day. They could lie in the sun and go for a cool dip in the Atlantic when the heat got uncomfortable.

They parked next to a tree to keep the car cooler in the shade and walked down a wooden ramp to the beach, where they laid out a blanket and anchored the corners with heavy sandstone rocks. Within minutes, Jack fell asleep. He was up so early in the mornings; it never took him long to drift off. Catherine was annoyed—Jack would be wide awake if he wanted to have sex—so she put her novel in the beach bag and went for a walk. She always strolled along the shore, up to her ankles in the water. It was a good way to cool off without getting soaked. Besides, this day was so hot the sand could burn the soles of her feet. She passed other sunbathers, like the typical heavyset middle-aged guy with the sunburned back and belly, the young skinny teenagers trying to make out unnoticed, dog walkers, cute little kids building sandcastles with their young fathers, and young moms standing with arms crossed like soldiers over their kids, scolding them in French. The kids were covered head to toe with sun hats, beach covers, or all-body one-piece swimsuits, and white spots of sunscreen stood out on their noses. Catherine whispered messages to all of them when she walked by. As an Islander, she felt like this was *her* beach, and that gave her the right to express her opinions.

Get some sunscreen on, you're cooked like a lobster. Get a room, and *God, I wish I still looked like that in a bikini! Nice sandcastle, but I know an easier way. Pour a bunch of sand and mold it from the top down, don't try building from the ground up. Much harder that way.* And *don't worry, your kids are not going to die of cancer after a short day or two in the sun. Let your kids enjoy themselves. This is Prince Edward Island in the summertime, for God's sake! Life doesn't get any better than this.*

By the time she got to the end of the strip of beach, Catherine was blistering hot. Turning around, she waded deep into the water. She made her way to a shallow sand bar and thought she could save some time going back to Jack by cutting across the water rather than trudging straight back to shore. She could see Jack heading towards her, in his old green swimming trunks and pale skin. His government job didn't grant him a lot of holidays in the summertime. He could've been one of the vacationers from Quebec, he was so pale. The only thing that gave him away as an Islander was that he wasn't wearing any coverups.

Jack met Catherine in the ocean, and together they waded out deeper. On this scorching day, it didn't take them any time to fully immerse themselves in the cool water, and they laughed and horsed around. There was no one else around them, so Jack played games and pulled Catherine's yellow, full-figured bikini top up. She liked the feeling of the saltwater on her rarely bared skin and wrapped her arms around his neck while he touched her and playfully teased her about how she looked, exposed and floating underwater. Catherine couldn't resist and pulled her bottoms off too. The lifeguard was far down the beach watching like an angel over the supervised section of Cabot Beach. They could play here for as long as they wanted to.

When the novelty wore off, Catherine pulled her bottoms back on and Jack helped replace her top. They started to head for shore, but the tide had been coming in and they found themselves immersed in deeper water than they expected as they moved between sandbars. They soon realized they had no choice but to swim. Pangs of fear shot up Catherine's body. She looked back towards the sandbar she had left earlier, but it was too far away for her to swim back to. She kept on swimming, easy, gentle, front-crawl strokes, no great technique, but instead some kind of amalgamation of what she'd been taught in swimming lessons as a young teen, and the rough strokes she'd developed over years of casual ocean paddling.

She got tired.

Catherine turned and floated on her back. Flipped over onto her belly and dog paddled. Tried to touch the bottom but couldn't. Panic rose in her like in a bad dream, and she begged Jack for help, but there was nothing he could do, he was swimming alongside her doing his best to make for shore as well. They both knew it would be dangerous for her to grab him, that's what often drowns swimmers—panicked swim mates—so Jack joked, trying to calm his lady down while he moved himself a few feet further away.

An increased dread overtook Catherine when she looked towards shore and couldn't see that they'd made any real progress. Nor was there anyone near enough who they could yell to for help. Dismayed, Catherine put renewed energy into her amateur strokes.

Jack said the unthinkable. "I think we're caught in a rip-tide. It seems like we're being pulled further out."

In all her years, Catherine had never experienced such overwhelming fear. The salty Atlantic was an ocean to be respected. Growing up on the Island, you heard about drownings; about people getting caught in the strong currents of riptides and pulled out to sea. But these tragedies were far removed from someone who loved to sunbathe on the beach and read silly novels and munch on barbecue chips. To be in such a dire situation instilled a humbling reverence for the majestic ocean and its lofty powers, and it imbued serious dread.

Is this it, then? Is this the end?

When Ryan was born, Catherine's labour was rather uneventful until the point where she felt the need to beg for a C-section. By then the labour pains were at their utmost intensity, but her sister-in-law was present, and Catherine caught the sister whispering to Ryan's father, with only the authority someone who had delivered two babies could muster: "It's going to get worse from here on."

Ha! Well, the adventure on the beach kinda felt the same. Catherine was already in a desperate situation, and someone she loved and trusted was telling her that things were going to get much, much worse.

This was the breaking point.

This was when people broke; they lost it when well-meaning others applied their fears over existing ones, in layers, like apples in a pie. During labour, this was the point when Catherine had to take control and talk herself through. If she hadn't, she would have lost her mind. At the beach, this was the point where she considered choking Jack if they ever got out of the blessed ocean. God-DAMN him! *Why can't the man EVER just say IT IS GOING TO BE OKAY?!*

This was the point when she had to still the rising fears and suppress an impending scream.

Her breath was coming in short, tired gasps and her arms and legs were lead weights. But Catherine had to push her terror away and JUST KEEP TRYING. She willed herself not to look any more at the interminable distance they still had to go, or out at the expanse of blue ocean that led to nowhere.

It was too beautiful of a day to die.

AS SHE INCHED along, stroke after impossible stroke, Catherine remembered a friend she met at a museum conference in Ottawa a few years back. She had only known him for a few moments, really, but they were at some social break-the-ice event, and they'd had the time to chat at a shared table as she sipped on her White Russian and he on his fancy-assed "tastes-like-grapefruit-costs-like-gold" craft beer. Somehow it came up that the guy had travelled a lot overseas, backpacking through Europe, and that at one point he got caught in a stormy lake somewhere. Perhaps his boat had overturned; Catherine couldn't really recall why he was there, in the middle of some expanse of dangerous water, fighting tremendous waves and battling God for the right to live his life. The salient part, the component of this tale of terror that Catherine now recalled while in her own terrifying predicament, was that the guy had told her that suddenly, when he was about to give up, he saw a man swimming next to him, encouraging him, telling him to keep heading for shore. Catherine's brief friend listened. He swam for his life. And when he finally touched solid ground, the man who had been swimming next to him was nowhere in sight.

"It was an angel," the museum guy said, raising his expensive beer in a toast.

An *angel*.

And because they were at a museum conference, and everyone who worked in museums learned quickly to believe in ghosts, Catherine nodded in a reverential, awestruck kind of way.

When she got home, Catherine didn't bother telling Ryan. He would have just said, "Duh, Mom. Of course!" and rolled his eyes.

Jack would have walked away.

That was the weird thing about Catherine's whole horrible riptide ordeal. When she and Jack finally somehow fell exhausted onto the shore, when their feet finally, gratefully, touched bottom after an agonizing sideways swim to pull themselves free of the riptide's grasp, she thought maybe she hadn't been that near death after all. Her muscles were rubber, her body cold, and she limped out of the water, yet she was able to stand mostly upright. She could breathe. Catherine was a woman of faith, she attended missions at her church, she never missed the Good Friday service. But as far as she could tell, an angel had not appeared and accompanied her during the struggle and overwhelming fear on that sweltering hot PEI summer day.

When she and Jack got their breath fully back, their plight annoyingly unnoticed by other beachgoers, Jack grinned and took Catherine's hand, led her slowly towards their patch of sand, and handed her a towel. They lay in the sun and pondered their struggle with the rip. After their salty skin dried off, Catherine sat up cross-legged, finger-combed her messy wet hair into a scrunchie and pulled a miniskirt and T-shirt over her damp bikini. Jack packed up the rest, and together they carefully shook the sand off their tattered beach blanket and folded it up.

It was just another day at the beach.

They drove unspeaking along the shore, through Malpeque and then French River with its clumps of buoys decorating the summer homes and cottages of families lucky enough to snug up near the pretty beaches. They passed saddle-bagged cyclists, riding dangerously close to the speeding cars on the narrow country highway. At Catherine's request, Jack pointed his black SUV towards New London, and they cruised over rolling, pleasant hills to Stanley Bridge and Cavendish. They melded into the tourist crowd and, maybe because of their earlier untalked-of adrenaline rush, Jack took Catherine to a cute seaside restaurant and bought her clam chowder. Jack didn't like restaurants. They were noisy and expensive. But this day, of all days, they sat unspeaking on an outdoor deck in the late afternoon sun and watched the tourists.

Because they could.

Ryan died in the ocean. All Jack had gotten out of Kate was that there was a storm, and their kayaks couldn't handle the waves. Kate hadn't reported seeing any angels, but Catherine hoped to heck there was at least one present. Or maybe a multitude, singing some catchy tune Ryan liked. She didn't want her only child to have been alone at the moment of ultimate transition.

It took Catherine a long time to believe—years, really—that perhaps angels do hang around even when folks don't think they do. One day it just hit her in the middle of the night. She wasn't alone during her almost-drowning. Jack was close by. And neither had Ryan been alone. His sweet Kate was with him.

Catherine lay awake that night and pondered the thought. She turned on to her right side and tucked her left hand under the band of Jack's underwear. She nestled herself against him and with her left fingers found that spot just below his hip where his belly met the top of his leg. It was one of her favourite Jack spots, and she fell asleep that way, thinking that he hadn't really tried to save her, but she was pretty certain he wouldn't have let her drown, either.

chapter *Ten*

Kate's key was stuck in the lock.

Last week she'd rented one of those short-term beat-up apartments you see on the news after a killer escapes jail and a body is found. Kate's new digs hadn't felt the bristles of a paintbrush in years, and all the flowers that were supposed to line the cracked cement-block walkway were dead. This seemed incongruous for Gozo, the most agrarian of the Maltese Islands. The flowers should be standing tall and proud; they should be blooming with the kinds of bright colours tourists fawn over.

In truth, Kate was surprised that anyone had bothered to plant flowers outside this downtrodden apartment at all. The soil was no good here, in this lonely place. It was dry, and lacked nutrients. Nothing could thrive in earth as neglected as this even if it wanted to.

If something is practically dead to begin with, if it has all the odds stacked against it right from the get-go, what would be the point in planting it and trying to make it grow?

Kate wanted to break down and cry, to let it all go, but she couldn't. People were eyeing her in the curious way locals examine people they don't know, people who are different from themselves. Kate's gaze lengthened and she caught sight of a grizzled man perched on a low cement wall across the street. She brought him into muzzy focus just as he took a puff on something she couldn't make out. A perfect smoke ring appeared, followed by another. Thick, grey, and cloudy, the vaporous rings hung above the street until they dissipated fully into the air and were no more.

The man's curious, dark eyes were locked on Kate.

Wildly, Kate half-considered crossing over to him and asking for a puff or two. How dangerous that could potentially be didn't even cross her mind. She was well past worrying about things that might be dangerous.

Straightening her shoulders, sucking up the last reserve of strength she had left, she wiped damp palms on the pleated miniskirt she'd been given to wear by the manager of the small café where she'd found work. The café was all the employment she could find on short notice. Already she'd proven her worth as a good server who didn't waste time on small talk. She didn't want to go home just yet. Going home would mean leaving behind the magical land where Ryan's fingers last grazed her skin, where his soft lips pressed, one final time, against hers.

Ryan had never been cool with Kate crying. Ever.

Fear? Weakness? Nah. No such thing. Ryan was all about the adventure. Nothing was worth crying over. Around Ryan, Kate had to put on her big girl panties and be a tough girl, even on the crazy adventure tours that she mostly loved but that sometimes scared her to bits. He teased her about being Aries, and being born in the Year of the Horse. Aries were not about being boxed in. Aries were all about breaking, like bucking broncos, out of the bonds that held them captive.

In truth, the Aries spirit in Kate loved the idea of cycling, riding four-wheelers, canoeing, kayaking, or swimming in cool mountain springs. Yet, lately, it had all become too much. The last few weeks, Kate had caught herself forcing too many false smiles at Ryan. Inside, she'd just wanted to scream.

Not once was she able to muster enough nerve to say *can't we just stay in and watch a movie?* Sometimes Kate just needed to recharge.

She was young but had already lost both parents, her mother to depression first and breast cancer second, the second tragedy happening when Kate was twelve. Kate's father passed while Kate was at university. Losing her father was part of the reason for the adventure trip to Europe. The kids were full of dreams, of life, of wanderlust, and Kate knew Ryan couldn't stand to see sorrow flood her eyes, in the way she drifted off in silence at mealtimes or stared aimlessly out of the window in the car. Travel and adventure were his solutions. In his righteous opinion, school and real life could wait.

Ryan had given up on school. He was not the studious type. He had gone to X, Saint Francis Xavier University in Antigonish, Nova Scotia, for one year, then decided it wasn't for him. He was not a partier—didn't spend his student loan on drunken binges—and he was certainly as smart as anyone else at the school. What he lacked was discipline. He would rather beat away on his drums or pick away at the guitar than write up some breezy assignment on one of the jazz greats. *I'll take a year or so off to work, even though it means I'll be away from you, then I'll figure something out,* he'd told her.

That was Ryan. His answer to everything. He would *figure something out.*

Dropping minimum-wage cheques into his bank account became a biweekly thing. The local music store was his new daily haunt. Ages old, the store was tiny and dark, crowded and overstocked. But it smelled of *music,* of leather cases and wooden guitars, of oils to keep guitars conditioned, and of sheet music nobody bought anymore because they could download every song they ever dreamed of playing or follow chords on an App. *Bliss.* While Kate studied at school, Ryan's bank account got stocked up really quick, since Ryan lived at home and hardly spent anything apart from quick coffees at the drive-thru. He gave some to his mom for groceries and poked the rest away.

Ryan's savings came in handy for this trip with Kate, the trip of a lifetime. Their travels were filled with adventure, just Ryan and his best friend.

But sometimes Kate got scared when Ryan got that sparky, animated look in his eye, the one that cried *I found a wild new adventure for us!*

The day they did a hot air balloon ride was the day Kate's last nerve was shot. Now, outside her door while she struggled with the lock, she tried to force the hard memory from her mind and focused on turning the key again.

"Damn it!"

Frustrated, Kate jiggled the stubborn piece of metal this way and that, but the key refused to budge, twist, or turn.

It reminded her of headstrong Ryan the day they took the balloon ride.

"Kate, come on, it'll be a blast! When will we ever have a chance to try this again?"

Not that she'd spoken out loud against the balloon trip. No, it was likely the sheer exhaustion on her face that alerted Ryan to her true feelings.

Settling back on one heel now, Kate let a small smile play over her lips. She remembered Ryan grabbing her that day, whirling her around the room like in some old classic Fred Astaire or Bing Crosby dance movie from the forties. After pushing Ryan away she'd fallen onto the bed, inwardly groaning but trying to paste on a smile for him.

It was just that lately her smiles had gotten smaller. That day, her upturned lips were barely upturned at all.

That's the thing with new love, she considered now as she pulled out the obstinate key and turned it over and over in her hand. *At first, it's insane—happy, happy, happy everywhere, inside and out. But then life starts to wear on you, and you start wanting to please yourself again. So, the things you do to please your partner become less and less. And the smiles ever so slowly settle back into yourself, like rain into the earth.*

Something else was on her mind these days now that she had way too much time to think. *Where'd you get the energy, Ryan? Was it put on, sometimes? Were you trying to outrun something? What was it you needed to prove to yourself?*

Every day it was something new. Lately he'd been spending time emailing a travellers' network trying to find a place for them to stay in Spain so they could do Hemingway's Running of the Bulls. He showed her images of people being gored—one man got a horn in the shoulder, another got impaled in the butt. Kate would never forget the shocked expressions on those crazy runners' faces—surprise, she thought, and a sudden *knowing* that what they were doing was absolutely senseless.

She wondered if the people in the pictures Ryan showed her had survived. She doubted it very much.

Ryan acted like he didn't care. He was all, like, *whoa, what a rush that'd be*. A little part of Kate wanted to go do the run, but the bigger part wanted to live, and there would be no guarantee of that in Pamplona, running on a lack of sleep and probably—she figured she might as well be honest with herself—cheap wine. Spain was Hemingway country. You couldn't go to the festivals and not douse yourself in buckets of wine.

Ryan seemed to think he was immortal. That he couldn't die. He was like those shish-kabobbed tourists in white T-shirts and fanny packs trying to outrun bulls. They likely thought they'd be fine until the last ghastly second.

Ryan was dead now. NOW he was dead. And he hadn't even gotten to Spain.

Sickened, Kate reprimanded herself for all the times she wanted to chicken out. She knew the ultimate truth. Fear didn't matter. It should not have ever been a *thing*. People are gonna eventually die anyway. Ryan should have had the chance to run with the bulls. That would have been exotic, the way he might've died there. Would've made a bigger impression.

And it wouldn't have had anything to do with *her*.

A sob almost choked her at the exact moment the lock gave.

From inside the beat-up apartment the startling ring of Kate's phone muffled the next sob, which clawed itself inwards in a quick sucking of breath. She never took the cell to work with her—the miniskirt didn't have pockets. Hell, it barely had fabric.

"Damn! Damn this crappy, rusted, bent-up old thing!" Kate couldn't get the key back out. She couldn't get it to move in reverse. "Breathe," she demanded of herself as she counted the cellphone rings. On number seven, the doorknob gave way to Kate's insistent, dry, unmanicured fingers, and released the rusted key. She walked on tiptoes through the door.

The phone stopped ringing just as Kate stepped inside. She fisted the useless key and threw it across the room. It skittered to a stop underneath a low table by the window.

Dejected, Kate dropped down on the bed and stared at her empty, shaking hands.

A shrill ring cut the musty air in two.

Other than Jack checking on Kate, no one ever called except the Maltese police.

"Worth trying again, huh?" she muttered. "Someone must really want to get a hold of me." She stared at the phone before she reached for it.

Kate tried to muster up some saliva so she could swallow. Her brain asked her hand to swipe right, so she did. She cleared her throat. A low quake started in her gut and rippled outwards in ever-increasing waves.

Trembling, she lifted the phone to her ear. "Hello?"

The lieutenant on the other end thought she sounded very small and fragile. He wished she would go home, back to Canada. Staying in a foreign village was not going to bring the young girl's boyfriend back. "Miss Cassidy?" he asked, his voice almost as timorous and uncertain as Kate's.

Ah, the police. Kate stiffened and, for a moment, couldn't bring herself to speak. She hadn't heard from this guy for over a week. There must be news. Maybe they'd found—

The lieutenant took a breath. Strength. "Miss Cassidy, a scuba diver who'd heard about Ryan's accident found a pair of sunglasses today. They were discovered not far from the area where Ryan, uh, where he went down. They appear to be the pair he was wearing in some of the photographs you, uh, shared with us. We would like you to come in to confirm this, to positively identify them."

Sunglasses. Oh, how Ryan worshipped those ridiculous, expensive sunglasses. He'd lost them at least seventeen times, he said the last time Kate helped look for them. And they always turned up, *surprise, surprise,* even now. Like Kate half-expected *he* would, someday. She cleared her throat again. In a way it was a relief it wasn't Ryan's body that had been found. Kate obsessed over having to identify him. *Probably he would be bloated*, she thought. *And weird.* She would probably puke her guts up when she saw him. Or pass out. Probably both.

"Oil drums."

"Pardon me, Miss Cassidy?"

"Oh, um, they were Oakleys. Brown." Kate lifted her opposite hand and watched, detached, as it shook. "They were called Oil Drum Oakleys. They went around, um, around the side of your head? So you could see better out the sides? Ryan, uh, liked them for their peripheral vision. Better to do sports with, he said. Are the ones you found brown?"

"Yes. Brown. Like in the photos you emailed."

"They had these thick arms on them. Strong. Strong arms. Ryan thought they would stay on his head better. But he was always losing them anyway. His mother, um, Catherine, she just about had a fit when he bought them. They weren't cheap. Ryan is, uh, was, stubborn as old blazes. He bought them anyway. And they didn't stay on real well." A nervous laugh escaped Kate's lips. "Go figure. So I guess they didn't stay on this time either, eh? Obviously. Like, duh."

A big sigh came through the line from the other end. "Kate. When are you going to go home? It could be a long time, if ever, before we find him."

Kate was glad the lieutenant had said *him*. And not *his body*.

"The found sunglasses," she breathed, inhaling shakily while touching a trembling finger to her hair. "Were they...I think you said...were they brown?"

69

chapter *Eleven*

Hot-air-balloon day. Irritable and cranky, hormonal as all get out, Kate had sulked all the way to the takeoff point. On better days she laughingly told Ryan to just ignore her moods when *period* time came around. He was a good listener on his more sedate days, so he pretty much did—ignore her low moods, that is—most of the time. Ryan was sweet and loving, on a forever endorphin rush, and besides, after four years of dating he had pretty much figured out his girlfriend's monthly highs and lows. So, for him, nothing about her behaviour on hot-air-balloon day seemed unusual.

Kate recalled the day very clearly. What Ryan was wearing (denim shorts and a T-shirt), his exhilarating smile (it reached his eyes, made them shine and dance, lent his whole body an enthusiastic glow), how the whole wild day played out.

She was still gathering her knapsack and water bottle from the window seat of the tour company's van when Ryan stepped confidently onto land. Through the glass, Kate watched him lift two fingers and slide the brown Oakleys down over the beautiful eyes she loved. Her gaze flitted ahead of him. In the farmer's field rented by the balloon company, she spied a huge basket sitting unperturbed despite the brisk, casual prep activity happening around its perimeter.

Attached to the basket, thick trailing ropes led Kate's eye to the deflated balloon under whose mighty power she was expected to fly. *A balloon! Like at a kid's birthday party!* Studying the dormant mass of colourful fabric spread out over the field did not help her nerves. At all.

"Whoa," and a low whistle, caught her ear.

Gathering her nerve, Kate stepped down from the van and stood near Ryan. Inhaling slowly, she leaned back against the side. "I'm gonna puke."

She cursed under her breath. It wouldn't do for Ryan to hear, although at this point Kate doubted he was even fully aware that she was within touching distance. She figured the only thing he really wanted to connect with right now was the big-boy toy that would lift him majestically up into the sky and sweep him gracefully over the earth.

He surprised her, for the briefest of moments. Just as Kate started to raise her shoulders in a put-on attempt at confidence, Ryan turned around and fixed her in his gaze. A huge grin lit him up from his soul on out. His sun-freckled face was about as radiant as Kate ever saw it. Before Ryan wordlessly jogged off to see if he could help prepare the balloon for takeoff, he raised a hand in salute.

Watching him go, Kate bent her right leg and rested the back of her foot against the van. Shoving her hands in the pockets of her shorts, she thought about something Ryan had said on the way out from town this morning.

"The way I see it, the more I learn the better I'll do back in Canada. Look at it this way—this is all a kind of experiential post-secondary training. I'll study and practice and then set up my own business, maybe in the Rockies."

"Oh, your mom will love that, if you set up out west," Kate drawled back at him.

His retort was quick. "Hey, at least I'll be on the planet. In the same country, even. She can come visit any time!"

It made sense to start a business out west, maybe someplace near where Ryan's dad was living. There wasn't much in the way of opportunities for adventure-providing entrepreneurs in tiny Prince Edward Island, unless one counted a few brief months in the summer when the place was overrun by tourists. There were no mountains to climb or white waters to dominate. Unless kayaking in the Northumberland Strait or in the Gulf of St. Lawrence during a storm counted. That could get pretty hairy. Little mini twisters sometimes popped up out of the great wide blue that surrounded the small eastern Canadian island. Baby funnel clouds. And that was apart from rogue waves that could swamp a kayak in an instant.

A tremor passed over Kate. She shivered. Ryan didn't notice.

Now, the sun-warmed van against her back, Kate watched the only man she had ever loved approach the balloon like an eight-year-old schoolboy on Christmas morning. He was like a floppy-eared puppy going after a ball. *Or a druggie seeking a fix,* Kate contemplated.

In the distance, Ryan shook some long-haired guy's hand, dropped his knapsack on the dusty ground, and jumped right into the fray to help. That was something that drove Kate nuts about men—as long as they were willing to help out, most seemed to become an immediate part of any group. Yet if a woman tried to join up, like, say, if Kate wandered over on her own to help with the balloon, she'd be as likely to be given a takeout coffee to hold as a rope to handle. Oh, the guys would welcome her assistance, all right. But they'd like her better if she had pulled on Daisy Dukes and a low-cut top that morning. Her strength was rarely of any interest. In Kate's experience, men in groups like this would simply humour her, and maybe offer to lend a hand if she was stubbornly trying to lift something beyond her strength. Sometimes Kate could admit that she liked that about men, that they helped her when she needed it. But most of the time, at least with Ryan around, it seemed important to just meld into the group. Ryan was affable, friendly, eager. He had everything going for him, including the right gender and an easy way of blending in.

Sometimes it pissed Kate off.

Edging over sideways, Kate dropped down on the van's sturdy running board without losing sight of her man. Edgy and tired, she couldn't pull up enough gumption to make her way over to the balloon and its focused crew. Bicycles, kayaks, ATVs—*hot damn, give 'er*. Hot-air-balloon baskets? This was one time when watching wasn't just preferred. This time, it seemed essential.

RYAN WAS STRONG. Healthy. Smart. Funny. Good looking. He had pretty much grown up alone with his mother, at least until Jack came along, which was only a few years ago. So he was more comfortable with "adult speak" than most kids. This was sometimes good, sometimes not so good. In school, his confident, forthright communication style was often interpreted by teachers as a lack of respect. He stood up to them, rarely backed down. As a kid in elementary school, he got picked on by one of the toughie west-end kids. There was some pushing and a lot of threats.

The principal looked at the bright side. "The other kids don't know how to deal with Ryan. He's too smart. His vocabulary is beyond theirs. They don't know how to socialize with him."

In those days, Ryan's teachers loved having him in their classes. He encouraged discussion and was interested in learning. Until it became clear that he had to dumb himself down in order to fit in.

He still did that, sometimes—dumb himself down. It depended on who he was talking to. Today was an exception. The guy flying the balloon was smart, an experienced pilot who'd logged over six hundred flights. The pilot and Ryan launched an animated discourse the second they met.

Within the hour, the balloon was fired up and ready to go. The tour company started rounding up the participants, but Kate bit her lip and held back. The water bottle she'd fished from her seat earlier was empty now, and her too-full bladder was demanding release. Cramps from 'surfing the crimson wave' cut her in two, making her bend over in pain and silently wish for a dose of the Midol she'd left back in their hotel room bathroom.

"Fuucckkk this." She couldn't decide which was more agonizing, the menstrual cramps or the bursting bladder.

Kate's frayed nerves made her want to cry.

She was sure it, her bladder, was as full of fluid as the balloon was, now, of hot air. Kate imagined the balloon inside her, a swelled-up, big, round, multicoloured stitched-up ball. Nauseous from her period, an added worry was that she was leaking. Everyone would know if she walked in front of them. All these uber-tough free-spirited guys would know when they stared at her ass, and anyway she was oh so tired to begin with. Tired of having to smile and act like she loved all of this. Tired of being afraid. Tired of trying to be someone she sometimes wasn't to impress this good-looking guy who was her companion, her friend, her lover. Tired of the fear that if she didn't perform, she might lose him.

So, she cemented herself to the steps of the van and fiercely eyeballed a guide who asked her to move.

Ryan called over a few times, but Kate didn't budge. Frustrated, the guide turned to him. Anxious to slip the earth's invisible ties, the tour company urged Ryan to settle this problem. The crew had dinner dates, families, normal lives awaiting them at the end of this day.

On the run, Ryan approached Kate. "Hey."

She looked up at him, mouth set in a straight line and frustrated eyes flashing.

Alarm bells started dinging inside Ryan. "Hmmmm." He did the mental calculations in his head. *Yep, her hormones are likely the boss of her today.* He blamed all of Kate's moods on her hormones. It was easiest that way. He would just nod and smile and the next day his gal would be good ol' Kate again.

He thought he heard her growl.

Uneasy, Ryan squared his hands on his hips, rocked over on one foot, and shot a surreptitious look of longing back towards the folks huddled in and around the balloon. Rustling sounds were coming from the intelligent pilot inside the basket. Evidently the guy was getting some final things in order. Outside, a few crew started gravitating towards lines they had to prep for release. A big guy sidled closer to the basket and offered an arm to one of the passengers, a grey-haired schoolteacher or government worker-bee type who looked far too ordinary to be climbing into a risky basket about to swing up in the air beneath something so fragile as a balloon.

Turning back towards Kate, Ryan paused, took a deep breath and held it, then swung around to take a second look at the unusual mode of flight.

"Whoa."

Simple but effective, *whoa* had been one of his favourite expressions since he first learned to talk and act dumb around most people.

The balloon, in all its rainbow-infused glory, was magnificent. Funny how Ryan could see its air-filled, pillowed beauty so well from over here, where Kate was. Underneath it as it was filling, he hadn't much noticed its beauty or thought about what it would look like in the air. He had been too busy thinking about sailing gleefully through the sky and sharing champagne with his girlfriend from what, three or four thousand feet? The balloon had filled above him, and by a kind of omission steered him away from considering how simply overpowering it would be, how stunning its presence when it was fully filled and ready to fly.

The world stopped for a moment. Ryan couldn't hear the guide gently encouraging Kate to wander over to the basket. He was deaf to the gentle breeze shuffling leaves in the nearby trees. But he could *see*.

Kate followed his glance. Yeah, the balloon was really something. Glorious. But overwhelming. Especially here, on this small island that was hardly fifteen kilometres across. Gozo. Kate believed in psychic experiences. She believed in imprinting. The islands had been brave, heroic, but a lot of young men had died here in these skies and on this land and in these waters during the Second World War. She had a *feeling*. And she was afraid.

Kate sucked up her courage. "I'm going home," she said. She toed a hole in the ground.

"What?"

Ryan heard her. He caught the word *home,* and in some deep cavity in his brain it registered that the word came from Kate. He forced his eyes away from the balloon in all its glory and looked at his girlfriend. Searched her, really.

Kate stayed focused on the earth beneath her feet.

"You'll feel better tomorrow," Ryan said with a shrug. "This is a once-in-a-lifetime thing."

"I don't mean this." Kate gave the world around her an impatient wave. "I mean all of it, Ryan. No more rock climbing, horseback riding, cycling through ancient ruins. I want to go home."

It was a first, this declaration to Ryan that their adventure trip wasn't really working out for her. Or more succinctly, it was the first time he heard her say it out loud. In actuality, she had dropped lots of clues.

Leaning forward, Ryan whispered to her. "Kate. Babe. Another day or so and you'll feel much better. You just need some lovin', that's all. A good night of bed business will put things back to rights."

Preening like a proud peacock, he stood back upright and smiled like he had it all figured out, like any problem in a romantic partnership could be fixed with sex. In some ways, it was true. He and Kate always felt closer after a night of vigorous lovemaking followed by a good cuddle. What Ryan didn't know was how many times Kate succumbed to his sweet touch *because* she longed for something closer. A more intimate part of him.

It had little or nothing at all to do with the sex. It was like she was always reaching for him, and sex was the way in.

After a lingering, sad look up at him, Kate stood up. The dam burst. Actually—both dams burst. At the same time she finally let loose on Ryan, on how tired she was of pretending that this crazy freestyle life he was leading her on was okay, she felt her pad filling. *It must be one of those fibroid thingies.* A wet warmness fell from her, and she thought she would have to change the pad real soon, but the futility of that simple act out here in nowhere-land fuelled her emotional outburst. There was nowhere to pee here except in the woods. They'd been told to go before they left. Toilet paper? Nope. *This* was unexpected.

The catalyst was frustration. It was powered by anxiety, and driven by the pain of menstrual cramps and an overfull bladder. Added together, they burst a bubble of discontent that Kate could no longer rein in. She let loose, expressing weeks of pent-up feelings.

Ryan attributed the outburst to hormones. Not seeing the point of diving into an argument he knew he could never win when she was in this kind of female temper, he spun himself around and strode away.

Kate sat back down on the steps of the van with one of the guides.

Her man drank champagne in the pretty blue skies above Gozo with a schoolteacher from Switzerland, and a hunky, bearded Italian pilot named Vittorio.

THE FIGHT DIDN'T go any further that day. Kate was quieter than usual and stared out the window of the van on the way back to the hotel while Ryan chattered on with the tour folks about the latest notch on his adventure belt.

That night, after a shower and a change of clothes, Kate let a deep ennui wash over her. It had been weird watching Ryan float like that, carried away in a silly basket underneath a puffy blue-red-white-yellow-purple marshmallow called a balloon. The balloon got smaller and smaller while Ryan's and the Italian's voices diminished entirely, carried away on the wind.

Kate's heart had begun to pound as anxiety took over. It grew so quiet in the field. The guide took a nap. Kate finally got to pee; she changed her pad privately in a grove of trees where the guide wouldn't see her if he woke up. She took care to pull her shorts off first, to reduce any chance of an accident. When she was done, she wrapped the soiled pad as tight as she could in layers of leaves and shoved it inside a spare T-shirt in her knapsack. Gozo had been soiled enough. The islands had proven worthy. She wouldn't leave her garbage on this land, no matter how remote.

At the hotel later that night, Ryan went down to the lobby to email his mother and Jack. He prided himself for being an expert on women. It was simple. That time of the month, you give them space. After he pushed "send," he played on the internet for a bit, looking up other countries and plotting more adventuring. Spain, Italy, Switzerland. Maybe even Germany. Cycling Italy was high on the list. Turino, Tuscany. Lots of hills. Great for the legs, and—he laughed—Kate's butt. Oh, how he loved to lay the palm of his hand flat against her tight little butt.

Back in their room, Ryan found Kate half asleep on the bed. He cozied up against her, pressed his knees up to the inside V of hers, and wrapped a muscled, tanned arm around her middle. A faint scent of peaches tickled his nose when he nuzzled his face in her hair; mingled with fresh goat's milk soap on her skin, it gave Ryan the feels and reminded him that they could roam wherever they wanted to. He would never feel rootless. Home was anywhere with Kate.

Touching his finger to the soft skin on the inside of Kate's arm, he let his eyes flutter closed, and inhaled deeply.

"I'm sorry," Ryan heard her murmur, her curved back warm against his chest. "I was a poor sport. I promise I'll go kayaking with you on Friday."

"That's great, babe," he answered in an excited, loud whisper. "You'll love it. It's unreal there. Gorgeous. Vittorio showed me from the balloon today."

Ryan nestled deeper into Kate, spooned her tight the way she liked him to. He sighed with happiness. He had known just what to do. Giving her some space granted her the time to settle back into herself. This snuggle proved it; all was well between them again. In the next day or so they would take their spooning up a level and dive into each other's bodies for a great night of sex. Kate's hormones would settle down. She would return to normal.

"I've got next month sorted out," he blurted out. "You've always wanted to see Tuscany, right? We'll cycle it, hang around Italy for a while, and hit the Running of the Bulls Festival in Spain. If we hang around long enough, we can ski the Alps this winter."

He didn't even notice her body tense up. Typical Ryan, he was snoring within seconds. It was a good thing, because Kate buried her head in her arms. She didn't want her guy to see her cry.

chapter *Twelve*

The sunrise on kayaking day should have given it away, the fact that something big was going to happen. What was it they said? *Pink sky at night, sailor's delight. Pink sky in the morning, sailor's forewarning.* Something like that.

One winter night a few years ago, over hamburger-macaroni casserole back home, Catherine told Kate and Ryan about a foreboding sunrise she'd never forgotten. She saw it the morning after Swissair 111 went down in Peggy's Cove, Nova Scotia.

Catherine recounted that remarkable fingers of colour were laying the stars to rest in that early morning sky, and they got her attention. Catherine was up early that day, heading for work as an extra in a TV series filming in Prince Edward Island. Catherine loved her sleep, but that 1998 September morning she was up with the birds, cruising down an empty highway towards an airplane hangar repurposed as a sound stage. She was going to be dressing as a girl with smallpox, complete with drooling sores, circa 1896, which was grim enough to consider.

Excited about the unusual day ahead, Catherine had flipped on the car radio. She sobered instantly when the announcer shared the awful news about the unbelievable tragedy unfolding in the frigid waters just off the coast of the famous scenic Nova Scotia fishing village. Then her eyes landed on the sunrise.

"It wasn't the usual expected orangey pink," she said to Kate. "It was blood red with a kind of sun dog effect. Vermillion spears of light were shooting upwards at both ends. It was stunning, but weirdly strange and fearful."

Catherine attributed her recoil at seeing the astonishing sky to the fact she rarely saw the sunrise. "Maybe this kind of portent to a new day happens all the time. Or maybe the shocking news about a passenger airplane crashing so close by gave the rising sun ominous, otherworldly layers. It was such a strange kind of beauty," she'd said in a thin voice, fading into the memory. "Twisted like the anguished metal of the lost aircraft."

On the morning of the kayaking expedition on Gozo, the dread that clawed into Kate's bones was reinforced by an unusual, solemn sunrise. One that was probably eerily like the breaking dawn Catherine had talked about.

The sky was red. Dire. Kate was drawn to it. She was compelled to take a closer look.

While sleepy Ryan clumsily brushed his teeth in the hotel's small bathroom, Kate slipped over to the sliding glass door to the private deck, wrapped her fingers around a mug of steaming coffee, and eyed the horizon. She pondered the ethereal sunrise while Ryan regaled her with tales he'd heard at a local pub. Mostly they consisted of where to put your boat in and where not to put your boat in. One site on the internet had suggested that tourists wanting to swim in local waters ought to stick with the locals.

Kate figured the same should go for boating. But Ryan was in this for the feeling of freedom the adrenaline rush would bring. So, when choosing a local paddling hole in which to dump the banana-yellow kayaks they were renting, he picked a bay that almost didn't make the map. On the northwest coast, it was quiet and serene, he told her, and he left out the part that a few years ago some kayakers from Sweden had gotten caught in bad weather and never returned. In fact, he had found out at the pub that some locals thought the bay was cursed. Only the bravest adventurers put their kayaks in there. So of course that was where Ryan wanted to go.

Ryan and Kate were not amateur paddlers. Tall tales from the locals might scare most tourists, but Ryan brushed them off like cobwebs on a window. Give him calm water and he'd beg for waves. He was so anxious to get going that he and Kate didn't even make love before they left.

That was the other thing Kate would always remember about that day. The incredible bloody sunrise was bad enough; add to it that they hadn't made love. It was a tradition of theirs, part of the routine, to make love on the morning of each adventure. This was another of Kate's concessions, but she never told that to Ryan. Not being a morning person, she wasn't so sunk on making love that she was willing to give up sleep. But initially, when this craziness all started with Ryan and the romance of adventure travelling and in anticipation of the endorphin rush ahead, she thought it was awesome. A real zest-for-life kind of thing. It was only after a while that she realized the energy her boyfriend put into loving her on adventure mornings wasn't about her so much as it was about marking the day ahead.

Oh well, she thought. *We kinda blew that tradition on hot-air-balloon day, anyway.*

On kayaking morning, they climbed into a newly rented SUV and hit the road. Kate couldn't shake the feeling of dread even after the sun turned a sublime coral pink and then a golden yellow and commenced its crawl high, high into the sky. Forcing it from her mind, she chewed a toasted bagel with butter Ryan bought her from a local coffee shop, and kept her lips zipped. Balloon day was haunting her enough.

Pushing any spooky negativity out of the way, Kate sat back more comfortably in her passenger seat and tuned in to an old seventies song while Ryan happily tapped his fingers on the steering wheel.

Once a drummer, always a drummer, Kate mused, trying to coax up a tiny smile. She tore off a piece of the buttery bagel and pushed it into her mouth. Chewing was one sure way to force herself not to say something stupid or hurtful.

She and her sexy guy were off in search of another adventure.

A FEW YEARS ago, Kate went with Ryan the day he saw an audiologist. He'd been experiencing ringing in his ears in physics class, when the room was quiet and his jeans-and-hoodie-clad classmates were studying or getting started on acceleration problems. The audiologist was supposed to test Ryan's hearing and then recommend a solution. Or at least a tempered solution.

Once hearing is gone, it doesn't come back. It won't heal itself the way broken skin will. If there is ringing in the ears when it's quiet, then hearing loss is already a thing. It's permanent. At the clinic, Kate and Ryan were told sternly that some people, by the time they reach their forties or fifties, experience such severe ringing in their ears that they end up being admitted to a psych ward. A *psych ward!*

"Some reward for a passion for music," Ryan had said with a lighthearted laugh. Forty or fifty was a lifetime away so he was only half concerned. The audiologist, an older ponytailed woman, crunched down on a lip and looked at Ryan sideways.

Typical Ryan, he was all ears and grinning when the audiologist sat him down and placed a headphone over one ear and a tight-fitting earpiece in the other. Happily, he responded to the beeps and tones, and when he was asked what problems he was experiencing, it was everything he had in him not to blurt out "erectile dysfunction." But the woman was sweet and grey-haired, and kinda reminded him of an older neighbour from the little house in Bedeque—well, not so much the sweet part—so he just smirked and paused for a moment before he answered. He directed the brightness in his hazel eyes towards Kate and sat there grinning for so long she almost piped up for him. But she clamped her mouth shut and wondered what he was thinking.

Finally, he said, "Well, it's like I'm hearing this shwoop-funnel-zssssttt thing." His super-animated hand gesture and quirky expression expanded his thoughts very accurately, and were quite priceless, really. "I hear it a lot when it's real quiet. It's like a spaceship taking off."

The audiologist was a good sport. She smiled and asked Ryan to enter her soundproof booth, a big metal box with a heavy door. Kate thought it looked more like a giant restaurant freezer. Ryan got the greatest kick out of that. Didn't seem at all concerned about his hearing, but wow, how he wanted that booth for his drum set. He was asked to repeat words like bathtub, popsicle, puff, and hash. Hash?

They obviously don't test a lot of teenagers here, or they probably would have excluded that word, Kate decided. Unless there were mothers involved, and this whole scam wasn't a sound test at all. Maybe it was a psychological test to see what kind of reaction the teen gave when repeating the word *hash*. Could he be stoic? Poker faced? She pictured Ryan looking up, reacting to the word. Being Ryan. She smiled. She heard him repeat it—*hash*. Didn't sound like he was laughing inside.

The refrigerator wasn't all that soundproof. Kate could hear Ryan's voice, albeit faintly. Like a whisper. *H...aaa... ssss...hhhhhh.* Nothing was ever as it was made out to be.

Turned out Ryan's ears were okay so far. Just a little dip on the graph at the end. A warning. They made an appointment for custom-molded earplugs, mainly for Celtic drumming on the sharp, loud snare drum, and left, Ryan expounding on the awesome sound qualities of the big bad box.

In the days, weeks, months ahead, he continued drumming, at home on the Pearl set and with the much-loved

Celtic College drum corps. Sometimes he wore the custom earplugs, sometimes he didn't.

Ryan wasn't one to worry about the future.

It was the here and now that mattered, after all.

RYAN WAS THE same about their adventures. The future would come in its own time, so why worry?

The little Gozo cove Ryan chose for their day trip settled Kate's stomach a bit, at least. She had to admit it had a special, serene beauty. Stark grey rocks hugged the soft cobalt-blue waves and, with the sun shining overhead, the little sanctuary would have easily passed for a deep jungle pool. Kate half expected to see naked swimmers lounging around on the warm, expansive rocks. She had to blink the thought away. There were no swimmers here, or sunbathers. Ryan's new buddy from the rental place told her that the locals didn't swim here. "Nor do they ever put their boats in these waters."

Kate stared at the guy for a while after he said that. If she had forced a look to Ryan, she would have crumbled.

Trust, she thought. *I have to trust my boyfriend. Right?*

They would paddle out into the Mediterranean, and Kate, the thinker, the history buff who had been encouraged and nurtured by Ryan's mom, who was formerly a museum curator, would set her imagination to work. She would picture the Spitfires and the Hurricanes soaring overhead, in dogfights with the Me 109s and the Junkers. They would paddle peacefully. The day would drift away in sunny solitude with the occasional cry of birds overhead and just the two of them communing with nature. It would all be okay.

Kate could tell that Ryan was a little disappointed. His stance was too still, too quiet. He was in thinking mode.

Too calm, he was thinking. *A lazy day*. Then he thought, *well, it will be good for Kate, at least.*

The rental guy had pulled in behind the SUV. He had at least eight kayaks behind his rig, being towed on racks on a homemade trailer. He was making a few deliveries this day, mostly paid rentals including the two yellow single seaters for the charismatic Canadian kid and his quiet girlfriend.

As he hauled the boats off with Ryan's help, he started in with warnings. "Any sign of a change in the weather, and you head back, you hear me?" He implored Ryan to take the warning seriously.

Ryan grinned from ear to ear and nodded.

A slow nausea worked its way up from Kate's belly. Closing her eyes, she meditated a moment, then took a deep breath and followed all the ritualistic preparations for the trip. As she was about to climb into her boat, she spotted a little grey heart-shaped rock.

That's got to be a good sign, she told herself. *See? It's all good. We'll be fine.*

Picking up the rock, she used a polar-fleece sleeve to wipe it free of clingy, loose dirt. Bending towards Ryan, Kate showed him the little rock before she tucked it deep into his pocket. Instantly, he blushed at the sweet gesture and whispered something naughty into her ear. Her heart softened, just a little.

The day is calm. We are happy. Everything's okay, Kate thought. She climbed into her kayak while the rental guy held it steady.

A few more moments and they were off, with Ryan in the lead.

Paddling peacefully along, Kate wondered whether some of the young Second World War airmen found love here on Gozo. But mostly she noted the rocks when they passed, flat-topped and smooth. They looked like good lovemaking rocks, warm and sunny and inviting. She remembered that she and Ryan hadn't made love this morning and wondered whether they might get back early and stretch out on a good solid rock. Get naked. Play. Laugh. Maybe afterwards she could talk to him seriously about their plans, about going home, about maybe going back to school.

Ryan was getting ahead. Kate dug in her paddle and followed along. On the shore, the kayak guy watched them a little anxiously, but the young people looked like they knew what they were doing. With one last look, he climbed into his truck and drove off towards his next delivery. He would check back in late afternoon, gather the kids' kayaks and hear their tales. His tire tracks left ruts in the dried mud while, on the water, Kate's and Ryan's paddles disappeared into little watery swirls.

chapter *Thirteen*

Kate wouldn't mind kayaking so much if she didn't have an almost unreasonable fear of deep water. She chided herself. It was a perfect, sunny day, and she was kayaking off the coast of exotic Gozo with the amazing guy she would love her entire life. She could have been working as a waitress back home at a tourist hot spot that overlooked the marina in Summerside, delivering club sandwiches and lobsters and steaks to the influx of summer tourists. Saying *no sir* and *thank you ma'am and* plopping mysterious blue crushed-ice drinks down in front of the visitors. Running with extra tartar sauce for their fish and chips. Wondering about the amazing lives they were probably leading.

The past two summers that's what Kate had done—served tourists on the pub's deck as she watched sailboats motor gently out past the breakwater towards the white wooden nineteenth-century Indian Head lighthouse, with its quaint Atlantic Canadian red trim. She stood above and apart as tanned crews in shorts happily hoisted the mainsails below, tugging on halyards and adjusting tension, pulling on jibs and tying fancy sailor's knots on the ends of lines so they wouldn't pull through the cleats. Their skippers would stand at the wheels or tillers with one knee on the bench seats; to Kate, they looked like millionaires (even the ones on the small boats) as they maneuvered their boats out to open sea or home to berths in the cozy marina.

Kate always wished she was on one of those boats, sipping some bottled mixed drink, maybe something red or pink. She could see herself waving up to the servers at the pub on her way out for an exhilarating sail, all the while anticipating the refreshing feel of salty spray on her skin. Always, her imagination was augmented by a perfect summer day, the kind God gives Islanders only a few weeks of the year—for sailors, it meant a splendid breeze out of the south so the sailboat would heel over just enough for Kate not to find it scary.

She would only sail on blue sky days. That was also part of the fantasy. Even though sailors chowing down at the pub told her the boats had lead-weighted keels so they would never go completely over, she had heard animated talk over post-sail beers on gusty days of something called a *death roll*.

She didn't want to know what a death roll was; its name alone was enough to conjure up terror. The sailing fantasy only included the good stuff. There was no room in it for images of flailing about underwater tangled up in the lines of a sunken sailboat. Kate preferred to let her mind drift to blissful things like sunbathing naked on the cushions in the open cockpit, and sighing with pleasure while a gentle breeze caressed her sun-warmed body.

Ryan would be there too, of course. Between sips of his beer, he'd be singing ancient sea shanties while he adjusted the main and played with the jib. Kate dreamed about holding the tiller, caressing the soft, polished teak between her fingers, steering absently while lying on her back with her eyes closed. She'd hear Ryan tread softly barefoot up to the bow with the spyglass to peer at another boat on the horizon. They'd eat an awful lot of barbecue chips, and she'd go through a ton of pretty-coloured drinks.

They'd sail into the horizon for forever and always.

This is what Kate thought about at work when her legs were so tired they ached, while some rich old American lady made her run up and down the stairs for malt vinegar and ketchup. This would be the future—Kate and Ryan waving at the jealous wannabe sailors up at the marina pub while they slid past below on some big slick Beneteau on the way to open sea.

Kate loved the sun; adored watching the seabirds dip and soar over the sparkling, diamond water. She liked to swim, but only when she knew she could touch bottom or reach the sides of the pool in a few easy strokes. She liked watersports but had to stop her mind from thinking about the unknowns far below. When she felt gutsy, she would peer into the murky blackness, but she would quickly shiver and avert her gaze back to the sun's pretty reflection on the water. She didn't like the unfamiliar. Or the idea of soggy lungs. She'd had pneumonia a couple of times, and she recalled with toe-aching fear how much her lungs hurt when she'd tried to breathe.

This day, kayaking day, Kate focused her thoughts on the beauty of the natural world around her. She was lucky to be here. In this moment, all was well. She caught herself smiling as she reached into the stroke. The muscles in her shoulders and back dug in as the sun heated her. At one point,

Kate laid her paddle across the bow and glided gracefully along so she could take off her lifejacket for a sec to haul off her fleece. Cocking an ear once she got going again, she listened to the whooshing sound of her paddles as they sucked at the little whirlpools of water. From Ryan's boat she could hear singing. It made her laugh. He was happy-go-lucky, her man. When Ryan was singing, all in his world was *good*. It filled Kate's heart to overflowing.

They didn't talk much, just shared occasional comments about the craggy shoreline or about the famous underwater caves they'd visit someday, or about the seabirds dipping and floating above and alongside them. The kayaking was unremarkable, comfortable and serene. Even their aching muscles were fine, just part of the thrill. Occasionally they rested their paddles across the boats' surfaces, above where their legs lay hidden underneath, and just looked around at the idyllic beauty. Those moments were Kate's favourite.

After a few hours, Ryan pointed out a sweet little cove for lunch. He pulled in first, Kate followed, and after they secured the kayaks they spread out a small picnic blanket they had stashed in Ryan's boat. Out came croissants, cheese, crackers, a cantaloupe, bottled water, and a knife. Ryan sectioned the melon and they ate quietly, then Kate tidied up while Ryan groaned and stretched and napped contentedly. When she was finished putting things back in the kayak's hatch, Kate dropped down next to Ryan and her thoughts drifted back to the young pilots of the Second World War. Offshore, seagulls were riding the breeze, floating carelessly over an ocean that, to Kate, appeared endless. She wished the pilots could have felt that way, could have enjoyed their flights way back when, instead of having to always be on alert for the enemy. In her opinion, flying ought to always be freeing.

"You haven't said about the bulls. Are you up for Pamplona?"

Ryan was awake. In his sleepy voice, he almost went unheard, Kate was so deep in her reverie. She gave the seagulls one last longing look, and lay down beside Ryan. Reaching over, she rubbed her hand along his muscled forearm. The sun's heat on Ryan's skin thrilled her. Kate loved Ryan's forearms more than any other part of his body because of the way the muscles pulsed and moved when he was drumming.

Ryan rolled over, propped himself up on an elbow, and looked at her, his pretty Island girl. For the kayaking trip, Kate had shoved a black baseball cap on her head, pulled a ponytail through the hole in the back, and pushed sunglasses up on her nose. Her cheeks were rosy from the sun despite a layer of sunscreen. A light sheen of sweat on her skin sparkled in the day's heat.

Ryan shoved his brown Oakleys up onto his head. Smiling, Kate reached out and tucked a few rogue tufts of his hair down. Ryan let her, and entwined his fingers through hers when she was done.

"We have to go home soon, Ryan," Kate said, imploring him to be serious and listen. "I really mean it. We're going to run out of money."

They had been on the go for months. Their funds were dwindling.

"We'll figure something out," Ryan said. *Real life. Pfffftt.* "We'll get jobs. We'll wash dishes."

She raised her eyebrows.

"Okay, so I'll wash dishes, you serve."

Groaning, Kate pulled her fingers from his and rolled over onto her back. "I'm tired of working as a server. Been there, done that. Bought the T-shirt."

Ryan got quiet. Dropping a finger into the sand, he started drawing circles. Around and around his finger went, digging a deeper and deeper hole. A seagull swooped low overhead, looking for scraps. Its hoarse call got Ryan's attention. Watching it float on some invisible current, Ryan considered what it must be like to be free. He cocked his head to the right when Kate went on, but he didn't lose sight of the free-flying creature in his peripheral vision.

"I want to go back to school, Ryan," Kate said. "I want a career, not a job. I don't know about Spain. I'm tired to death of living out of a suitcase."

Ryan didn't answer.

"Look," Kate added, a little softer. She watched the seagull circle closer and closer, "This trip was a great idea. It really was. We ran away, and it dulled the ache of losing my dad, you know? Like we wanted it to? But life, it feels like it's going on without me now. My friends are moving on to bigger and better jobs and I'm still just a server. Continuing on at school will open up the door to choices, choices that will lead to a career. A career means money. Money means freedom."

Ryan listened carefully. He was starting to get that their dynamic was changing. He had noticed that things were a little off after the hot air balloon ride adventure. Something was happening to him and Kate that he didn't like, that made him wary. Grabbing a fistful of sand from inside the circle he'd traced out with his finger, he watched it trickle through his fingers as he spoke. "Yeah, Kate, it's just that—home? I'm not ready yet. I'm not ready to go back to living inside that little box. I can't breathe there."

Stilling his body so even his breathing was hushed, Ryan tilted an ear to the ocean. Ever so gently, tiny wavelets lapped up against the beached kayaks, all rhythmic and dreamlike, creating the most perfect kind of music and adding to the hazy melancholy of the sun-drunk post-paddle lunch break. It seemed they were whispering Ryan's name, calling him, begging him not to give up his freedom. Home meant an inevitable long, cold, snowy winter; it meant monotony. There wasn't even a soul home to play music with. Most of Ryan's buddies had stuck with university or college or gone out west to work in the oil patch.

"You want me to go home to live with Mom and Jack again. Are you even serious right now?" After a second, he turned his head away from Kate and mumbled, "It's not my home, Kate. It's theirs. Not one part of that place feels like home to me."

Kate sighed before firing a rebuttal. "It won't be for long, Ryan. Just until you figure out what's next. Okay?"

Above them, the seagull gave up its search for scraps and winged itself off to a nearby cliff. A moment later, it was out of sight.

Staring at the empty sky, Ryan groaned. A renewed weight settled on his shoulders. He sank back onto the sand and closed his eyes.

Arguing with Kate about going back home was painful. Why couldn't she just let him be free?

It was so much easier being free.

THINGS GOT QUIET. When Kate and Ryan disagreed about something, it rarely came out in a fight. Generally, they just retreated into their own corners or Ryan would change the subject. But for now, things just got quiet. In the air, as well.

Kate looked around. The little cove they had pulled into was pretty isolated. Large, unclimbable, leaden grey-scale cliffs emerged from the sandy base on three sides. There was no walking out of here. The sky was becoming an ominous grey, only a few shades lighter than the cliffs. Like a gremlin, a shadow passed over them, cooling their heated bodies, and Kate sat up, wrapped her arms around her knees, and shivered. The unsettled feeling she had dismissed, pushed away, returned. At first, she blamed it on the disagreement about going home to Canada, but the ominous morphing of the once blue sky into gunmetal grey didn't help settle her nerves.

She looked over at Ryan, who appeared lost in thought and unusually subdued. Extending an arm, Kate touched him again. The warm, real feel of the boy she loved jump-started a sudden urge to expel the negative feelings that had come between them like a tomb. They could worry about tomorrow *tomorrow*.

Be a good sport, Kate chided herself. With a giggle, she climbed on top of Ryan, bent at the waist, and with her lips she tickled the cozy spot she adored at the side of his neck. In true Ryan fashion, it didn't take much prodding to encourage a smile. Kate could almost see his worried thoughts dissipate like a clearing fog.

Ryan's eyes danced. When Kate, the love of his life, kissed him, the real world just fell away. Oh, the sweetness of it all. *Magic*.

Kate allowed the tip of her tongue to gently touch Ryan's. Barely. He opened his mouth wider, expecting more, deeper probes, but she moved swiftly back to his neck, to those little biting kisses that always got him laughing. She kissed him from the bottom of his ear down to the much-loved hollow between his neck and shoulder, sucking there for a moment before Ryan laughed and pushed her away.

"Jellyfish," he called her, chuckling until the chuckle turned more serious when her hands slid beneath his shorts.

Soon they would have to pack up the picnic. It looked like it might rain. But for now, they played.

Kate thought that probably the curse was broken. She pushed the bad feeling aside.

Quick swims in the nude cleansed their lithe bodies before Ryan helped Kate into her pretty yellow kayak. As Kate settled her feet against the foot braces inside, she noticed that in the absence of the sun the little boat's finish looked dull. It took a hard, deep breath to fight a wave of claustrophobia when Kate reached for her paddle. Not far away, the deepest part of the ocean was no longer sparkling; now it was starting to stir, as if invisible demons underneath were waking from long, eternal naps. A second inhale, then Kate smiled bravely back at Ryan—her signal to him to push her off the beach back out into the water.

Naturally adept at managing a solo kayak, Ryan slid easily into his by bracing his hands on both sides of the seat and sliding his legs inside and underneath. A quick shift of his butt changed his weight and moved the kayak forward. After a quick glance at the imposing black thunderclouds snaking closer and closer above, he attacked the water and followed his alluring, sun-kissed Island girl out into the ocean. Because of the frighteningly fast change in weather, they decided it best to head back to the bay where they'd met up with the guy who rented them the kayaks. It had taken a few hours to get to the cove where they'd had lunch and made love.

Ryan craved adventure, but he wasn't foolhardy. The approaching storm was intimidating. Probably it would just bring rain and maybe some thunder and lightning. He knew Kate was terrified of lightning, but instinct also told him that they were in two small boats. There was a sailboat out around the point now, probably hightailing it for safe port. If lightning were to strike it would more likely be attracted to the sailboat's metal mast before it posed any threat to the paddlers. Still, they ought to paddle hard. They had a large point to get by. Underneath the surface were sharp, slate-hard rocks. Best to get by that point as soon as possible in case the wind came up and drove them too close to shore.

Ryan watched Kate as she paddled expertly towards the outcropping of rocks. His heart swelled with love for her. Sure, she was mental at times, but he could handle that. Nobody was perfect. She could be moody, sure, but hey, she'd been through a tough time with her dad passing away and all. He needed to be patient with her, take care of her. Now that both Kate's parents were gone, he *really* had to take care of her. A momentary nagging worry pushed its way inside, but Ryan fought it back. He would figure something out for their future together. All would be well. For now, they just had to get through this sweet, blessed storm. The rainbow would come.

chapter *Fourteen*

They'd been back at it, working against the current, for about an hour and a half when the wind really picked up and the rain started coming down in sheets. Kate looked back at Ryan who, with all his muscled drummer's forearms, was struggling against the wind and heightened waves. The brown Oakleys were spotted with raindrops; he had pushed them back atop his head. The sun was gone so the expensive lenses were no help to him now. Later Kate would remember tufts of hair sticking out from under Ryan's glasses. She would picture her slender brown fingers tucking them back in around his sun-freckled face.

The sailboat over yonder, urged on by the wind, was now a tiny speck in the distance. Beyond it, the sky lit up. An electric charge had emerged suddenly but not unexpectedly out of the darkening sky and thrust its jagged dagger into the ocean, just beyond the racing sailboat. *Shit*, Ryan thought, *bet those sailors just crapped their ever-lovin' drawers.* He said a silent prayer for the occupants of the tiny boat. He'd heard about a boat sailing in the Bahamas that got hit by lightning. It lost all power, all fancy GPS navigational tools and such, but managed to limp back to port. Nobody on board had been hurt, but they sure as heck were scared.

Heck, lots of sailors get caught in storms, he thought. *Most live to brag about it. Some...don't.*

Kate was still paddling furiously, digging into the swirling foam with all her might, hard enough that Ryan let a small smile escape at the sight of her taut, rippled muscles. He was relieved that she hadn't seen the lightning. Good thing. She would have freaked.

Ryan couldn't tell from behind Kate, but she was freaking anyway. She didn't need to look up to acknowledge the lightning, she knew it was there. Thunder roared across the sky, God's bass drum announcing a warning to take heed. The first crash jarred Kate into "annihilating fear mode," but she got her shit together and channelled her terror into "survive against all costs" mode. Somewhere along the line of her life she'd read not to fear fear; it might have been in one of those well-thumbed little books of adages people tuck into baskets near their toilet. The little saying stuck with her. Kate needed that kind of manufactured comfort just to survive Ryan and his wishes and dreams and his ain't-gonna-let-the-grass-grow-under-my-skinny-butt lifestyle.

The thunder was a reminder to Kate to pay better attention, to Ryan, to herself, to her life. It was like the universe was crying out to her, admonishing her for all past sins. The roar of the sky, the crashing of the heightened waves, was ungodly. The world was tearing apart at the seams all around her, catching Kate completely off guard. Another roll cracked across the sky, this time louder, closer—the mystical glass that is heaven shattered with a wail and fell around them, fracturing the last tenuous hold Kate had on her wits.

She fought the engorged waves with a terrorized full-body shudder and an otherworldly, disembodied scream.

Ryan couldn't hear Kate over the dissonant roaring and crashing, but he could tell by the way she tried to hunch her entire body into the tiny kayak that she was out of her mind with fear. He watched helplessly as a mighty wave almost knocked her over. It soaked her with its cool might and seemed to startle her back into herself.

Kate whipped her head around for just a split second to look helplessly at Ryan, whose beautiful, tanned arms were navigating the paddles the same way he handled drumsticks, digging in and urging a steady heartbeat. He did this with whatever he played—drums or guitar or water or air or life. Judging from the all-in way he was forcing the kayak to move forwards, his mind and body appeared entirely focused on the immediate peril, although his eyes were looking elsewhere, off in the distance towards the tumultuous horizon. Kate twisted her body back around just after Ryan looked back at her and then quickly past her to the right. Following his intent gaze, she sighed in relief when she realized they had just about made it to the point. She knew there were hidden threats ahead, but she tried not to think about them. The rocks had seemed serene and safe in the sunshine. They didn't frighten her as much as an endless black bottom did. But she knew Ryan thought differently. She could sense it in that quick look that narrowed his eyes, in the way he was paddling forcefully through the mounting waves of seawater.

Above the rocks, perched safely on land, a group of seagulls braced their feathered bodies against the wind and stoically watched the two humans battle nature. It registered somewhere deep in Kate's brain that they were the only witnesses, the only living creatures to see her and Ryan fight the water that day. Lone observers, each would raise one leg, pause, then switch out for the other in a kind of precious natural balancing act that Kate found unbearably eerie. The seabirds were far too silent. And far too accepting.

Likely they had seen dying before. Probably they instinctively knew that the water battle playing out before them was someone's end of life experience. It was unsettling that they didn't say anything. That they just watched.

Kate's boat was rocking fiercely. She had no choice but to look away from the strange audience of birds.

Another twenty minutes of fighting with the waves made Kate wish they had chosen to overnight in the little cove. From shore at the beginning of the storm it was easy to picture a positive outcome; it was a whole other thing to think good thoughts while mired smack dab in the middle of it. They thought they'd get through. Kate and Ryan had human spirit on their side, which got them thinking they were immortal. Not that they put it into words out loud or in their heads, on this adventure or on any other. It was just a feeling they got sometimes when they were in the thick of it all. That they would survive. Or maybe it was more that they *should*. Maybe it was more about entitlement. They were kids, really. Survival ought to be a given.

Kate, soaking wet and starting to shiver, and so exhausted she just wanted to lie down and sleep, started thinking back to the beginning of it all. To the futility of arguing with Ryan. To the loneliness of wanting something different for them, something Ryan didn't want. To the sighing that came with giving in.

She paddled with a fury that came from that, from the frustration of not wanting to be out here in the first place in a dangerous cove Ryan wanted to dominate for its lonely, mostly untrespassed waters and for its solitary, expansive sky. She dug in with a fury that made her dog-tired arms beg for mercy and her aching shoulders scream.

Oh God, I just want to take it all back. I just want to be a little girl again, safe in my mother's arms, safe from the hurts that come with loving someone who puts me at war with myself.

The thunder crashed again. This time, coupled with the excruciating physical pain and mental anguish of trying to keep the little lemony kayak afloat, and making no progress at all past the rocky point, Kate gave into crying. She mouthed Ryan's name a few times but didn't have the energy to call out to him, and she cried that she wanted to go home, she—just—wanted—to—go—home. She was tired. So very tired! Ryan couldn't hear her, so it was okay. He wouldn't know she was weak and that her fear had taken a cold, hard grip on her being. She let herself sob outright as the futility of the last few hours overtook her.

Balancing in the dips and valleys between the waves was getting harder. The waves—*are they growing?* The still-rising swells made it tough to see across to the horizon. Absurdly, Kate thought Ryan was likely having a blast. "You want a rush? Well, you've fucking got one now!"

Suddenly a mammoth wave hit Kate's kayak and spun her around, only to be followed by another, which caught her broadside. The second wave hit her port side just after a bolt of lightning struck, so that while Kate was roiling underneath the giant wave, she could barely hear the screaming thunder. The gods were really angry today. Thrashing around under the water, trying to free her feet and legs from the kayak, Kate wondered absently whether the cries were coming from all the young pilots whose lives had been cut short over these waters so long ago. Those fliers must have been so angry at being forced to give up life when they were so young, trading their youth to fight in a war they thought would never end. Kate was certain she heard them cry out, those sweet young boys, while she was struggling under the sheer power of the momentous wave. She swore she could hear every voice, harsh and hoarse, desperately crying to be heard. She swore she could see every single one of their baby faces.

A ghostly arm was there, in the water, strangely. It reached for her, grabbed at her. Kate, thinking it belonged to one of her ghosts, swung wildly at it, tried to propel herself away, until she saw the worried eyes in the beloved face that belonged to the arm.

Ryan. The boy I love.

Tanned and strong, confident and powerful, Ryan gripped Kate fiercely as he kicked them up to the surface. Kate would have the bruise for many days after, would study it and will it to stay with her forever. But like all bruises, it would eventually turn a deep blue, and purple, and then a sickly mustard-yellow, then a pale lemon, and then it would simply go away. She would sob for hours the day she could no longer make it out on her left bicep. The bruise was

Ryan's final grip on her, and it heartlessly went the same way as him.

Faded into memory. Gone.

They rose to the surface together, gasping for breath the way they often did when they brought their lovemaking to a close. Kate was thankful Ryan couldn't see her tears through the rain and the unforgiving, relentless water. She feared the ghosts could, and maybe the seagulls could as well, but she was quite certain they would never tell.

Wordlessly, Ryan urged Kate to his overturned kayak. He placed her hand securely on a black bungee strap on the bow and interlocked his fingers in hers for a moment until he was sure she had a solid grip on the boat. He looked with absolute certainty into her eyes for what seemed like an eternity but which was, in actuality, just a sliver of time, the briefest of moments. Then he let her go. Just like that.

They were running out of money. It wouldn't do to have to come up with $2500 to pay for a lost kayak.

Kate's boat was being pulled towards the rocks. With a strength borne of necessity, nudged on by the waves, Ryan pursued it, stroke after stroke. He could see it; it was only about twenty metres away. He would swim to it and float it back to Kate. If they had to just hang on for a little while longer, well, they would. They would cling to the kayaks and sing sea shanties until this storm passed, as it undoubtedly would, and soon. Already, Ryan could see a glimmer of light beyond where the little sailboat had been. He thought maybe the monster waves were easing off. In the distance were faded colours—steady, strong, surreal.

Am I seeing a rainbow?

Hope.

But then another wave laced with superhuman power crashed over him like a thick, concrete wall, and a big black rock rose up to greet him, and just before Ryan was rudely thrust into the rock's jags and crags he noticed staunch, proud seagulls watching from far above the water, lording their power over him, and—how weird—Kate's ashen pilot ghosts were suddenly all around, floating, their features hazy and confused.

Just as Ryan's head met the rock, he wrinkled his eyes in bewilderment at the young guy closest to him, and after a singular blinding pain that made the world go black, it was over.

Life.

Gentle water churned by God had become a wild ocean with undeniable power, the kind of power that forced souls to relinquish all attempts at control. The kind of power that demanded respect.

Sometimes the sea demanded offerings.

And sometimes it got what it wanted.

chapter *Fifteen*

It took the authorities a long time, too long, to contact Catherine in Canada. They had no cooperation from Kate on this part, and with no body and no ID from the missing boy, and a hotel room paid for by Kate, they had very little to go on. Kate was the accountant on this journey; she was the banker, the treasurer. She and Ryan had pooled their funds, but it was she who carried the credit card. Terrified to face Catherine, apart from the designer card Kate had sent despairingly by express post, she chose to remain silent.

Ryan's mother had been Kate's sort-of mother, too, for a while. Catherine was good to Kate. But ... Kate had wanted the adventure trip to end. She had pretty much willed it so. And with the loss of Ryan, it was over. She'd gotten what she wanted. This unbelievable ending was her fault. She couldn't control the kayak, she got swamped, she wasted precious pre-storm time by making love with Ryan in the little cove on the beach, and she hadn't talked him out of putting their kayaks in at a dangerous cove avoided by locals. She sulked about being tired, and lately most of her conversations with Ryan were about *her* wants, needs, and desires. Ryan was just sweet, affable, friendly, happy-go-lucky Ryan.

I'm sorry, Catherine. But how can I face you after what I've done?

By the time the brown Oakleys were found, Kate got up the courage to allow herself to speak. She did it by writing Catherine's name on a small piece of paper. The letters were almost too tiny to read, as if she had been afraid to write them. Maybe Kate hoped they would disappear, like she wished she could. At any rate, she gave the paper to the nice lieutenant, and then she nodded at him. She wasn't sure why. It was like that time when an electrician at work died, and Kate went through the line at the wake saying *thank you* to all his family members. He was Acadian, so there were lots of family members. The Catholic kind. *Thank you, thank you, thank you,* she had said to the family, all serious and imploring as she held their hands and nodded. That day, she'd told herself on the way out to her small snow-covered car that it was okay to say thank you because she was indeed thankful. The guy had been nice. Friendly. He was always upfront with the pub staff. When he was having a bad day, he turned his baseball cap sideways so the brim pointed insolently out over his right ear. So they would know when to leave him alone. No secrets, no guesswork. It was a brilliant idea; it communicated his mood more clearly than most folks ever communicated, and it worked.

The Maltese lieutenant had felt sorry for the young girl. She had hung on to her battered kayak for hours in the salty water. She was screaming her boyfriend's name when they finally fished her out and loaded her into their patrol boat, although by then her scream was no more than just a slight whisper.

"Ry-an...Ry-an...Ry...an..."

It was all they got out of her that first day. She'd tried to lift her arms and point, but her arms were so done-in that the gesture was barely noticed by the police. Kate's lips were blue despite the heat of the day, and her skin had an accompanying sickly ash-blue pallor. They'd headed the boat towards the marina so they could take her to the hospital, and she had just faded away into the greyness of the blanket they'd wrapped around her in the boat, exhausted eyes trained on the rocky point by the cove, and on the quiet, serious seagulls above.

Kate knew that only the birds understood where he was, the young man with whom she had planned to spend her life. As the boat motored quietly back to safe port, she silently implored the seabirds to tell, and then she turned to the dead pilots and asked for their help too.

She believed in those things, in the wisdom of cats and dogs and of other living things, in the earthbound spirits and the ghosts who come back for occasional visits, and in the spirits' accompanying mysterious-yet-familiar scents of lavender and onions and cigarette smoke. She begged them to tell, but then the boat eased into a cautious turn and the rocky point disappeared, and the day was over for Kate, and more than just a day was over for Ryan.

There would be no more making love, on the beach or otherwise.

chapter *Sixteen*

Ryan got a kick out of his mom. He had always enjoyed her eccentric side, and even embraced her belief in all things supernatural, except maybe sometimes when he was an impressionable thirteen or fourteen and his friends were around. Then he preferred she just keep quiet about the whole *you've-walked-through-a-ghost* thing (*that feeling like you've walked through cobwebs,* she told him). And the stories of mysterious footsteps on the stairs, and doors closing by themselves, in the Bedeque house? Better left unsaid, back in the day. Their old paperboy, who just happened to be a friend of Ryan's, once told them he saw an old woman rocking in a chair in their sun porch. That got Ryan to half-start believing. He made a mental note that now that he was on the other side he ought to look that old woman up. He thought it'd be really cool to just check in and say hello, like introduce himself, at least. He wondered if she would know who he was. He wondered if he could find her.

Not that it seemed like anyone else was around...

"I'm kinda all alone," he whispered, hunkering his shoulders forward into a protective curve and looking curiously around. "Like, completely alone." Where were the serious young pilots Ryan had spied just before he, uh, died-crossed-over-passed-moved-on?

Yep, so far Ryan was the only spectre on the block, unless you counted the fact that he could check in on still-alive folks with just the briefest thought (he mostly stayed by Kate). He had a feeling that might someday change, but he didn't waste time worrying about it too much at first. This was an experience to be savoured, the ultimate kind of freedom! It was kinda cool to float about this way. Checking in on people was freaking awesome, and the crazy newness of this surreal existence made Ryan a giddy kind of insane.

Adventure! I love adventure. I crave it! Who am I to worry about what's gonna happen next? Change will come in due time—I hope.

The second time Ryan reluctantly left Kate, it was to see his mom. He found Catherine in her office, alone.

I guess Jack is at work, thought Ryan. He did his *I'm curious* nose-wrinkle thing. A snuffling sound was coming from his mom, whose head was bowed over a pretty piece of pale pink notepaper decorated with a border of perfect roses.

"Hey! You crying?" he murmured in wonder. The only time Ryan had ever seen his mom cry was a couple of days after his parents separated, when he was three and she confronted his dad in the parking lot of his dad's work, a home-building-supply place. Ryan and his mom only talked about it once, when a hard memory hit Ryan in the gut. She told him she'd found out Ryan's dad had drained all the money from their joint account. A hundred bucks or so. She'd been trying to get together enough change to do laundry.

He didn't want to be nosy, but when Ryan leaned forward, he could see that his mom was indeed crying; at least, her shoulders were shaking in time with the snuffles, so he thought he would take an even closer look. He was rather surprised to see his name at the top of the midsized page she was working on. *My dear Ryan,* he read.

Reflective, he dropped cross-legged onto the floor and watched his mom's long, elegant fingers write in cursive script with a silver-embossed pen he knew to be her favourite. She was a history buff. If his mom was writing a letter to be kept, it didn't surprise Ryan in the least that she would refuse to use the computer. Too impersonal.

Another thing surprised him. If she was so tuned in to spirits and the afterworld, then why couldn't she sense that he was there, watching over her? Her only son?

"Like...ouch," he breathed. "What's up with that, Mama Bear?"

He decided that she was still too wrapped up in her pain to feel him just yet. She needed to let go a little bit, to create some space for him. Ryan would stay near but would let his mom be; he would just check in once in a while until she was ready to feel his presence. For now, he would just be with her, take comfort from her. Comfort her.

From...well, from a distance.

Looking around, Ryan soaked it all in: his mom's bulletin board (covered with inspiring quotes and pictures—did they really inspire her, or were they there just for colour? She'd seemed sad and lonely a lot of the time); her giant "If ye break faith, we shall not sleep" First World War Victory bonds poster left over from some exhibit at the museum where she worked; her tiny framed photos of Ryan as a boy playing hockey; her stuffed Eeyore; the poster of the Seacow Head lighthouse where she and Jack used to meet for dates when their romance was new; old film posters; and little rocks and shells collected from the beach to remind her of the joy of a Prince Edward Island summertime. A slight twinge that could have been ennui passed through Ryan. It caused him to close his eyes in wonder.

Music. There was music in the room.

Ryan chuckled silently. *Of course there is music in the room. Where my mom is, music is also.*

Some husky-voiced blues singer was singing about love and loss.

Honeybees and apple trees, you left your sting in me.

Next time you leave me alone, I'll lock my heart and hide the key.

After a while Ryan could see that his mom was almost done with her writing. She seemed to be crying less, and the page was getting full. Afraid she would fold up the paper, he got up and leaned over to see what she had to say to him.

My dear Ryan,

It has been two weeks since the dreaded card came from Kate to tell us you'd been lost. Jack finally found Kate and talked to the police, and they tell us there is not likely any hope that they will find you.

I find you. I find you everywhere.

My darling boy, I seek you and I find you. You are in every song, in the chili and biscuits Jack and I had for dinner last night (the hot, fresh-from-the-oven biscuits that you and I always soak with melted butter), in the cats' longing eyes and in the motors of their purring, and in my hopes and dreams. You are in the movies I ache to discuss with reverence for the filmmakers, and in the messy room you left behind. Did you know I found socks underneath your bed? Three. None of them match. Maybe I will find their partners someday. I found them when they clogged up the vacuum.

The other day I went outside and stood underneath your tree. You know the one, the one you said has a different rustle from the rest. I think you and that tree shared some mighty secret. The day I stood under it was freezing cold, one of those days so cold that the air does not move, and you fear the branches might just up and crack, and suddenly a breath of air shook it. I swear I heard a rustle, a rustle of leaves, yet it was winter and there was not a leaf on the tree. I knew the air—the rustle—was you. I just knew.

I will never forget the night you and Kate left. The last time I saw you, you said goodnight to me and started walking up the stairs to your room. I think you hugged me. Did you hug me? My last glimpse of you was of your tousled black head going up the stairs. Something seemed off. Different. I didn't know you were going away that night. If I had known, I might have kissed you goodbye.

I might have held on to you a little longer.

If you hugged me.

I hope you hugged me.

DC the old uncle cat knows you are gone. Sometimes I think he goes looking for you. He sleeps on Jack's lap. I feel that he is missing you. I feel that he needs comfort. Or maybe he is the one offering comfort.

I will keep writing to you if you don't mind. I would rather believe you are just away and will be coming back someday. It's better than thinking the impossible. That you are, as Kate wrote, lost.

Love always and always,

Your Mom

Ryan paused for a moment and considered his mom's words to him. He might have passed through that tree. Things in this "dimension" were still a bit fuzzy. He made a mental note to check in on his mom more often. Maybe she did sense his presence.

"Or more likely it is just wishful thinking," he murmured, wistful.

He was surprised how much he could still *feel* now that he was on the other side. Looking at his mom now, he missed her and wished he could chat with her about what had happened to him, about the accident and about how it was so cool that he could just *think* about her or Kate and suddenly be with them. He figured his mom was more curious than ever about life in his realm. He knew she believed there were different frequencies that people couldn't necessarily tune into unless they had real intuitive powers.

"Like a fan," she had explained to him. She once told him that like different speeds on a fan, there are different frequencies in which to exist. Normal speed is life on earth, medium speed is where the earthbound spirits hang out (*like me*, Ryan thought, almost gleefully), and top speed is what some people refer to as heaven. Catherine believed that the earthbound spirit frequency operates at a slightly higher frequency than the one on regular earth. That is why one can see ghosts floating—they are on their own level, higher than earth's regular level. Catherine also believed that time doesn't exist, that humans arrange time in a linear fashion so they can keep their lives straight.

Ryan knew his mother believed lives are all superimposed over each other.

"Picture a blueprint," she'd told him. "Many templates exist that can be laid over that blueprint. One is the 1920s. One is now. Maybe one is the future, say 2060. If two are happening at once, it explains why you might see someone you call a ghost walk through a wall. Maybe in their lifetime there was a door where that wall is now."

Ryan had thought she was a bit nuts, his mom. Loco. Now he wasn't so sure. He hoped she would go back to one of her psychic buddies so he could try to break through to her, so he could let her know he was okay, that he no longer felt tired or hungry, although the *thought* of a fajita sub loaded with extra banana peppers still made his mouth water.

～～～

JACK NEVER REALLY supported the whole psychic thing. Catherine had told him when she met him that one of the reasons she'd been alone for so long was that she was a bit eccentric, that she saw and felt things on a deeper level than most people.

The otherworldly psychic stuff that Catherine sort of half-believed in was far beyond Jack's pragmatic mind. She couldn't get him to go to church, so it wasn't likely he'd buy into the supposed whispering of ghosts or the telling of the future. She thought he ought to, though. He just fought it. Like, once when they were in bed together, reading, Jack got a whiff of an unexplainable floral scent that was hovering around the pillows.

"Do you smell that?" he'd asked, wrinkling up his nose in that cute way of his that made him look like a little boy even though he was in his fifties. "Flowers?"

She smiled knowingly. "It's probably the fabric softener sheets." Wink wink.

He looked at her curiously. A few moments later, the scent disappeared as quickly as it had appeared. Jack knew it didn't make any sense, that it had no known origin. It was real and was centred on the pillows. It tickled their nostrils. Jack and Catherine smelled it as sure as they could Catherine's perfume, Contradiction by Calvin Klein.

Lavender. Sure as a whisper of a breeze in a country garden.

Catherine leaned forward and brushed her lips across Jack's cheek. "We had a visitor. Now do you believe me?"

His mystified, lengthy stare quieted her. She settled against her pillow, opened a novel, blushed happily, and whispered a muted "hello" to their unseen nighttime friend.

A few weeks after the loss of Ryan, Jack offered to take Catherine to see a medium. It was a momentous stretch for him, but he found it excruciatingly painful to watch her recede into herself. She was losing weight and she rarely slept; she just took short naps here and there. She had stopped making their bed in the mornings, and sometimes she forgot to feed and water the cats. Hardly a word crept from between her lips, which made Jack's quiet nature even quieter; he struggled in the increased silence. He had always rather relied on her to do their speaking for them.

Catherine furrowed a brow when Jack brought up the medium. "Thanks," she managed, unable to fully hide her surprise. Jack offering to take her to a medium meant that Jack was willing to *pay* for a medium. Hmm. That was almost more shocking than the idea of seeing a medium endorsed by Jack. *Almost.*

She didn't act on the unexpected offer right away. She was a woman of faith, in God and in heaven. Consulting so-called psychics was frowned upon by her church. In the past, though, over the years, the rebel side of her weighed the options and responded to the curious side. In those days, she'd gone despite the church's opinion on the matter.

Some of the mystics she saw back then when life hurt less were right about a few things although none of them had ever alluded to the fact that Catherine was going to lose her son.

Out of a sense of decency, maybe, she considered. *Didn't want to cause me pre-heartache heartache.*

Back in the pre-loss days, Catherine dove into tons of books and YouTube videos about the "other side." They were fascinating! Heck, she'd been totally freaked out by more than a few unexplained experiences in the museums she'd worked in over the years. And not just her. Surrounded by dark, musty Victorian artifacts, tons of people, when led or lightly prodded, admitted to hearing voices and seeing ghosts and having strange experiences. Lawyers, doctors, respected, educated, supposedly sane folks opened up about such things when they were in a place where ghosts were pretty much expected to hang out.

Yet now, if Catherine were to visit a medium and Ryan didn't show up, well that would just be too much. For the moment, she simply preferred to believe that her son was out there somewhere, that he dropped by occasionally, and that he was somehow *okay*.

chapter *Seventeen*

Months later, there came a day in early summer while Catherine and Jack were having lunch at the kitchen island when hard footsteps on the front deck got their attention. Seconds after, a knock came at the door. Catherine was flipping through the pages of a magazine, trying to get motivated to do a few story proposals, and Jack was reading the paper. It was a Friday, and a bunch of advertising flyers had fallen from the paper to the floor when Jack opened it. Catherine was blatantly ignoring them; she just let the newsprint ads lie where they landed, splayed across the floor at their feet like fallen leaves. Bending to pick them up just seemed pointless. She simply couldn't muster the energy.

Jack didn't bother picking the flyers up either, until the knock came on the door. He was slacking off in his housekeeping—going back to his old ways, Catherine presumed. His post-divorce-from-his-wife bachelor life.

The knock belonged to Chelsea, a Celtic College drummer and one of Ryan's best and oldest friends. Jack invited her in.

Chelsea told them that when word first hit town that Ryan was gone, the old gang got together, picked up some beer, and gathered up guitars. For starters, they just picked away at mellow songs, but as the alcohol moved through their bodies and loosened their tongues, they started to talk. They remembered Ryan for how gung-ho he had been about drumming, and how he was the guy that always made everyone else laugh, and how he was able to defuse tensions when things got out of hand. They shed tears and they raised their bottles to him, and they worried about how Kate was doing alone in Gozo. They wondered why she hadn't come home. None of them were close to her—she was not a drummer, nor a piper. But they knew her from high school. She and Ryan did everything together. The more airy-fairy of the gang called them soulmates.

"We're all still reeling," Chelsea admitted quietly to Jack and Catherine. "I can't imagine how Kate must be feeling."

Turning his back to the women, Jack bowed his head, tugged the kettle away from the wall, and took a long time filling it with water.

Watching him, Catherine raised an arm in Chelsea's general direction and gestured towards the back door. "Let's talk outside," she suggested in a low voice that came out sounding like velvet on gravel. *Breathe,* she ordered herself inwardly. She did that a few times, breathed in and out, before she followed Ryan's friend outside. They settled in comfortable deck chairs placed haphazardly underneath a canopy of leafy trees, sheltered from the occasional cool gust. Swishes of air propelled the branches with their happy new leaves into motion; in the distance a dog barked, and a motorcycle zipped loudly through a faraway street.

Green tea was Jack's remedy for what ails ya. Green tea and long walks in nature. He brought them the tea in warm, earthy pottery mugs so they could wrap their fingers around the mugs and draw comfort, or use them to simply just hang on to. He thought Chelsea's presence seemed to be giving Catherine a lift. It was good to hear that the kids missed Ryan, that somehow, he was still a part of their lives. She was smiling, at least.

Jack wasn't looking close enough. The lines around Catherine's lips were tense, taut. Her eyes were focused on Chelsea, yes, but they were still and unmoving. Almost un-blinking. Dark. Serious. Unlit.

"We're going to Maxville in a few weeks," Chelsea was saying, curling her knees carefully up onto the chair and nestling the tea more securely in her hands. "To the North American Pipe Band Championships."

Ontario. Catherine had gone to Maxville with the pipe band when Ryan was younger. They tented in a farmer's field and woke to a cacophony of bagpipes. Many bagpipes, all practicing different tunes. It was something you got used to, the discord wrought by pipers and drummers on the competition field, all warming up at the same time, facing the trees or only partly visible off in groves somewhere. Each had an uncanny ability to tune the others out. Catherine sometimes wryly wondered if the skill would hold them in good stead in boardrooms in the future.

"Jacob is getting married," Chelsea announced nervously, switching the mug to her other hand. She was watching Catherine for clues. Say more? Or shut up and let it go?

Unlike the others, who had been given their pipe band pieces to practice over the winter while they were away at university, Jacob had gone out west to work the oilfields. He made money hand over fist, as a labourer at first and then as a truck driver.

Chelsea waded in deeper. "He met a girl out there. He's bringing her home to the Island. They'll have enough money to build a house, pay most of it off, and buy SUVs. The rest of us are placing bets that she's already pregnant. They can live in PEI and Jacob can work in Alberta. Three weeks on, three weeks off."

Unlike Ryan, Catherine added silently. Remembrance and loss hit her so hard that she visibly winced and curled her shoulders over her chest.

Chelsea paused. "Are you okay?"

"Yes, fine," Catherine whispered. Inside she thought, *No grandchildren. There will never be grandchildren for me. No tiny fingers curled into mine. No yellow sand buckets on the beach.*

Chelsea pushed a sweaty red-blonde tendril off her freckled forehead. "It sure is hot here out of the wind." Puckering her lips together, she cocked her head to one side, fixed Catherine solidly in her gaze, and dropped a bomb. "Me and the gang from the pipe band, we'd like to have a memorial service. For Ryan," she added unnecessarily. "We want to say goodbye."

Jack was leaning against the wooden deck rail sipping his tea, watching the two women, and looking over at the cats every now and again while they stalked birds. Oliver had a squirrel friend over by the woodpile he liked to taunt, too. At Chelsea's declaration, though, he just about fell over.

Catherine went rigid, and intensely pondered a crack in the nearby patio table's tempered glass. She half expected the glass to shatter. It had happened to her mother's table—supposedly the heat of the sun warmed up the glass to the point where it spontaneously shattered. Her mother had written the company that manufactured the table, hoping for a replacement. *A child could have been killed,* her letter had stated. *We'd like a replacement, please.*

Two of those words echoed in Catherine's head now, just bounced off the empty caverns of her brain, her skull, like one of those old Atari pong games they'd had when she was a kid. *Child...replacement...replacement...child.*

If only.

Chelsea was talking too fast, turning her teacup around and around in her long, manicured fingers. Catherine thought her nails looked nice. She'd never been able to get her nails to look like that. They were always cracked and chipped. Life as a writer. Hard on your nails. Chelsea's nails were a delicate peach colour. *Probably match her bathing suit,* Catherine caught herself thinking. *It's important on Prince Edward Island in the summer. One's nails have to look good on the beach. Or wrapped around a Dark and Stormy drink glass that sweats all over the table.*

Chelsea cautiously waded further in. "We were thinking maybe it would be cool if the drum corps played the fanfare at the service." She stopped turning the teacup around, and looked over at Jack before peering nervously back up at Catherine.

Still leaning against the rail, Jack uncrossed his ankles and then crossed them again. Old Uncle DC dropped a mouse at his feet and looked up expectantly, either hoping to receive praise or counting on disgusting Jack in exchange for his freedom. Jack's concerned eyes were now fully on his lady. If he saw the mouse, he didn't acknowledge it.

Catherine did see it. She stared at it. The sight of its limp body got her head spinning. She wondered if the poor thing would be reincarnated into a higher being. A dog, perhaps.

Maybe Ryan will come back as prime minister.

Chelsea cleared her throat and shifted her legs in her chair.

Catherine glanced back over at her and copycat cleared her throat.

She looked down at a cracked nail. Scratched aimlessly at a mosquito bite on her wrist. And murmured, "Okay."

She was thinking about the fallout of a bunch of boisterous snare drums being played in unison in the church. The acoustics. All that stained glass—they'd about burst with derision and disapproval. Ryan would find it funny. His grandmother's senior friends all hunched over with their hands over their ears ... Catherine imagined Ryan whispering in her ear.

"Chill, Mama Bear. Let it go."

She let her lips curl up at the corners, in just the tiniest way.

Jack relaxed, just a bit.

Chelsea reached out and laid her strong young hand over Catherine's neglected weak one. "Catherine? Catherine, we're not going to forget Ryan. He will always be the drum corps' ghost."

chapter *Eighteen*

It seemed bizarre to Catherine to be going to a memorial service for her son when she hadn't seen his body, and so hadn't solidified him in her brain as really being gone. She was taking Kate's word for it—and, well, the word of the Gozo police. She supposed they were legit. She wondered if her son's body would ever be found. She was of Irish ancestry, and she shuddered at the thought of Ryan floating out to sea suffering the same fate as some of the Irish back in the 1840s, Irish whose ships foundered in storms and sank during the journey to the New World. They were seeking relief from the potato famine, and just like Ryan, they were also seeking a new, adventurous kind of freedom.

What goes around comes around.

When it was time to leave for the service, Catherine's younger sister Abby had to pull out some cheap shots. She brought her little girl, Grace, to the house. They found Catherine in the bedroom, dressed but unable to will her body to move. Wringing her hands, Catherine was sitting on the bed peering out of the door. She was afraid she would break down in front of people who knew her.

Grace tiptoed into the room. At four years old, she didn't really understand the whole heaven thing. All she really knew was that Ryan had gone away forever and that everybody was sad. She was confused—they all seemed pretty excited after Ryan left on what Grace's mom called "a crazy trip." There was a lot of angry-laughing back then; a lot of mutterings like, "That crazy Ryan," and "Leave it to Ryan!" But now they were sad. They said he wouldn't be coming back.

Grace's analysis of people was generally cut and dry. Aunt Catherine was sad, like, all the time. She had seemed so before, and she was worse now. Maybe God could help. And although Grace believed God was everywhere, she was pretty sure God's favourite hangout was church.

Her small fingers reached for her aunt's hand and wound around the larger, thin fingers. "You look pwetty," Grace said. "Will you sit with me in church?"

Strength. Catherine found it in the earnest, moist eyes of a four-year-old. An image of a yellow sand bucket on a beach floated somewhere within her.

Grace held her aunt's hand all the way to church. Her mommy had asked her to. She said it would make Catherine feel better about Ryan. Since Grace liked Ryan—after all, he had let her play his drums—she felt she should help. Holding her aunt's hand seemed like the right thing to do.

During the service, the first time Catherine almost lost her composure was when she saw the pipe band all sitting together. They were about twenty-five strong at this point, practicing together just about every day for the North American championships in Maxville. They were sharp and sophisticated in their red-and-green plaid millennium kilts, black tunics over black dress shirts, green silk ties, and green wool socks over which black Ghillie Brogues were carefully laced. Most of the large church was filled. Many of Ryan's past teachers were present, sitting stiffly just in front of the small staff of the little music store where Ryan had worked. Catherine's parents' friends were there, trying to hide in the back rows, doing their duty by showing up.

The second time Catherine almost broke down, after working so hard to stay in control of her emotions the first time, was when she saw Kate's few relatives. There was just an old great-aunt and great-uncle left, a couple in their late seventies. They looked so small and diminished that Catherine almost, fleetingly, forgot about her own pain. The couple had a real thing for happy-go-lucky Ryan, who had kindly shovelled entire winters' worth of snow out of their driveway every season since grade nine. As a thank you, they'd dropped countless dinners in front of him, meat and potatoes or soup and biscuits, even though he wasn't a real meat-and-potatoes kinda guy. Sometimes spaghetti hit the spot. He liked the great-aunt's homemade sauce because it always came heaped with scrumptious round meatballs.

It was clear to Catherine now that the older couple was desperately worried about Kate alone over there in Gozo, hanging on to some stubborn fictitious thread of Ryan that didn't exist. Slumped shoulders and dark circles shadowing their eyes telegraphed their fears on this difficult day.

The third time the breakdown really threatened— Catherine fought it as hard as she could—was when she was listening to kindly Father Ken talk about Ryan. The gentle priest hadn't really known Ryan that well, since Ryan was no more the youth-group type than he was the meat-and-pota-

SUSAN RODGERS

toes type. But good old Father Ken, as Ryan had called him, had done his research. No doubt Chelsea helped organize the service. The young priest talked about Ryan's love of music, his quest for adventure, his friends, Kate, and life. The usual stuff.

What got to Catherine was just that—the everyday stuff. Ryan was going to miss it. All of it. The *living*.

The *actual* breakdown came when the drum corps got up and went to the small choir stand next to the green-carpeted altar and picked up their Celtic snare drums. Some of the band avoided Catherine's eyes in the front pew, but Chelsea had gumption. She looked right out at Catherine and smiled sadly as she adjusted her drum on its front harness and poised her sticks over top.

The drum fanfare would have made Ryan laugh. It was far too loud in the little church, obnoxiously loud, even, and the tempo was way too upbeat for the solemn atmosphere in the austere building. Catherine had to cover her mouth and try not to laugh as she watched the drummers play, as she watched their youthful hands fly over the drums. Stunningly synchronized, back sticking and paradiddling to perfection, they were majestic in their kilts and formal ties. Oh, how Catherine had loved watching her son play that fanfare, and oh, how Ryan loved to play it. How proud he was! How like a rock star to the younger kids. The corps was always in sync, almost perfectly. Drumming in the corps gave the musicians a kind of freedom that went way above simple entertainment. Drumming in unity gifted them a soulful kind of purpose, too, a shared kind. A deep, wise, youthful kind of friendship and solidarity emerged out of training hard to be the best. It came from being yelled at when they weren't good enough (*tough love*, Ryan said the lead drummer called it), and from character built like blocks on the day-to-day, month-to-month, year-to-year discipline of learning how to succeed.

Grace, her small hand in Catherine's, sat straight up so she could see. She'd told all of them she was going to be a drummer someday, just like Ryan. Ryan was so proud of her. Tickled, mostly, all smiles back when he first wrapped his cousin's small hands around a set of smooth, balanced drumsticks.

Lined up at the front of the altar now, the drum corps had left a space open for Ryan right next to the instructor, on the right where he'd always stood. The missing-man formation, they called it, like the flypast for pilots lost at war, held each year during the city's Remembrance Day service.

The drumming was awesome. But the missing-man thing was too much.

Grace let go of Catherine's fingers. Leaning forward, she braced her two little hands on the top of the pew's rail in front of them.

Catherine let out a moan that only Jack could hear over the deafening drum line, and she melted sideways into his strong, quiet arms. Next to them, Abby gathered Grace to her and let her own tears fall, while Kate's great-aunt and great-uncle entwined fingers as they had at so many funerals.

When the drum corps finished playing, some people in the church (okay, the pipers) forgot where they were and let out a collective roar that shocked the older people in the back. Even Father Ken let out a cheer. The pipers gathered their instruments and joined the drummers. They struck up their pipes and marched slowly out of the church, allowing that old favourite sacred hymn, "Amazing Grace," the honour of saying the final goodbye.

Father Ken smiled as he watched them go. Grace looked up at her mom in wonder—after all, it was *her* song they were playing.

Jack took a firm hold of Catherine's elbow for the lonely walk past the churchgoers to the street outside. *Leave it to Ryan*, he thought with a sideways grin. *He always wanted the solemn music in this old church to shake from the rafters.*

RYAN WATCHED IT all go down. Of course! The music spoke to him. His mother's anguish beckoned him. He raised a fist and hollered "Yeah!" If Catherine had looked up, she might have sensed him punching his fist in the air, jumping up and down in the choir loft above the back of the church. He was ecstatic to hear his beloved drum corps and pipe band again. It would only be later that he would sit alone in the church, hear the music in his head, and ache to play with them just one more time.

chapter *Nineteen*

Kate had laid the brown Oakleys on the windowsill. That way they were in the room but not really a part of it. She could see them when she wanted to, but never really have to touch them to move them if they got in the way. Sometimes she would lie on the bed in the darkened one-room space and stare at them. This usually happened after a long shift at the café when she was too tired to move or to focus on the television. Which was mostly programmed in Italian anyway. She would lie there and stare at the sunglasses and imagine Ryan wearing them, maybe pushed back on his head so she would have to straighten out the stray tufts of sun-kissed hair, or the usual way, so that when he looked at her, he looked like a movie star.

Heck, she would tell herself. *Everybody looks like a movie star when they are wearing sunglasses. Just Ryan ... his smile, his energy ... he actually could have been a movie star.*

Could have been ...

Kate wondered about the memorial service, about how it had gone. She figured Jack would eventually send a note. Once he'd tracked her down, which wasn't all that hard in the end based on an old hasty email from Ryan that had a loosey-goosey itinerary in it, Jack was good to stay in touch.

His preferred contact was email, usually brief and to the point, as if he wasn't sure how much Kate could handle. She usually digested his news for a few days before getting up the nerve to write back.

"Dodged that bullet," Kate sighed, as she drew a brush slowly through her hair, her back to the mirror because she couldn't bring herself to look at her wan face and dark-circled eyes. *A memorial. Not my thing. All I'd see would be that look in Ryan's eyes before he let go of me to go for the other kayak. The fear look. I never saw fear in his eyes, ever. Until then.*

It was the last she'd seen of Ryan. Vital, alive, his sunburned face and the messy black hair she loved dripping wet, water droplets falling from his nose like rain off a yellow dandelion on a damp early summer morning. Held captive by terror then, she hadn't taken enough time in that briefest of moments to search his face for details, the kind of details you look for when you suspect it might be the last time you will ever see a person you love.

In her dreams she saw him, sometimes. Kate was one of those people who dreamed many stories in her head all night long. At least, she was the kind of person who remembered that she dreamed. Ryan never seemed to recall his dreams. This was one of Kate's new curses, now that Ryan was never coming back. Dreaming. The dreams sometimes, gloriously, brought him back to her, the smell of him, the sight of him. But more often than not they just brought fresh memories and pain and a mystical Ryan she could never touch.

The night before the memorial, Kate had dreamed that Ryan was teaching her how to kayak. She was in a class of people that included some of his old Celtic drumming buddies, but mostly was made up of strangers, people from Europe she didn't know. Everybody was focused on the task at hand, and Ryan was going from one paddler to the other, leaning out of his kayak, fine-tuning their grips. When he came to Kate at the back of the class, he pulled up on her left side, reached over and, with his strong, sun-browned hand, gently adjusted her grip. He had turned his body around so that he was covering her left hand with his. Their bodies were opposite each other. He had smiled at her as if to say *just let me help you a little.*

Heaven.

To see Ryan's smile again, the one that made his eyes all soft because the smile was meant just for her ...

Waking up had been rough. The dream world had a magnetic pull; coming back to reality was like fighting off an invisible enemy. Why would Kate want to be awake and alone when just moments earlier the guy she loved was right next to her, close enough to touch? Showing her how much he loved her with his gentle smile? Kate's nose tickled—a musky guy scent awash with a salty ocean sea breeze lingered in the dark room. She looked around, as if expecting to see her man standing nearby. She hung her head as reality came into sharper focus.

She'd pushed herself upright, swung her legs over the edge of the bed and sat there staring at her toes, her body curled over into a dejected C. *I ought to be happy*, she thought. *I got to be with him again.*

Telling herself that, she'd padded to the small bathroom, flipped on the light, and dropped down onto the toilet. By the time she came back to bed, tears were falling onto the carpeted floor, too few to leave a damp circle of sorrow, yet too many to stop. It was impossible to have Ryan within her grasp and have to let go—again.

"I wasn't ready yet!" Kate cried into the night, her anguished eyes focused on the Oakleys in the windowsill, her hands fisting and worrying at her sides. "Not yet. I never got to say goodbye!"

Like clutching a sunburst...

...that turned to rain.

Melting onto the bed and crushing a pillow to her chest, Kate sobbed until the heavy curtains were edged in gold and the room brightened. The street outside was waking up. Somewhere, a child laughed. A bicycle flew by her window, its rider flicking a charming bell that lost its twinkly essence as the bike cruised down the street. The sounds offered a twisted comfort. The world was moving on without Ryan, as it had when Kate's parents left it.

How dare it?

How DARE it?!

Letting her eyes close, Kate had tried to sink back into a muzzy, disturbed sleep. "I just need to slow my mind down. Breathe in, breathe out..."

There was this Scottish guy at work, one of the cooks. His Scots brogue was so thick that Kate often had to ask him to repeat himself. He hummed jigs and reels while he flipped eggs, which made Kate think of Ryan and the pipe band. Heck, Ryan would have liked this guy—Colin. If Ryan were around, he'd be sitting at a stool by the counter at the café, drumming with a knife and fork, oblivious to disapproving stares. That was Ryan; everything was a drumstick.

Add in hummed jigs and reels, and boom, may as well throw on a kilt, close his eyes, and march onto the competition field at some Highland games somewhere.

Colin was an able-bodied guy, strong across the shoulders and tough enough to handle the drunks when they came into the café and teased the servers. He'd had to kick one out last week, a gnarly biker who laid a massive hand on Kate's thigh, high on the inside. It scared Kate to be touched that way, and scared her even more when she realized she couldn't handle the guy herself. It pissed her off when Colin came to her rescue. It pissed her off even more to know that she needed him. This weakness thing of hers, this fear thing ...

Maybe if I hadn't been such a baby in the storm that day, Ryan would have made it to shore. He could have stayed in his kayak, kept on paddling. It was me that should have died, isn't that the way life is supposed to go? The weakest first?

More tears. They racked her body, made it spasm, until Colin came back to mind and Kate could settle enough to lay her wet cheek on the damp pillow and sigh.

Colin was so Scots, all harried and happy. He talked about his family late at night when the only people in the café were young lovers and tired cops. Kate and the other server on shift, often a leggy Italian teenager named Francesca (they called her Frannie), would putter around filling salt and pepper shakers and ketchup bottles while Colin prepped breakfasts for the next morning and rambled on about home. Frannie and he would get into discussions over the weather in the hills, the type of livestock his parents had on their farm, what the schools were like.

Haggis was a favourite topic. "It's like a sausage that tastes like spicy oatmeal," he told the girls. "Wash it down with neeps and tatties and a wee dram of whisky."

"Cooked in a sheep's stomach. That's the part I can't get past," Frannie would rebut, giving the counter a dramatic wipe to punctuate her point. "Although the onions and spices intrigue me. Onions and me, we go together like peanut butter and chocolate."

Kate rarely spoke, she just wiped her cloth around the coffee machine absentmindedly, eyes unfocused, head tilted to one side, thinking things like, *I could go to Scotland even though it's cool even in the summer.* And *Colin's parents live on a hillside and raise sheep, maybe they could use a helper.* She smiled when Colin and Frannie got into a discussion about schooling in different countries—about the only thing the two feisty friends ever agreed on was that school was boring everywhere.

Kate learned, much to her surprise, that Colin hated the bagpipes. Despised them, more like it. But he loved Scottish soft drinks, and he brought them lots of it, mostly Irn-Bru, a smooth orange creamsicle, in Kate's opinion, with three times the sugar content of Canadian pop. Colin and Frannie argued like brother and sister, but they also laughed a lot on those nights, which made the time pass quickly. Kate drank at least one Irn-Bru a night and tried not to picture Colin's hairy legs in a kilt.

When Kate left work the day of the memorial service back home, Colin had followed her outside and offered her a fag—a smoke. She turned and looked at him for a moment before she declined. He was edgy, nervous, switching his own cigarette from one hand to the other, so she stayed put, her small purse swinging from her right hand as she peered at him, wondering what he really wanted. As it turned out, he told her about a group of friends who were getting together the next day to go cycling. They were all young people working on Gozo for the summer. They were planning to bike out to some of the old ruins near the city. He thought Kate might like to go. Being a brash Scot, Colin told her she ought to get on with her life and learn to have fun again.

She was floored. Kate had become the kind of girl who did nothing but work. She woke up in tears every morning, confused, anxious, wondering where she was and what had happened to her life. What happened to finishing university? What happened to marrying Ryan, having children, buying a sailboat? She knew Catherine had wanted more children. Kate had hoped she and Ryan could provide some grandbabies for her. It sucked enough that Kate's dad wasn't around to walk her down the aisle. Now there would be no aisle to walk her down anyway.

Pissed at Colin for being so outspoken, spots of red high on her cheeks, Kate spun around and took a few steps away from the café.

Colin squashed his smoke on the ground, under his dusty brown work boots. He spoke while he was bending to pick the last bit up so he could drop it in a rusty coffee can. "I'll 'ave a bike for ye. Just meet us here for a wee bit o' breakfast at seven."

He had turned to go back inside, then changed his mind. "Sweetheart—your boyfriend died, and that's shit luck. But there's not much point in both a ye being lost."

The door closed behind him; he caught it with a hand and slowed it before it clanged, for which Kate was grateful. The door was notoriously loud, and these days, loud noises startled her, so much sometimes that she found herself ready to scream or cry when they happened unexpectedly.

Kate had stared inside the rusty can where Colin dropped the cigarette butt. A bunch of butts were in there lining the coarse sand like markers in a cemetery. Colin's fag was still smoking. Squinting, Kate focused on the smoke's faint, dusky trail, watched it float up into the air and disappear. She couldn't imagine participating in life in any way other than survival at this point. She thought for the hundred-thousandth time about the memorial service back home and wondered how Catherine was faring. Kate often caught herself thinking that somehow all this loss must be easier for Ryan's mother than it was for her. After all, Catherine had already been starting to let her son go. Kate was just at the beginning of loving him.

"I'm not going biking with Colin," she decided as she lost sight of the cigarette's smoky trail. Wheeling around, Kate strode off to her dingy cave.

That night, another unsettling dream had come. It held Ryan out to her, teased and taunted, as if he were the carrot and she the stubborn donkey. Restful sleep was lost, as lost as the enticing touch and feel of Ryan.

What was the use? Sleep was elusive. With a rebellious growl, Kate slipped out of bed and headed for the café. She had the coffee pot on by the time Colin and his buddies landed for heaping plates of fortifying eggs. On her way there, she had paused and turned back towards her place. After struggling with the rusty lock, she got the door open, strode over to the windowsill, and grabbed the brown Oakleys. Her heart churned when her fingers wrapped around their worn plastic, but she settled them on her nose and stubbornly pushed them back, looking for a comfortable fit. It was a gesture she would repeat again and again that summer. The Oakleys were too big on her petite face, so big in fact that she looked like a space bug.

Colin had the decency never to mention the sunglasses. They were so oversized that they had to belong to the dead boyfriend. He accepted that Kate needed them. He never saw her without them from that day on, and the one time that she couldn't find them for a few hours 'cause they'd fallen under the seat in his car, a good part of her seemed lost as well.

It became a regular thing, the cycling. At first Kate rode at the back of the pack, alone. Once in a while Colin slowed down enough to let her catch up so he could check on her. But soon she grew to rely on the hard exercise since it did a damn good job displacing the searing pain in her gut. The harder she worked, the more sweat Kate forced out of her aching body, and the deeper the pain of losing Ryan got pushed. Soon Colin had to work to keep up with Kate. He fed her more of those days, cycling and hiking, before starting her on half-marathons and triathlons.

I can breathe again, Kate realized one day while she easily glided past a road-race competitor huffing away out of the top of his chest, about to drop out. "More, more, more," Kate demanded of Colin. More adventure, more exercise, more of this new kind of pain. As long as she didn't have to get in any water, she went for it.

And she always wore the Oakleys.

chapter *Twenty*

Ryan got the biggest kick out of Kate wearing his sunglasses. As far as these new athletic endeavours of hers went, he wasn't really all that surprised. He'd known she had it in her to be a dedicated athlete, but he was sad that it had taken his crossover for her to discover it herself. As far as the sunglasses went, well, he had always loved her. So, of course he thought she looked real cute in them. He knew they drove her nuts, always falling down her nose (especially when she was greased up with sunscreen) but he felt as close to her as she did to him when she wore them. What he didn't like about them was that Colin, that so-called Scots guy who couldn't carry a jig or reel if he tried, and who would never be caught dead in a kilt, had affectionately started calling her "Bug."

One day Ryan got real tired of watching Colin tease Kate. The two had been sitting on the top of a picnic table drinking Gatorade while they waited for some of the Scot's friends to finish the canoe leg of Kate's first relay race. Kate was next up—she was always the cyclist or the runner—but she had at least a half hour to wait. Colin was teasing her, trying to get her to open up to him. He rambled on about a bunch of crazy flights he'd been on in his lifetime, some very hairy, and with his robust Scots expressions he actually managed to coax a laugh out of Kate. Ryan, in all his new-found freedom, couldn't stand to watch. It hurt to see his gal on a journey towards finding happiness again. He knew she and Colin were just friends at this point, but the flirty banter between them was too much to bear. So, when Ryan saw the beginning twinges of a true Kate smile, and heard her first laugh since his crossover, he turned his head and left.

The relay race wasn't far from the little cove where Ryan and Kate had set out kayaking on that fateful day. He doubted if Kate, in all her newfound glory with Colin and his buddies, even realized how close they were. Ryan was rather miffed, and his heart hurt, so he put his mind on the accident and instantly brought himself to his body. It was weird looking at himself that way—tangible, his old way of living—so he only made this visit once in a while. He did it to ground himself, to remind himself that his new "sorta" life contained a kind of freedom that couldn't be obtained through life on earth, with its bonds and fetters and social injustices and bills that had to be paid by working sucky jobs.

Ryan would take this new life any day. He kept discovering things he could do, like think about a movie he wanted to see and instantaneously land in a theatre (or a drive-in if he preferred to watch under the stars while reclining on the hood of someone's car) or hang out with his friends while they barbecued and tossed back beers at his favourite north shore Prince Edward Island campground. Sometimes he spooned Kate in bed late at night and held her while she cried, which was less and less these days. He could *be* wherever he wanted! It was awesome. But the novelty was starting to wear off. Ryan's friends were talking about him less and less, and they'd started writing their own songs on guitars instead of playing the tunes he'd written with them. They'd eat their burgers right in front of Ryan (*heartless!*). The intoxicating whiffs of untouchable grilled beef made him roll over in agony. Kate was spending evenings with Colin and his friends now, and Ryan knew he'd go ballistic the first time she'd allow the Scots guy to spend the night.

People were moving on without Ryan. Could he just end this whole strange game? Appear suddenly, yell a great big, "Surprise, it's me!"?

On days when loneliness kicked in, Ryan did the body-visit thing. Lost, wondering if anyone was still really missing him, it helped to connect with who he was. Nobody was actively looking for his earthly body these days, but Ryan did look in on the lieutenant from time to time and saw that his file was still sitting on the guy's desk. *Phew!* Ryan figured the police would keep checking the shore in the hopes that his body would turn up. That would be a day for celebration. Sort of. Maybe it would mean that Ryan would get to go somewhere else, wherever he was meant to be. He wasn't afraid. Just lonely, at times. He had never been the kind of guy to stand on the outside looking in. Ryan was used to being the centre of attention, the guy who made people laugh. The guy who *did* stuff, who really lived his life.

This floating thing had its cool benefits, but at times it was starting feel a little lame.

When Ryan went to visit his body, he never got too close. He could see it from a distance, floating, floating, floating, with its green T-shirt almost non-existent thanks to the hazards of saltwater and sea creatures. Twice, boats had narrowly missed him, but he didn't know that. He watched himself drift out to sea, just a dot in that great expanse of Mediterranean Ocean, prey to the elements. His body was wearing down, along with his resolve to experience this, the greatest of all adventures.

One quick look, and he'd think-zoom himself away.

Ryan was as alone and lost as his last physical tie to the earth. Lately he had started to pray, in a way. He had always been a somewhat spiritual person—how could he not be, living with Catherine? She was a woman who once talked about becoming a missionary in Kenya in her older years. For certain she would spend large chunks of her senior days in church. When Ryan got bored, he made jokes about "going towards the light." In this weird dimension there was light everywhere; Ryan's world was illuminated always, and never truly got dark, even in the dark. There was always an element, a sense, of light.

Yep, the floating days had some perks.

Sometimes he wondered if he was in purgatory. Was he being watched, judged? Was God listening to his guardian angel plead his case (*"he's really sorry about not sharing his popcorn that day at the movies."*)? Ryan had lots of time to think about the life he had lived. He analyzed every second and sometimes voiced his thoughts out loud while he paced the isolated sandstone cliffs back home in Prince Edward

Island. "Was I a good person? Was I kind to others? Was I a light or did I bring people down?"

Selfishness had always been a part of Ryan's being. He was a self-centred kid. Catherine had doted on him, spent what little money she had on his hockey and then his curling, and then on drumming, drumming, drumming—on private lessons and on trips to competitions and on an extra pair of special wool socks the day of the Christmas recital, when Ryan forgot his at home in Bedeque. Catherine was a giving person when it concerned her only child. Ryan, although grateful, had come to expect that of her and of the world around him. He hadn't always stopped to think about what other people thought or felt in a given situation. He just *was*.

One of the biggest struggles Ryan had faced on earth concerned an old buddy of his—Conor. Conor was partially responsible for getting Ryan through the tough junior high years, like when Ryan was just figuring out that he needed to wash his hair and body more than once a week, and that he ought to have some variety in what he wore to school.

Like, Conor was the one who told Ryan to listen to his mother and use the clothes hamper. "Or your jeans are never gonna get washed and you'll have to wear the pair with the mustard stain three days in a row. Whaddaya think Sophia in English class would make of that? Huh? Loser! Don't be a douche!"

Conor was the oldest kid in his family. He was so much older than his other two siblings that his parents seemed to have kind of forgotten about him. So, he lost himself in a myriad of tiny harmful ways that his friendship with

Ryan seemed to abate. Conor was Ryan's introduction and acceptance into a cooler world, the world of hockey jocks with nice clothes and pretty girls who did well in school. The two boys became inseparable when they were thirteen. Ryan was learning to play the drums in the school band, and Conor was a guitar prodigy. They dreamed of the big time, like maybe opening for the Red Hot Chili Peppers (*those old guys*) or having a bunch of screaming fans tattoo their names on their bodies.

The thing that went wrong with Conor, perhaps because he had been basically on his own for so long, was that he became even more self-indulgent than his drumming buddy. The boys' band, ShadowRab, was everything. They wrote songs, they jammed for hours in the barn in the backyard of the Bedeque house, which they'd insulated and carpeted, and they got better on drums and guitar super quickly. Their singer and bass player were dedicated members of the band, too, and the four boys were joined at the hip. ShadowRab won all the local Battle of the Bands contests and, as the music got better and better, the boys who were like brothers started to fight like brothers. Ryan and Conor had strong personalities. Both were talented, and both had great visions for the band.

Things started to unravel when the band's local success increased, because egos got in the way and those two self-centred kids hadn't learned to compromise. Conor started to treat the other band members, and especially Ryan, with disdain and the kind of abuse he laid on his well-meaning parents. Conor's way was the *only* way. Some of that came from always being told he was a guitar prodigy.

Ryan pondered this during the floating days. *When you're told you're great before you even have a chance to get started, where do you go from there?* Conor needed to fail and learn. That was how he would develop humility and strength.

Ryan didn't know what to do about Conor. All he knew was that band practice had become insufferable. Their rehearsals weren't so much about getting together and writing music and figuring out riffs anymore. They had become war zones and battles of superiority; only where Ryan argued his points, Conor towered over him and heaped abuse. One day when Ryan and his mom were at the movies, they found Conor in the lobby in shorts and a T-shirt. It was January. Minus heaven-knows-what outdoors. Conor'd had a fight with his parents and, since the movie theatre was nearby, he'd crawled out of his window and hightailed it to shelter. Ryan's mom felt sorry for him, so she took him home. She figured he needed to cool off. Over the next few days, the story came out that Conor's father had thrown a table at him. Conor swore he'd been abused. But Catherine, in talking to his parents, figured out that Conor had physically pushed his mother around. Thus, the father had stepped in. Conor stayed with Ryan and Catherine for a few days until Conor's parents found him at another friend's house one afternoon after school and took him home.

Things went downhill from there.

The boys managed to keep it together for another couple of years, for the love of making music with the band. As they got older and entered high school, other temptations got in the way. Conor got his hands on Triple C cough medicine tablets, and booze, and it escalated to Ecstasy. The other boys tried *happy weed*, which Jack called marijuana, but rarely, and they stayed away from the more nefarious stuff. Conor had a girlfriend who got tired of his abuse and dropped him—and that was the beginning of the end. He hid rum and vodka in a loose floorboard in his bedroom, and drank so much combined with Tylenol that his parents had to rush him to the hospital one night to get his stomach pumped. At school, he started to spend time alone. The boys in the band tried to help him, and even went to the guidance counsellor to report his substance abuse and seek help in dealing with his anger, but it just made Conor toxic. He blamed Ryan for everything, and Ryan got upset enough with Conor's slander and abuse that in the end he shut him out. About four months after that, Conor took his guitar and left. Rumour had it he was heading for Los Angeles to break into the music scene. Two months later his parents got word that he had killed himself underneath some random pier. Ryan thought he was probably doing homage to Anthony Kiedis of the Chili Peppers. One of the Peppers' biggest hits was about shooting heroin under a bridge, and the loneliness that comes from living your life as a slave to drugs.

Catherine had always been secretly relieved that Ryan didn't go down the same dark road as Conor. She maintained that keeping an open line of communication with your kid was the best way to keep him on the straight and narrow. She had often counted her blessings about how lucky she was. She didn't take any real credit for Ryan, because she felt she had made a lot of mistakes with him. But people told her the kids hung out at her house because they felt safe and comfortable there. The last time she'd seen Conor he had come to the house to gather up his things—amps and guitar strings and pedals. She'd pushed aside his long brown hair so she could see his eyes and given him a hug and told him she loved him, and because she couldn't think of anything else to say, she'd said, "Drugs are not the answer." He had nodded and left. But he was a sad, sad boy by then, because the breakup of the band had destroyed his spirit, and Catherine knew that and Ryan knew that. But they were powerless to help him, and the things he'd said and done to Ryan had cemented the loss of the boys' brotherhood.

These were the things Ryan thought about on his loneliest days, on the days when he wondered if some mystical trial was going on and he was being judged. He went over and over and over in his mind whether there might have been anything he could have done to help Conor. He pondered the nastiness of drug addiction, and wondered which really came first—Conor's self-destructive, narcissistic, controlling personality, or the drugs that preyed on those qualities, ballooned them, and turned him into a monster. After all, Ryan considered, Anthony Kiedis had kicked drugs and found yoga and spiritualism and he even went on an enlightenment trek and met the Dalai Lama. The boys' hero had survived—at least as far as Ryan knew, Kiedis was still clean.

Could Ryan, just a kid himself, have helped Conor? Was there something different he could have done? *I dunno*, Ryan considered sadly while he paced the red cliffs. *Probably not.* He thought maybe when his judgement finally came, some spiritual entity would give him the answer, the secret to helping someone on a downward spiral. But for now, Ryan would just have to wait, and wonder.

Occasionally, Ryan thought he felt the presence of another in-between soul nearby. He would whip his head around and strain his neck to see. But there was never anybody in sight. He had known lots of people who crossed over besides Conor—relatives, and a kid from school who'd died in a car crash. He'd heard horrible stories about where someone who may have killed themselves might be. Where Ryan had ended up wasn't a bad place. Just lonely. In Ryan's heart, he believed that Conor had the potential to be a good person—they had been close friends at one time. Secretly he hoped that the in-between person whose energy sometimes buzzed by him might be Conor. "I wonder if we can get our hands on some drums and a guitar." That always cheered Ryan up. He imagined the songs they would sing and the music they would write. Maybe someday Anthony Kiedis, or Chad Smith, the Peppers' drummer since the 1980s, would show up. They'd jam for a while, then Ryan would hitch a ride with Anthony to go check out the Dalai Lama. Get some answers, maybe, about life and where all this was going.

These are the things Ryan tossed around in his noggin when Kate was with Colin. Friendships and music, the things he missed the most. Those and his mother's smokin' homemade chili, and hot freshly baked melt-in-your-mouth biscuits dripping with butter.

chapter *Twenty-one*

Ryan decided one day that he'd had enough of watching Kate firm her body up with all that exercise. She looked fabulous, as she always had, and he thought she was getting a little bit obsessive about the whole cycling and running thing. It didn't seem that she was thinking about him as much anymore, especially with that Scots dude lurking around her so much, so Ryan decided obstinately to spend some time with his mom. He figured that was what boys did when they felt sad and lost, they visited their moms. Moms were usually last on the list to visit for freedom-loving, adventure-seeking, much-in-love-with-their-girlfriend sons, but somehow Ryan figured Catherine had always been cool with that. She adored Kate and didn't have a daughter, so it was all good. But now? Ryan needed his mom.

He decided to try extra hard to force some kind of communication. His mom was in tune with these things. He felt certain that somehow, she would know he was there.

Ryan found her snuggled up under a blanket in her office in the new Summerside house. Jack was a real stickler about the heat. Or the bill for the heat. Ryan was glad he could no longer feel cold. Or hot. By the looks of Catherine, huddled deeply into a soft white blanket, Jack's sympathy towards her regarding the loss of her son did not extend to notching up the thermostat. "Come on, Jack," Ryan muttered disdainfully. "You're a great guy, but let my mom get warm, would ya?"

Catherine was on the computer, surfing the internet like in the old days. Looking over her shoulder, humming happily, Ryan decided that his mother was researching publishing ideas, searching for new magazines to query that might take some of her stories. "Cool," he whistled between his teeth. "I'm glad you're out of your rocking chair and back to work, Mama Bear. Productivity, that's the key to getting over me. Keep your mind busy. Your brain firing."

One of the cats wandered into the small office and questioningly angled its head at Ryan, who plopped down on the floor to play, his heart swelling with love and devotion. When the second cat bounced in and landed in his lap, Ryan burst into song. "You see me, you see meeee," he sang while he untied a shoelace for Oscar to swat around. Catherine, halfheartedly manipulating the computer mouse, heard the cats playing. She caught their questioning *rrrrrrppppps?* And *mmmmmmrrrrrs*. But she didn't turn around. If she had, she wouldn't have seen Ryan anyway. The frequency he was living in was only accessible to animals. "God knew we'd need some company to help us through the lonelies," Ryan murmured with a wistful frown tossed in the general direction of his mother.

He laughed. "You cats!" Especially Oliver with his tawny-faced innocent acceptance of life. "Geez, I get a kick out of you!" Catherine might have been a little freaked if she *had* turned around. Oscar was leaping over Oliver as if his legs were on springs while the littler guy batted his sharp claws at Ryan's outstretched fingers. The antics of the young cats seemed to suggest they were playing with a fictitious being—but since the household had always rather assumed Oliver and Oscar were a bit touched, Catherine probably would have shrugged off their behavior anyway. For sure Jack would have. The old stickler only trusted things he could touch and see. Like thermostats.

Old Uncle DC wandered in and sat like he always did, in a big lump that said *I ate way too much high protein kitten food*, and watched the goings-on in a rather somnolent, detached manner. Ryan eyed him with wonder and considered what the older cat might be thinking—*man, where ya been? Yeah, you used to ignore me most of the time, and you were crappy at feeding me, if ever, but at least your bedroom was warm. Everybody mostly just ignores me now and your bedroom is friggin' freezing. Thankfully it's a sanctuary away from these two youngsters. An old cat's gotta get some sleep. Thank God for Jack, who gives me a platter of milk or yogurt when he remembers. Oh, and by the way, this captivity thing sucks.*

Ryan laughed and wished he could really communicate with DC. The old cat had been in the family since Ryan was seven, and he missed the fat furball. A mental note to check in on the cats more often mellowed Ryan, and he felt a bit better about his aloneness in the sorta-life days. As his more optimistic nature pushed down the *meh* feeling, he was grateful for the perks of this bizarre version of life. He couldn't feel Oliver's sharp claws. It was uncanny, knowing he was being scratched and poked, but never bloodied.

After a while, Ryan glanced up at the computer monitor. When he did, Oscar caught him off guard and sprang right through him, *rather joyfully*, Ryan thought. "I'm not a game!" He grinned wholeheartedly at the cat. The whooshing that came with the spirited jump through his chest was super wonky; a startling high-pressure inhale followed by a slow, relieved release left Ryan gasping. The cat-ken batted buoyantly at Ryan's face, paws flying and *mmmmrrrrrrrppppps* questioning. Oliver tilted his head in a *whooooaaaa, dude, happy weed* kind of daze. Seemed like a cloud of pungent smoke could follow the little guy around and not raise an eyebrow. His expressions were priceless, all dozey and chill and easy. *What'd you do in your last life*, wondered Ryan with a grin.

Some cat.

The images on his mom's computer screen begged Ryan's attention. Something was a bit—off. He let the cat-kens beat each other up and stood so he could look over his mother's shoulder. Instantly he looked away, and then back again. *Hey, what the*—what was his mother looking at? On the screen, women in lingerie, some in very compromising positions, smiled seductively out at him from velvety couches and lacey beds.

"Yeesh," whispered Ryan. "What are you up to, Catherine?" The website Ryan's mom had leaned forward to take a closer look at was headlined with the word *erotica*. There was a shot of a couple, naked from the waist up, in a suggestive embrace. The caption read "Jessica and Luke love making love—you and your partner can, too." Reading on, Ryan could see that the gist of the web page was to take the stress out of the bedroom and find new ways to rejuvenate a couple's sex life. Like butter on a sizzling hot pan, he jumped back. "Holy cow!" Apparently, Ryan could find out things about his mother in these floating days that he wasn't really prepared to know. He tilted his head. His mother was smiling, not a lot, but her lips did have little upward curls at the ends. She was into what she was seeing and reading. It was the first time Ryan'd seen her really smile since his cross-over. Her eyes were wide and she was shaking her head, but she was obviously amused.

Ryan glanced back to the screen. One mouse-click by Catherine and a loving couple jumped into full view. Catherine hit "play" and they started to move, backed by music. A video. Catherine sat back and watched. Ryan didn't. Before his mother had a chance to double-click on another couple, he whipped his head around and squinted at the spaced-out cats leaping and playing in front of him. "Too much information," he said to them in a high-pitched voice, his hands in front of his eyes. Confused and unsure, he backed up a few steps and left Catherine to her research by thinking himself on the lifeguard stand at Chelton Beach.

It was pleasant to sit there atop the wooden stand without the annoyance of an irritating army of mosquitos biting his skin. The beach wasn't busy—kids were back in school for the fall and the tourist season had abruptly drawn to an unwelcome close. There were still seniors and newlyweds on holiday, though, probably avoiding the hot beach weather, high season traffic, and rambunctious, tired children. A few couples were wandering the sandy beach, dipping their toes in the still-warm tidal pools, or gathering shells to take home to friends and neighbours in Toronto or Boston.

One woman, in a bikini that was so small that her breasts spilled out over the cups, jiggled her way to a cozy beach quilt and flopped down to soak up the mid-September sun. Ryan sat on the little tower and watched her, then smiled and dipped his chin to acknowledge her self-confidence. "Good for you," he grinned. "Humans miss way too much beach time 'cause they're scared of what they look like. They're afraid they'll be judged." At the same time, he sent the woman a telepathic message to spend some time shopping online for a bikini that fit, well, better.

His eyes narrowed. Awareness bloomed. "That's a chocolate-covered turd," he admonished himself, forcing his gaze away from the woman with the too-small top. "I just complimented this gutsy, self-assured woman, and followed it up with an uncharitable thought that she should go shopping for a better bikini. While judgement might very well be awaiting me."

He groaned and buried his face in his hands. The unknown was debilitating.

Strangely, the woman reminded him of Kate. Kate was stunning in a bikini. His favourite was a deep chocolate brown with pink straps. Her sweet breasts offered just the right amount of cleavage to run his fingers along, to tease her. With her messed-up curly Island hair, in that swimsuit Ryan felt Kate could have been a model. Looking back at the woman in the overflowing bikini top, Ryan reminded himself that Kate's skin was markedly firmer and would probably remain so for life. After all, she was adventurous.

She worked hard to stay in shape. And she was young. She had lifestyle habits that would hold her in good stead in the years to come.

A low breeze on Ryan's left got his attention. Craning his neck sideways, he spied a balding man with faded beige cotton trunks and a towel in his hand walking down the wooden ramp to the beach. The guy perched lazily next to the woman. Ryan watched her happily reach over and lay a hand on the man's thigh. The guy opened a beer from his lady's cooler and offered her the first sip. They were a geeky-looking couple. But Ryan was touched by their obvious feelings for each other. He wanted to yell out at them the name of the website his mother had been looking at. But maybe they weren't in need of a virtual sex therapist. They looked like they were probably doing just fine in the bedroom on their own.

Eyeing the couple's beer and the sweet contentment that flowed between them, Ryan licked his lips and sat longingly back against the wooden slats of the lifeguard stand on the near-empty beach. He could see the quaint white-with-red-trim Seacow Head lighthouse from where he sat, standing sentinel on a red sandstone point to his right, stretching tall and stately up into the sky. Beyond that, a slim sailboat cut through the surf with buffeted certainty. Perhaps it was headed to New Brunswick, which was far away but visible on this clear blue sky kinda day. To his left Ryan could see flashes of sunshine on the windshields of cars, campers, and trucks crossing the Confederation Bridge, Prince Edward Island's just about thirteen-kilometres-long link to the mainland.

He leaned back and closed his eyes. The massive bridge gave Islanders a sense of security. They could leave PEI whenever they wanted to, like if there was an emergency in the middle of the night—a head injury, maybe, after a car accident. Sometimes patients were flown out by LifeFlight helicopter, but families would follow by car. Ryan knew a few of these folks. Ryan wished he had a bridge to—well, somewhere, he wasn't sure where. A permanent link to a hustling, bustling life somewhere peaceful and happy, where he could visit with people he'd known who had passed on before him. Maybe Conor. But then—what about Kate, his mom, his Celtic College pipe band buddies...the cat-kens? He needed to keep checking in on them to be sure they were okay. Could he do that once he crossed some unknown *bridge*?

His mother—he wondered what she was up to, looking at those provocative images. She went to the big Catholic Church on Sundays and cared about what people thought of her. And, being Catholic, she lived with no shortage of guilt, for just about everything. These images on her computer would likely eat at her brain until she turned herself into a pillar of salt.

Today was a blah day. All around him, Ryan was being handed reminders of "couple hood". Kate had Colin hovering over her. At his mother's house, loving couples practicing the art of sex via computer tutorials were not what Ryan expected to see. Even these older folks sharing a beer and holding hands on the beach were in Ryan's face, showing him what he was missing. His brain was saturated with memories and lost hopes and dreams. Ryan opened one eye and peered below him. The geeky guy was rubbing sunscreen on his lady's practically exposed breasts. He was whispering in her ear, obviously something naughty, judging by the way she tittered. With a big, heavy sigh, a sudden realization hit Ryan hard, like the Maltese rock that had sucked the life out of him in that pounding surf. There would be no more touching Kate in that beautiful soft tanned spot between her breasts, or anywhere else on her lovely body, for that matter. There would be no more soaking up the sun, no floating on the ocean, no hot air balloon rides, no cycling, no running just to feel the wind in his face. There would be no more hugs from his mom.

That was a lot of *no mores*. And there were more. No beers, no guitar by campfires, no drumming 'til his fingers bled. No more highs from playing in a pipe band. *No more, no more, no more.*

No more lovemaking. Ever.

The world was still beautiful, especially his beloved Prince Edward Island with its red soil cliffs, patchwork green farmland, salty ocean air and sandy seashell-ed beaches. But Ryan had to admit that for all the adventure he had sought and loved, and the freedom he desired from responsibility and stress, he was now more trapped than ever. He was now just a bystander—untouchable, unreachable, *unlovable*.

Loneliness, sudden and sharp, gutted him. Its jagged slices were becoming too much to bear.

Ryan wrapped his arms around himself, closed his eyes again and prayed for the pain to disappear. To vanish, like the lives of those he loved who'd left his grasp the day he died.

chapter *Twenty-two*

With her right forefinger, Catherine spun the tiny propeller of the toy metal Spitfire airplane she kept on her office desk. It reminded her of the young flyers who trained in Summerside in the early 1940s. She and Kate once had a hearty chat about the air base and its history. A little nugget that had been gifted to Catherine, a relative's Second World War pilot's logbook, had ignited an insatiable flame of curiosity. The days when Air Force uniform blues took over their town, many local families got involved. They took in flyers, gave them rooms to live in. They hosted dances and gave up some of their local women to romance—to men from all over the world. They gave up their boys to the fight.

Ryan had joined in the discussions, but his interests were more Spartan. He preferred ancient history. Catherine called him her *old soul*. In some ways wise beyond his years. The Maltese Islands had been added to the kids' travel itinerary because Kate was determined to see it, to absorb the tough spirit that kept the locals going during repeated overhead dog fights. It was a time that weighted the people who lived there with more death than anyone deserved to witness. They were just ordinary villagers eking out simple existences until the war devastated them.

Neither Kate nor Catherine had imagined they would lose their own beloved young adventurer on Gozo during peacetime. Sometimes Catherine, always thinking too much about otherworldly spiritual things, would picture Ryan as one of those young Spitfire pilots. He died on an island that was no stranger to losing young men in the prime of their lives, fighting for liberty.

Maybe Ryan had been there before. Maybe he had a tie to the land and sea in the Maltese Islands that he could not escape.

Catherine still hadn't been able to bring herself to contact Kate. Email was too robotic, plain—you couldn't *feel* through email. By telephone—well, there wasn't much point. Catherine and likely Kate, too, would just break down and cry. She often pictured the two of them on either end of the phone, gasping and sobbing. It wouldn't do much good and nothing important would get said. So, she just waited. One day Kate would come home, and they would cry over Ryan together.

She gave the little propeller on her desk another spin. Watched it lose its life force, and move slower, slower, stop. She wished again and again that she and the kids could have said their goodbyes. That she could have had the chance to wish Kate and Ryan well on their journey.

She knew that was why Kate had yet to call her. She knew that was why she stayed on Gozo, working in some café. Because she was afraid to face Catherine. Because the indomitable spirits of the island rocked her, somehow. The dead pilots caressed her and eased her pain. Ryan was now a part of the island's tragic history; he had tenure there. He died young; his spirit was deeply rooted in the land and in its wild, comforting sea.

Jack had done the best he could to support Catherine over the last few months. But since she had gone so deep inside herself, life had become a day-to-day existence. He brought groceries home every few days, just enough to feed them for a day or two, as if neither of them had the strength to make a decision so important as what to eat in three days. That was generally the extent of what they talked about: food, and sometimes house cleaning. They did not talk about Ryan, or Kate, although Catherine always checked to see if Kate had emailed Jack. She read the brief emails, but it usually took her a few hours to get up the guts to do so and a few hours to slide down the mountain on the other side. She dreaded the day the email would say that Ryan's lost body had been dredged up by some fisherman. For now, she could almost convince herself that he was just still travelling.

The lack of communication between Jack and Catherine had worsened over the last few months. What had really changed from before, however, was that Catherine had given up the thoughts of leaving Jack that had permeated her mind beforehand. She didn't have the energy to consider starting a new life right now. Before, she had tired of Jack's incessant passive defensiveness. He always seemed to think she was picking on him. She couldn't mention a single complaint or vent about something that bothered her or needed to be done without him somehow getting quiet or rolling his eyes or just sighing and turning his head. He was a good man, the driveway got shovelled and the grass got mowed, but a woman needs a place to vent and if it's not to her partner, then where is it? For a woman working in a solitary environment, it was like trying to meditate inside a volcano. Catherine was going snaky from frustration. She kept so much inside that her stomach roiled.

All. The. Time.

Yet she continued to live inside that big box of hers.

Trapped. Alone. Sad.

Their sex life had diminished rapidly. They'd always had good sex, and Jack had been very patient since Ryan's accident. He treated Catherine with kid gloves. He rubbed her gently, she allowed him to do that, although she always turned her head away from him. They would fall asleep like that, his hand on her soft fur or cupped lovingly over a breast. But he hadn't had much satisfaction otherwise. He tried, and occasionally Catherine allowed him in, but mostly sex ended up just being another source of frustration for the two of them.

Flipping through the erotica websites was truly an exercise in research, for sex and in consideration of future paycheques. Catherine didn't have much get up and go when it came to writing and working these days, but Jack had been hinting lately that money was soon going to be a problem if she didn't start bringing some in. He wasn't overly concerned that she was so quiet. He rather liked silence, although lately the silence was more like dead air. Jack missed Catherine's bubbly, sometimes wacky discourses. Instead of trying to start an easy chat, one day he simply expressed to her that money was getting a bit tight. She had wondered, because he didn't buy as many fudgey-chocolate cookies or tortilla chips and salsa as he used to. He was just buying the essentials these days. Her stomach clenched harder, and she wrapped her arms around her belly. Didn't meet his eye.

One morning Catherine felt a little better than usual because she had dreamed about Ryan—they'd been together, just sitting around talking, and it felt like he was close to her somehow. So she summoned some energy, laid a blanket over her lap to dispel the mid-September early-morning cool, and started searching for new erotica magazine options to query.

The erotica idea had come out of the craziness that was her fractured mind these days. A few years ago, she'd been in a secondhand bookstore with Ryan, and they'd spotted a book about writing women's erotica. Ryan teased her mercilessly that day. She was a writer, after all. Catherine was a hero to him. Ryan figured his mom could write just about anything, although he thought if she tried to write science fiction or fantasy the resulting story would be completely wacko since she didn't know a thing about those genres.

Catherine first started investigating the erotica magazines because she hadn't been having any luck with her usual freelance standbys. She had a couple stories to finish for a few of them, but she couldn't think of any new ideas. This happened, sometimes, even when things were good and she didn't feel challenged as a writer. Now, in her somewhat uncaring I-just-don't-give-a-shit-anymore present state of mind, the idea of using her imagination to come up with boring new story ideas seemed as dull as eating potatoes every day for supper. How many different ways could she put potatoes on the table? Boiled, mashed, roasted, baked, fried...blah blah blah.

Catherine needed to put her record on a new loop. She needed a spark to light her up and get her motivated. She wanted to braid the tail of a wild horse. Hell, the tails of a herd of wild horses! So, just for fun, she'd tuned in to the erotica sites.

At first, she was really just curious, more than anything. Being the good Catholic, she'd never looked at these types of sites before. She'd certainly never bought the used book that day in the bookstore with Ryan! But even then, her curiosity was piqued. Truthfully, she might have bought the book if her son wasn't watching over her shoulder.

"I suppose now I can buy whatever I want," she figured rightly, saying the words aloud to an uninterested, dozing Oliver stretched out on the desk in front of her. "Sad. And weird."

At first, the sites Catherine visited under a general search for erotica were rather nice. The images were artistic, beautifully posed and lovingly lit with the soft glow of radiant light. They celebrated the physical manifestation of love within a couple's union. But the deeper she looked, the more shocked and surprised Catherine became. She soon discovered that there was a very fine line between erotica and pornography. Some of the images and videos were downright disgusting. In some cases, she was grateful that viewers had to pay a subscription fee to become members to watch full-length videos, because the short freebies that she researched were, well, disturbing. *Watching whole videos will be downright sickening*, she thought.

She went back to the photographs. Some were quite lovely. Pictures featuring women in casual reclining poses with their blouses separated to reveal just enough cleavage to be considered beautiful. Photos of sultry-faced, blue-eyed, tawny-haired twenty-somethings with perfectly rounded smooth breasts. *Probably airbrushed*, Catherine thought. Those shots didn't bother Catherine. She compared herself to those women and thought she had pretty nice breasts herself for a woman in her forties. The disturbing shots were the ones of the girls with their legs spread open and their fur shaved off so the viewer could see everything they had down there. Some of the women were touching themselves. This aroused a strange, complex set of emotions in Catherine. She was so intrigued, repulsed, disgusted, and yet turned on that she didn't bother to wheel around to look at the cat-kens, who were going a little berserk behind her. The cats did that sometimes...odd.

The images of men didn't do as much for Catherine as the pictures of women. This bothered her. She didn't think it had anything to do with hidden desires to be with a woman, as she had heard some women harboured, but instead she figured it just reminded her of her own body. She caught herself thinking that Jack would probably like to come home some evening and find her in bed, or on the bed, naked, with one hand on her breast and the other—down there. Legs open.

Heat rushed up into her cheeks when she thought of this. "Whatever," she mused aloud. "Call it research."

She continued contacting the erotica magazines to see whether there might be something she could write for them. She was so deep inside her mind anyway, so removed from church and society these days, that the only person she figured she would hurt would be herself.

Erotica was supposed to be beautiful. Some of the written stories Catherine studied were blatant, outright porn. They contained descriptions that repulsed Catherine and would probably disgust most people. Some would likely even bother some of the guys out there in the real world. Bizarre, irregular Lesbian encounters, husbands watching their women have wild sex with fantasy men—Catherine read some of them, and then closed those sites and continued searching elsewhere. Some websites were actually pretty good. Some were even Christian-based and encouraged couples to have a healthy sex life as a benefit to marriage.

I suppose that makes sense, Catherine thought, sitting back. *After all, a healthy sex life is written about in the Bible.*

On the better sites, women modelled tasteful lingerie, and in these shots the models' heads and breasts were lightly airbrushed to prevent recognition.

The more Catherine read, the more she secretly started to wish Jack would come home early. She smiled and sent query emails to three of the new magazines she found that day. It wasn't until the next morning that she realized she hadn't thought about Ryan as much as usual. As far as Jack went, well, they still didn't speak much. But the nights after Catherine did erotica *research*, they shared late suppers they cooked together. *Very* late suppers. The *post-coitus* late kind.

Jack figured his good luck was not worth questioning. He didn't know what had shifted, but he accepted it gratefully. He welcomed the change with a smile the size of Ryan's the year before when the pipe band won the North American Pipe Band Championships in Maxville.

For the first time in forever, Catherine started going to bed without her stomach hurting.

chapter *Twenty-three*

A few days later Jack said to Catherine, "Things are always beeping at me."

It was a Saturday morning. Jack had been outdoors cleaning up around the yard while Catherine slept in. This was a routine they maintained almost from the beginning of their relationship. Jack was an up-at-five-o'clock kinda guy, and Catherine needed (loved?) her sleep, so Jack always found something to do in the early mornings while Catherine put in earplugs (in the new house every sound resonated, a cupboard door, the shower, the metal paint bucket Jack used to scoop kitty litter in the mornings—she could hear his toast popping) and dozed 'til eight or nine. On this particular Saturday, Jack had the lawn mowed, the birdhouses filled with seed, the first leaves of fall raked into see-through bags, and the shed organized into sections by the time Catherine got up. Some of Ryan's things Jack pulled out and delicately placed into the back of his car, awaiting disposal. They hadn't talked about this, but these were things Ryan had never touched since Jack's introduction into the family. Old goalie pads, a ramshackle hockey net that Jack disassembled, broken hockey sticks. Ryan hadn't played hockey since he was thirteen, on his mother's suggestion that it was getting too rough and he *oughta try something else*. He had taken up snowboarding instead, and had only broken his wrist that one time, doing the trick that was way out of his league.

While Catherine showered, Jack made what he called "cowboy eggs." He cut out the centre of a slice of toast and fried an egg in the middle of it. He always put lots of butter in the pan first, but only because Catherine always growled at him for using oil. Oil on bread equals *gross*! Catherine would never admit to loving the cowboy eggs, but this was a part of Jack she adored. That he cooked funny things like cowboy eggs. Jack was a *do-er*. He made the neatest meals, meals that never ascribed to any rules about cooking. The cowboy eggs came from him riding the rodeo circuit when he was Ryan's age, even though the eggs likely had nothing at all to do with the rodeo. Jack's way of sentimentalizing the old glory days, Catherine figured. She pictured him in weathered leather chaps and a dusty hat, longer hair tickling his shirt collar, muddy boots kicking up dirt. A beer in one hand and a rope in the other. Cowboy eggs. An old rodeo guy. That was Jack.

"The girls must have loved him when he was a teenager," Catherine told Ryan and Kate once. Kate blushed sweetly (the girls still loved Jack) and Ryan grinned, happy that his "single" mom finally had a "friend."

Catherine was infamous for long, drawn-out showers. "Best time for a writer to write," she'd say. "A whole novel once downloaded in my head when I was in the shower. Every word!"

Jack was patient. He cut up slices of apple and placed them on Catherine's plate. Made it all pretty by tucking orange slices in between. Didn't slide the cowboy egg onto her plate until she slipped onto the stool at the kitchen island. Set the maple syrup by her place so it would be ready (she'd pour it over the bread part). Poured her a small glass of cranberry juice, watered down, of course, to cut down on sugar. Vacuum-pressed her a coffee. Timed it to the second.

With this kind of painstaking care and attention, Catherine didn't dare ask for more favours than just butter in the pan, although she drew the line at Jack putting a pat of butter over her jam on the side of toast he made for her. That was one of Jack's little idiosyncrasies, that he didn't follow the unwritten rule where the butter always goes on the bread first.

But that was Jack. Overall, his breakfasts were worth waiting for.

After cutting up her cowboy egg, Catherine scrolled through the news on her phone while she chewed (she used to read the horoscopes but that didn't seem to make sense anymore, since they hadn't warned her about losing Ryan).

Jack looked up from scrolling through the weather on his phone. He was obsessed with the weather App. That's when he said it. "Things are always beeping at me."

He was looking at Catherine rather curiously, as if he wanted her to explain why. She straightened up and cocked her head, listened for beeps. She smiled. Jack was odd. He would hardly speak for days, and then—poof—this. He came up with the most ridiculous things at the most mundane times.

"The microwave, the timer on the stove, the dryer, the clock radio, now even the new washing machine beeps when it's finished."

Hmmm. "Honey, I think that's a buzz," she replied with a hint of a smile.

Jack reflected on that for a moment, then nodded in agreement.

"Things are always buzzing and beeping at me."

Catherine put her phone down. Looked at the remains of her juice. Blinked. "So, what do you want to do about it?"

"I think we should buy a sailboat."

Catherine's heart jumped. Kate and Ryan used to talk about getting a sailboat someday. There was that, and then there was the fact that sailing meant being out on the ocean, in the Northumberland Strait. Logistically Catherine knew that Ryan's body, wherever it was, was very far away. But she also knew that she would always think of him aimlessly floating somewhere, if she were out on a boat looking into the water.

She put her fork down and sat back. Looked at Jack with sinking shoulders as the nascent light in her eyes dimmed to almost zero.

He shrugged. Took in a breath. "Sailboats are peaceful things," he tried.

"We're amateurs," Catherine managed to sputter. "What about rigging the thing? Repairs?"

"I know Joe. Joe will help. He's had a boat down at the dock for years."

"What about money?"

Jack leaned both elbows on the kitchen island. Stared at Catherine, waited for her to look up so he could peer into her eyes. He assessed her for signs of flight. She was white knuckling the edges of the counter, but so far she was hanging on. Listening. "I'll sell some land. I heard Linkletter's son is getting into potatoes. He's already asked me about that parcel I own in Wellington."

Jack must really want to start sailing, thought Catherine. He had always, always maintained that he would never sell any of his land. Besides, land prices on PEI right now were the pits.

Little did Catherine know; Jack had an ulterior motive. Sailing, which Jack knew Catherine enjoyed, would get her outdoors, and help her overcome her fear of the ocean. She would begin to look at the water in a respectful but less fearful way.

The chances of them running into a body were infinitesimally slim.

Too slim, Catherine frowned grimly, thinking of Ryan's body indiscriminately floating somewhere in the deep, dark Mediterranean. *Will we ever be able to really put Ryan to rest?*

There were a few weeks left of the sailing season. Already local owners who had enjoyed the summer were considering trips to the New England states to purchase bigger boats. Jack's friend Joe had a line on a quaint, classic twenty-seven-foot C&C that was going up for sale. The owners, an Acadian man and his partner whose kids wanted to bring friends sailing, had already bought a proud thirty-seven-foot Beneteau with more sleeping space.

Jack gave him a call.

Soon they were invited out for a sail to test drive the C&C. Joe brought his wife, Brianna, a kind redheaded woman who was no stranger to initiating conversation, and the four of them took the boat out for an inaugural journey. Catherine didn't look into the water any more than she could help it, because when she did her heart started to pound and she thought she was going to throw up. Brianna, figuring she was seasick, offered her new friend an anti-nausea bracelet. Catherine declined, respectfully, and tried to enjoy the fluid glide of the pretty white boat over the water in Summerside Harbour and out in the Strait. Jack gave her little jobs to do, like footing the jib and tidying up lines. They drank beer and cranberry coolers and were grateful to their affable friends for the fun sailing lessons and happy chatter, which filled the silences taking up so much space between them.

Next summer they would take a trip to the Bras D'Or lakes in Cape Breton. Maybe in July they would overnight in Shediac, New Brunswick, and later in the summer sail in the race to the Confederation Bridge. They would spend all their spare moments sailing, and Catherine could begin to let Ryan go.

Catherine knew Jack's intention in buying the boat. It was simple, and as old as time. *Get 'er back on the horse that threw 'er.* Old rodeo guy indeed.

They got back to the dock safely after that first sail, and genuinely smiled at each other for the first time in a while. Joe and Brianna invited Catherine and Jack out for beer and wings at The Lucky Bar on Water Street and, despite the tacky dollar-store décor, they went. A few people they knew popped by to say hello.

The entire day, not a soul had the guts to bring up Ryan's name, even though it was written in every set of moist, questioning eyes and in every caring, breaking heart.

That night at home while Jack brushed his teeth and Catherine scooped kitty litter out of the box in the corner of the upstairs bathroom (Jack did the mornings and Catherine did the nights), they named the boat. They called it *Hope Floats,* after one of Catherine's favourite Sandra Bullock movies. Heck, Jack would have let Catherine call it *Pigshit* if she wanted to. Or *Arsehole,* like he called most drivers on single-lane Walker Avenue outside their quiet cul-de-sac. She'd let him buy the boat. She'd gotten on it with him. In Jack's books, that was what it meant to heal.

He joked about having sex on the sailboat. Catherine forgave him because it gave her some story ideas for one of the new erotica magazines.

The day had been okay, overall. Considering.

The night was downright memorable.

chapter *Twenty-four*

The first time Kate allowed Colin to stay overnight was a disaster, plain and simple. Some of Ryan's things were still tossed here and there around the little apartment, for fear that if they were moved a part of him would be gone too. It was silly, Kate knew, but by moving those things—a pair of flip-flops; a bunch of papers he'd printed off the net about the Running of the Bulls in Pamplona, Spain; his shampoo, soap, and shaving things in the bathroom—he would leave her, bit by bit, one object at a time. Ryan himself had placed them, left them. His grace was on every bit of those everyday things; apart from Kate, he was the last person to touch them, to squeeze the tube of toothpaste, to stick his tanned toes in the flip-flops.

Sometimes Kate grazed a finger over them, over the strap on the summer shoes or over the plastic of the toothbrush. She tried to feel Ryan's fingers under hers when she really needed his presence and so delicately laid her hand on them, and sometimes she laid her head on the sandals or on the papers when she needed to cry for him.

Colin understood her angst when she cried out to him and begged him not to move the sandals from the floor on Ryan's side of the bed. So, he withdrew his hand and let them be. But as nice a Scot as he was, it was really hard to imagine that Kate had kept Ryan's shaving cream, shampoo, and soap. Toothbrush and toothpaste? *Weird. Seriously weird.*

Colin alternated between shameful bursts of deep jealousy, like should he even be envious of a dead guy? And feeling weirded out that she still kept the dead guy's things around. *That* was simply morbid.

Kate ought to be getting over him by now.

In the end, Colin's desire for sex with this woman he had come to adore won out. He pushed all other strange thoughts from his mind, and tentatively, intimately brushed his lips over hers. Kate let him, but only because she could close her eyes and picture Ryan on the bed next to her. It worked for a while, maybe because her mind remembered Ryan's essence and the feel of him, but every guy's touch is different, and so when Kate ran her hand up Colin's forearm and was shocked by feeling a hairy Scotsman instead of her sweet, tanned drummer, her eyes burst open, and she pulled away. It wasn't yet dark, and that drove the knife in deeper, but Colin was into it and Kate didn't have the heart to be alone *even so,* so on the outside she smiled and pretended everything was okay while inside she cried like a baby and counted the seconds until Colin finished and enough time went by so she could send him home.

She faked her orgasm and turned her face towards the wall so Colin couldn't see the tear that finally leaked out. It wouldn't do to let him see the watery trail crawling slowly down her soft, lonesome cheek.

chapter *Twenty-five*

One night, completely out of the blue, when Catherine hadn't been thinking about Ryan (at least not at that moment), she had the most insane release. She attributed the mind-blowing orgasm to writing those articles for the erotica magazines. She wasn't writing fantasy crap, or wishful sex stories, but instead was trying to write about the beauty inherent in a loving relationship, the female and male bodies as art forms, the natural desire to reproduce. Her articles were tasteful, educational, and inspirational for new couples as well as for marriages stuck in a demoralizing down-cycle. Her research was thorough and professional, and she had quickly learned which websites to avoid for their porn content and which books to order for their pedagogical style.

There was something empowering about writing erotica. The stuff worth reading screamed equality. Age, race, appearance, status—those things were equal. Many sorts of women were stars in their own sensuous stories. Catherine's narratives and articles always featured some inner version of herself instead of some twenty-year-old blonde goddess. That one small resolve was empowering. Catherine always straightened her back and raised her head, just a little, when she was writing for the erotica sites and magazines.

At first, she would find herself blushing while she worked, but then after a few contracts (and payments) she gladly accepted that part of herself, and she looked to the heavens and thanked God for allowing men and women to love each other intimately, powerfully, physically.

Lo and behold, Catherine only had Jack to practice on, so rock and roll! He floated in his own little heaven.

At first, Catherine was still shy and reserved. *He's my experiment. Let's keep this in perspective.*

But she soon learned that through their physical intimacy grew a slow, delicate, deeper love for each other. Building blocks. She had always thought it was more natural for it to be the other way around. Love should come *first,* through the little things they did for each other during the day (more him doing things for her, lately). That way she would feel closer to him, and thus be a more willing participant in their lovemaking. It was astounding to her that by participating in the lovemaking first, they would grow closer as a couple. A real woman-in-her-forties revelation.

Jack had always known that. It just took Catherine a while to figure it out.

The crazy orgasm came as a complete surprise. Catherine did okay with Jack, she always "went off," as he called it; he was a gentle, caring lover whose soft caresses drove more than just her crazy cats to ecstasy. But there was something about that night, a few nights after they'd pulled the sailboat out of the water and parked it under the trees in their yard for the winter season so Jack could sit in the cozy lime-and-lemon-hued dining room, sip his mint tea, and stare contemplatively at his big toy during the sure-to-come Nor'easters that winter. The night of the big O, sailing and the planned trip to Cape Breton next summer were on Catherine's mind, since Jack was already planning for it in his obsessive research way. For once he was not afraid to talk, so suddenly there was hope beyond just the next immediate twenty-four hours, and it offered release. Along with it came some kind of peace—not total, encompassing peace, but at least the most peace Catherine had felt since Ryan's unexpected death robbed her of any kind of hope for tranquility.

On the downside, the release ushered in by that magical orgasm came with tears, purifying, gut-wrenching, anguished, fist-soaked tears. It was like some angry demon that had taken over her soul since the loss of Ryan absolutely hated the peace Catherine had so recently started to ease into, and wanted NONE OF IT. It demanded escape, and with its almost violent retreat some deep hidden recessed part of Catherine tore free. It came in a sudden, heartbreaking, Niagara Falls whitewash of tears.

The big O brought with it the most incredible relief Catherine had ever dreamed possible, well-earned after losing Ryan and earned too for the tough years before that of trying to prove her worth to the world, to Ryan, to Jack and, mostly, to herself. The cry that was her initial release had transmogrified into Catherine's very own personal wailing wall.

Jack didn't really get it, or maybe he did on some level, because he didn't run, which was a shocker when Catherine thought about it later. This was a guy who never stayed in a room to finish a discussion. Once any topic got even a wee bit heated, Jack turned and left. While the big O cleansed Catherine in great hulking sobs, Jack held her, although he was as useless as she when it came to trying to stopper the pain that poured forth.

Embarrassed, Catherine choked in his arms as she tried to stop, but her body wouldn't let her. Her demon was crying out to be free. It was begging, beseeching, and then—becalming.

Going, going—

Gone.

Catherine gave in, let the big O carry her away to some unknown place where she could cry out her anguish in peace. Jack held her, fearful at first, before he settled into her.

Catherine couldn't see, and really, she wouldn't have wanted to, but Jack's eyes were moist with his lover's grief.

The big O had long subsided by the time Catherine's body lay weak and limp in her man's arms. She needed a tissue, but neither she nor Jack saw fit to retrieve one. Surely if they moved, something sacred would be jarred and perhaps lost.

This, Catherine caught herself thinking, *THIS* is what I am writing about. *This* is what living, what LIFE, is.

They were as one, inextricably entwined, irrevocably alive.

The night of the big O, Catherine nestled deeper into the musky cave of her good man's arms, feeling protected and secure for the first time in forever. She and Jack were sailors that made it to safe harbour, after doing thirty knots against the current in a storm.

They would be okay—if they could just keep each other afloat.

chapter *Twenty-six*

Ryan had always had a special kind of faith. Special because it came from everywhere, which is the best kind. You couldn't grow up as the son of Catherine and not retain some kind of spirituality. He'd usually attended church with her on Sundays, but they weren't the all-pious-say-grace-at-mealtime types. In the last couple of years, Jack contributed in his own breezy way—his church was nature. To him, the Father, Son, and the Holy Ghost sign of the cross was said "spectacles, testicles, wallet and watch." He'd borrowed it from some old movie about nuns. Or maybe it was a Monty Python thing, Jack was always spouting the irreverent dialogue of those crazy Brits.

Ryan had hung out with the kids in the youth group but didn't make it a thing to spend his Friday nights being indoctrinated at the parish hall. At Easter one year, he and his mom got seats in the back row at a drama presentation at the non-denominational community church, and another year he went to sleepovers at the Church of the Nazarene, where music was a big deal and he could play the drums. And where the cute girl from his tenth-grade English class hung out. He diligently researched the Bahá'í faith, which seemed to believe that all churches and prophets led to the Bahá'í.

The thing is, at first this whole dying thing had seemed like the greatest adventure of all. With just the blink of an eye, you could be anywhere you wanted to be—even where you shouldn't be, sometimes. Ryan was careful now when he dropped in on Kate, choosing his time in Gozo with great attention. He didn't like seeing her with the big Scots dude—that was destroying him. He would wait for Kate forever.

But he wasn't certain she was waiting for him.

Ryan couldn't go back. There was no dial he could twist to change the frequency in this bizarre new game. Yet, it seemed there was also no way to go forward. He couldn't think himself into floating through a tunnel with golden light and a host of waiting departed ancestors at the end. There was no rainbow bridge he could cross into a beautiful meadow filled with frolicking pets. There was no new body his soul could step into around the corner; no 1930s jazz club or 1950s rock-n-roll tour he could physically manifest his body into. He could visit them, sure, and he did, with gusto! Sitting on the crossbeams of a club's rafters offered the best view of all—or sometimes Ryan hopped around the stage, taking up space beside the drummer and playing along with him or accompanying Elvis on the air guitar. What a rush! There was nothing like it! And it was merciful—music helped Ryan *forget*.

Ah, the strange floating days. A trap! A seemingly endless, mystical, surreal, heartache of a trap!

Prayer occupied a lot of Ryan's time.

Pleas for forgiveness for all the little wrongs Ryan figured he'd ever done in his life ("I am too narcissistic. Everything is always about me, about MY desires"), or voicing a
desire for some kind of unstuck future got emphatically sent
to whatever spiritual deity Ryan figured would listen. Sometimes he prayed from atop the lifeguard chair on the south
shore of Prince Edward Island at Chelton Beach, watched
the sunrise, and sometimes he was still there when it dipped
down beyond the peaceful horizon somewhere over New
Brunswick across the Northumberland Strait. Other times
he found a comfortable red sandstone rock at Cavendish, or
in Darnley or Thunder Cove on the north shore.

The "teacup rock" sandstone formation was a favourite.
So many tourists taking pictures, wandering down to find
the famous rock with its narrow base and wide top. They'd
climb stupidly over the rocks while Ryan cringed and held
his breath. Once he whispered in a boy's ear, "Don't climb
underneath the rocks on the cliff because the sandstone
is unstable and sometimes it gives," which the kid found
out the hard way because he didn't listen to Ryan and he
climbed anyway, and yeah, a rock gave way and crushed the
kid's leg. Lucky he wasn't killed. "I mighta had someone
to talk to, at least," Ryan considered glumly, but watching
the mom cry and the dad worry and the sister scream was
enough for Ryan to shove his loneliness away and pray for
a safe and quick recovery for the kid. At least the day was
exciting. Ryan helped the EMTs by whispering in their ears
which dirt road to take that would get them closest to the
kid; it took a few tries, but he finally found one whose spirit and mind were open enough to hear him. Thank God. It

took hours but they finally got the boy off the remote area of the beach to a waiting ambulance above.

Beaches were awesome places to pass the endless days, even in the freezing, gusty winter, when Ryan could traverse the ice built up along the shore in magnificent, craggy, statuesque patterns. Floating on ice cakes and jumping from one to another (largest to smallest—might as well make it interesting!) was a favourite pastime. Strolling the high cliffs with a coyote or a silver fox was amazing—so cool to see where they go, what they eat! Sometimes gross, but whatevs. Nature. Wow.

Hands down, though, summer topped winter for the sheer pleasure of people watching. Hanging around tourists while they built their uneven, yet still majestic, sandcastles on the beach was epic. What freedom they thought they had, those families from Toronto or Montreal or New York or Boston. Their entire holidays, one week or sometimes two if they were lucky, consisted of stays in overpriced cabins near Cavendish, or maybe in Brackley or Stanley Bridge, and laden-down trips to the beach towing floaties that were dangerous on a windy day 'cause they could so easily get tossed over or blown out to sea (*but why would they know that? They live in cities*), and meals of expensive lobster rolls and overpriced fish and chips.

"Or cheeseburgers...oh God, what I would give for one last cheeseburger grilled by Jack..."

Thinking about it one night in early summer, Ryan licked his lips. "Maybe this isn't heaven after all," he wondered aloud. "Maybe it's..." Ryan pushed the heinous thought aside and stopped sliding pictures of cheeseburgers through the old-time movie in his mind. He went back to watching flip-flop-wearing tourists craft sandcastles.

With boundless enthusiasm and focused attention, they bent over their sandy creations. Some of the work was pretty good—Ryan sauntered around all the castles in the evenings, the best time to view such outdoor art, when the sun was going down and thus created a magnificent play of light and shadow in the miniature doors and archways. The brand-new sandcastles had stairs, and little carved-out doors, and seaweed lining their perimeters. Some had min-iscule shells and tiny stones marking walkways and win-dows, and others, if they were close enough to the gently lapping waves, even had rivulets of water in their moats.

Most fun was listening to the super creative little kids. One little blonde girl sang a story the whole time she patted sand and placed seashells; her tale was so vivid and real that Ryan decided she was retelling a past life from maybe the fourteenth or fifteenth century, when she was, who knows, maybe the daughter of some king? She was absolutely cer-tain about where the horse barns were and the family cem-etery and even a river by the woods, and she was only about six, so she was way too young to *really* know those things. When she tried to build a church steeple, Ryan knew for sure. He just wished her older brother would listen to her, because they got into a fight about where to put the church and the girl was inconsolable when the brother kicked over a low shell-lined "stone" wall. Seemed some inside soul-part of the little girl missed her past life, or the people in it, even though she didn't really understand.

Oh, the mystery. "Will I ever really understand, either?" Ryan whispered to the sea breeze. "Will any of us?"

As the tide came in each evening, the magical little castles with their fantasy lives disappeared, one grain of sand at a time. Sometimes when this happened Ryan couldn't stay to watch.

Sometimes he made himself stay.

As the days passed by, so too did summer holidays. Dreams born and shared on the beaches on divine Prince Edward Island went the way of the castles—memories swallowed up by tides and time.

chapter *Twenty-seven*

This couldn't be all there was. These were just weird, in-between days. There must be a magical future awaiting Ryan, one that would dissolve this dreary, lonely phase in his sort-of life.

Ryan had discovered through trial and error that some folks sensed his presence. It was a little disconcerting. They would get a sudden chill when he walked by and, if he was too close to them, they would shudder. To Ryan these reactions were just another slap in the face, more reminders of how alone he really was. On sticky, dog days of summer, the beach was crazy busy during the daytime. In the evenings he could take his solitary little wander and more easily avoid running into people. Once he had gotten up the guts to actually walk through someone. For him, it was an odd feeling, more psychologically edgy than anything. Reminded him of the day Oscar the cat-ken jumped through him. *Whoosh!* His unsuspecting test subject, a young dude around Ryan's age, hardly reacted at all, although a strange expression passed over the guy's face and he wiped his arms off a few times as if they were covered in sticky cobwebs. Ryan thought about how unsuspecting people really were. Cool extra-dimensional things were happening around them all the time, and they weren't even aware! If they paid attention to the little things, the subtle nuances of their beings, they would know something really surreal was up.

On one particular evening, only a few sandcastles dotted the beach. There was also a nude sand-mermaid sculpted by some creative wannabe Picasso. Its breasts were unevenly sized, one an apple and one a grapefruit, and its expression was a wide-eyed frown, warped and unflattering. Someone had stuck—and stupidly, uncaringly left—a beer can in the sand nearby. Despite himself, Ryan laughed. Truth be told, it wouldn't have surprised him if the weird sea-sand creature was made by some of his friends. It was a Sunday, stinking hot, so the beach was busy all day. Tourists and locals left all kinds of human trash—more beer cans, pop bottles, and some chip bags that, buffeted on the wind, were colourful homages to their inattentive people.

Ryan even spotted a child's sneaker. "That kid's mom is going to be pissed when she gets home," he chuckled, remembering how scatterbrained he used to be in the living days.

This evening, wandering amongst the spotty litter carnage on one of the most beautiful places on earth, Ryan absentmindedly noticed an older man walking towards him. Tall and strong-boned, the guy was silhouetted in the liquid melon, pink-orange glow of the setting sun, so that his features were darkened and not readily distinguishable. As they approached each other near one particularly arcane sandcastle decorated with plastic straws and potato chips (and currently surrounded by two fighting seagulls bravely picking off the salty chips), Ryan stepped aside so that his presence wouldn't in any way startle the gentleman. As he did so, Ryan glanced over at the guy. The man was crowned with white hair, snowy white, in fact, longish, so that it curled around his ears and fell in waves almost to his shoulders. He was sixty-something, Ryan figured, probably a rich American judging by his well-made beige cable-knit sweater and creased cotton pants rolled up past his ankles. Rather distinguished, he strolled with his shoulders back instead of drooping discouragingly forward the way Ryan was walking. The man was carrying leather deck shoes in his right hand, and his skin seemed rather unweathered for anyone who might have spent any length of time on the beach. Ryan figured he had just gotten in, had probably driven the three hours over to the Island that afternoon after landing on a U.S. flight in Halifax, perhaps. Probably he had a rented sedan waiting for him in the parking lot above, a Lexus, or even better—a luxury SUV like a Range Rover.

As Ryan looked at this man, he became perplexed. Not only did the guy seem a little out of place here amongst the sand dunes, but there was something off about him that took Ryan a few moments to figure out. It was breezy there next to the Atlantic Ocean, so much so that the sand whipped softly around people's ankles and gusted sporadically up into their faces, so that they occasionally had to shield their eyes with upraised forearms. Ryan realized that the blowing sand was not bothering this man. Nor was his snowy hair in the least affected by the ocean breeze. Not a strand even so much as flickered in the wind.

Ryan's gaze shifted to the guy's feet. *He is not leaving a single footprint!*

The man's bare feet were not marking his path in the damp sand where the sandcastles were built. Other visitors sauntering this close to the surf had put on shoes to keep their feet from getting wet and cold. But this gentleman seemed unconcerned.

These things were remarkable to Ryan. He had been wandering alone for what seemed like forever, which was a long time to be left alone with one's thoughts, too long a period to go without touching or being touched by another human being or snuggled by a beloved pet. Too long to go without truly feeling the sand between your toes, or the soft ocean breeze in your hair. Too long to go without passing a word or sharing a thought with another soul.

Ryan's gaze drifted downwards, and he stared, baffled, at the man's feet, where a piece of seaweed blew *through his pale ankles*. With a gasp, Ryan took a step back and darted a look up into the strange man's face. So bizarre, so surreal— *the snowy-haired man was looking, with his ice-blue eyes, directly into Ryan's hazel peepers*. It seemed to Ryan that the older gentleman was peering intently into his soul.

It scared the living shit out of him.

The older guy was also surprised but didn't appear to be as shocked as Ryan. He guffawed with pleasure at having found a new friend.

Reflex. Ryan thrust his hand out and then, grinning, pulled it back. In the end, he decided he was thrilled beyond words. "Yeah, uh, oops—old habits are hard to break." He wondered if his voice sounded hoarse and croaky. He hadn't often spoken aloud in the last while.

The beach walker tossed his curls and laughed. "Yeah, I'd like to—shake your hand—but we'd likely just end up waving at each other like a couple of idiots."

Not as distinguished sounding as he looks, Ryan considered. *He has a decidedly East Coast accent.* Once Ryan got over his surprise, he decided the guy must actually have been a beach bum, a windsurfer or something. Probably he had died at work instead of on a board. That would explain his cotton pants and expensive sweater.

No-footprint-guy offered an introduction. He had a laidback way of speaking, almost a drawl. "My name's Dave. Good to see you—"

It took Ryan a while to respond. He stood, confused, with his hands on his hips, his face a spectrum of emotions as he sorted through this unexpected situation. "Ryan," he finally choked out. Flustered, amazed, and most of all, grateful, Ryan gawked at Dave. A whole range of emotions flooded his head; he got all fuzzy, out-of-control, woozy. He plopped down on the sand and landed on his butt. A soft wavelet touched his toes with what felt like a sense of runaway glee.

Ryan pulled his legs up and loosely hugged his knees. Looked up. "Am I dreaming? Is this a dream?"

Dave chuckled and shook his head, then happily lowered himself down beside Ryan. His face was easier to make out now that the sun was no longer behind him; Ryan was relieved to see the laugh lines running out from the creases of his eyes.

"Am I the first earthbound soul you've met?" Dave asked. "How long has it been since you crossed over?"

"Too long," Ryan groaned. "And yes. Uhhh—there are more?"

"Son, you've probably come across some, but in my experience, most are so wrapped up in themselves and in the lives they've departed that they are not approachable or aware."

This was news. Ryan braced himself and prepared to learn. Relief washed over him like one of the lacey whitecaps offshore. Finally, answers.

He hoped.

They talked like old friends for hours. Dave explained to Ryan that he'd met a number of others during his time in what Ryan called the floating days or the in-between days. He hadn't often met new souls, like Ryan, but had been fortunate enough to spend time with souls who had some experience and knowledge about what happened to them and, more importantly, what they felt was *going* to happen to them.

Ryan tripped over his words, trying to get his questions answered. One thing he decided for sure at this moment was that there was indeed a god, or a god-like or Divine Source entity. He felt this because he had spent so much time praying and now it seemed Dave had been sent to give him some answers. Maybe all that prayer had somehow helped Ryan evolve.

It was such a sweet, simple joy just to have someone to talk to. Dave was a gift.

The older man said that he could only remember parts of his life now. His earthly experiences were fading from his memory. He said, "When that starts to happen, it is a sign to souls that they are finding peace about where they are, who they were, and who they left behind. They develop an intuitive knowing that they will be fully crossing over soon, or going 'home,' as other soul-people call the mysterious place where they would all end up."

Dave went on to explain that eventually Ryan would be ready to let go of the things—more specifically, the people and places—keeping him earthbound. Dave had gleaned from knowing others the order of how this all worked. Those who were not quite ready to make the full crossover stayed for a while, until they finally realized they would not be forgotten by those who truly loved them, and that their loved ones would be okay to journey on without them. These were generally younger people. He said the seniors usually crossed right over directly after they died, probably because many of their loved ones had passed before them and they were more anxious to see them than they were worried about those they were leaving behind.

"But some people are very confused about their death," he continued. "So, it takes these folks a lot longer to make the full crossover. Decades. It simply takes them longer to adjust." There were those who were angry, really angry—who felt cheated out of life. They stayed and caused havoc on earth, frightening people by using their thoughts to smash windows and throw paintings and slam doors.

"Eventually they settle, too, though," Dave said. "Their memory banks clear over time, and they move on."

Dave had died a few years ago. He made his transition after the Cessna he was piloting took a frightening nosedive into Lake Ontario.

"What'd you do in your human life?" Ryan asked him.

"I made and sold surfboards," Dave answered with a wink and a chuckle.

"Ha!" Ryan laughed and clapped his new friend on the shoulder, even though Dave couldn't feel it. It just seemed like the right thing to do. "Just so you know, you still give off that vibe, man."

Dave grinned widely and lightly fingered his chin with his thumb and two fingers as the memory of who he was in the physical plane took hold. His eyes sparkled and dimmed. "Some things are hard to let go."

Ryan wasn't sure, but he thought a wistful sadness passed over the man's ruddy, pleasant face. "Guessing you surfed on the boards you built, too."

"Yeah, man." Dave's eyes lit up. He waved an arm at the ocean before them. "Not here, though. These tiny waves are like rippled chips. They're meant for casual dips."

Laughing, Ryan wholeheartedly agreed.

Dave told Ryan that the crash was now a foggy memory, for which he was rather grateful, because whenever he thought about it a crippling fear overtook him, likely the same fear he had felt just before dying. He had visited Prince Edward Island once, as a child. Its beauty and tranquility had always captivated him, and throughout his long career he always swore he'd go back; he'd take his family to the east coast on a vacation. But he never had. His job got in the way. His kids grew up and married, and his wife left him for her dentist because Dave spent too much time focusing on his business and travelling the world to surf the next big wave. None of those things mattered now. Time slipped by in the blink of an eye, and now that he realized how absolutely ludicrous his life goals had been, some element of healing clicked into place—some kind of vibrational step on a ladder, Dave supposed—and he finally gave himself a break, stopped hanging over his wife and kids, and decided to bask in the glory of the fabled little Island.

"You probably came across other souls on this little patchwork Island, and particularly on this beach," Dave said sternly to Ryan, his avid student, who was listening intently while he absently let sand he couldn't feel run through his fingers. "A lot of them come here during their transition. This place helps them begin to let go of their ties—Prince Edward Island is as beautiful and healing now as it was when they were living. Only now I guess they know to really enjoy it. Usually when they get here, they've passed a test in their in-between journey. You couldn't see them because you weren't there yet. Psychologically. Emotionally."

Ryan recounted a day when he had aimlessly wandered between the castles built of sand and the sand sculptures, a day when a child spoke to him. The little boy had walked by, small fingers firmly clasped in his father's, seemed to look Ryan in the eye, and said a simple, "Hello." The experience shocked Ryan, who looked behind him for someone else the child was probably talking to.

"So, he had crossed over too, then?" Ryan asked his new friend. "Or could he see me while he was alive? It was obvious his father couldn't. Had his father passed too?"

Dave explained that it had been his experience that living children who were very young could indeed see those who had crossed. "Pets, too," he added.

Ryan nodded and laughed. "I go home a lot to play with my cats."

Dave adjusted his seat in the sand. "My theory is that it's all about innocence. The young are not jaded by life yet. Their uninitiated minds still believe in the abstract because they haven't been taught not to believe. Yet."

Thinking of Grace, his young cousin, Ryan nodded. He yearned to make some kind of connection with home. He would go visit her.

But for now ... he and his new friend talked all night.

Eventually the lazy rose fingers of dawn broke on another serene and beautiful earthly day, washing the land and sea with splendid untainted elegance. Ryan felt such peace at the sky's pink hue on the sparkling, diamond sea that he closed his eyes and tilted his head upward. More than ever, it seemed that a sort of god was there, somewhere, calling him, waiting for him, and he felt such reassurance in Dave's presence and in the promise of pure energy and love that he lost himself for a bit.

Dave didn't know for certain what would happen to them, but he had seen people begin to lose their earthly memories of material possessions and jealousies and fears, and that omnipresent search for something better. And that was when those people began to disappear. They always had a peace about them when they went. Dave had never actually witnessed a crossover, but it seemed people knew when they were about to go. They always said goodbye in some small way, but never verbally. They always appeared a little luminous, had a kind of a natural sun-kissed glow about them. They seemed happy—before they went away.

Dave and Ryan promised to meet at the end of every day right there on Cavendish Beach. Together, they would watch the sun go down. During the day, they would continue to visit with their loved ones, studying them and mentally preparing themselves for the goodbyes before the anticipated journey ahead. Both men were still so attached to their earthbound lives that it seemed it would be some time before their final crossovers. They would have lots of time to get to know each other, to talk of the things that mattered, which were Dave's family and Ryan's mom, and—his Kate. They never talked about their *things*, just their people. It was the people that mattered.

The people, after all, were love.

chapter Twenty-eight

Little Grace lay in her small child's bed, curiously studying Ryan, who sat on the edge, his big feet and long legs resting out of place on the fuzzy pink princess rug that covered her red oak floor. Dawn was breaking through Grace's eastern window, and in the silent home Ryan could almost hear the sun squeak and stretch as it nudged open another day. Neither of them spoke for the longest time, as they contemplated each other's existence. Ryan fingered the tiny, heart-shaped grey rock he'd pulled from his pocket, the one Kate had given to him at the little cove in Gozo the day they'd gotten into so much trouble.

He looked up at Grace, who was frowning.

"I miss you when you'we not awound," she said.

"Hmmm. I see. I miss you too." Ryan grinned. He was overjoyed that, as Dave had led him to believe, she could see him. They could converse! Holy crap! Ryan thought wildly of all the time he'd missed—if he'd realized this was possible, he would have gotten out of his own head and paid much closer attention to kids.

"Are you staying fow bweakfast?"

"I don't think I can, little Grace. I wish I could." Oh, eggs, bacon, hash browns...Ryan REALLY wished he could stay! That he could taste ... salt. Grease. Butter!

Grace lay back against her pink lace pillow, looked up at him. He sighed, rubbed the smooth rock between his hands to soak up its energy, and held it out to his young cousin. "This," Ryan said, "is for you. It's sacred. You need to keep it special, in a very safe place."

Grace elbowed her way up and took the rock from Ryan. Studied it at length; turned it this way and that and ran a tiny finger over it. Ryan was grateful their hands hadn't touched. That would have been weird, had she noticed that her hand went right through his. He had held his breath, hoping that she could in fact hold the rock, that it wouldn't drop right through her hand. He'd told Dave that he intended to give her this gift, and the older man assured him that her innocence combined with his sincere intention would make it real to her. He had seen it happen.

The rock had been rubbed so often by Ryan as he thought of Kate and their fateful day in the kayaks that its once sharp edges had softened, and it was so smooth to the touch now that once Grace felt comfortable, she immediately and delightedly rubbed all her small fingers over it. That, and the fact that it was a gift from her cousin Ryan, made it very sacred indeed.

She held it close to her chest and smiled up at him. "It's a heawt," she breathed.

It took Ryan a while to regain his composure enough to speak. The rock was the only tangible physical connection to Kate he had left. But this was important. By giving

Grace the rock, he was assuring himself that he would not be forgotten, at least not in the near future. Grace held on to things. She would carry that rock with her everywhere, at least for a while, and maybe, if he was lucky, by the time she forgot about it, he would have completed his crossover.

A stirring from the master bedroom next door brought Ryan to his feet.

"I have to go, sweetheart," he said, and with careful intention brushed a thumb across her soft cheek, even though he couldn't feel her skin beneath his finger. It took everything he had in him not to reach out and grab the rock from Grace's small fingers. He swallowed painfully as he looked at it there, sublimely innocent. He hoped it wouldn't cause the little girl undue pain, if someone were to find it and ask her where it came from. Or for her to remember this experience, years later, and think she was crazy. He wondered if anyone had ever visited him like this when he was small.

Grace wanted a hug but Ryan explained that it wouldn't be possible. He told her he was sick, sort of, kinda like when they'd all had the flu one time and had to just wave at each other in church rather than shake hands like they usually did. She bought the fabrication and gave him the sweetest little wave and smile he'd ever seen. He was too choked up to speak, and left the room so that when he thought himself somewhere else, she wouldn't freak at his sudden disappearance.

Grace's mother Abby was on her way to the washroom. They sort of collided in the hallway while Ryan was looking back at Grace's room, and she freaked when she walked through him because she thought she'd walked through a spider web. While she was screaming and swatting at the nonexistent webs, looking for the spider that usually came with such sticky things as spider webs, Ryan FREAKED at the fact that his aunt was wearing a T-shirt and little panties with *Sunday* written in candy-floss colours across the back-side.

Groaning, he squeezed his eyes shut and thought himself at his mother's house. He sat on the edge of her bed for a while, watching her sleep while he thought about Dave, and Grace, and Kate's little heart-shaped rock. A bud of excitement formed inside him as he thanked God for answering his prayers, and for once he wondered peacefully what *home*—after he crossed fully over, beyond—was going to look like.

chapter *Twenty-nine*

Abby thought it was sweet of Grace to say Ryan had given her the rock. *You know how kids are,* she told her husband. Ray was concerned. It seemed a little odd that all this time after Ryan's death Grace would come up with this story about some random rock. Abby told him that probably Grace had dreamed about her cousin, and that was why today of all days she found this little rock in her room and decided it was a gift from Ryan.

That day, Grace spent her craft time at Sunday school learning how to draw hearts. It was a big conquest for her, but the little girl wanted to colour some in and then hang them in her room. She wanted to remember Ryan, so she surrounded herself with hearts. The daycare staff thought Grace's cousin must be a nice guy since Grace seemed so devoted to him. Grace showed everyone Ryan's rock, but she wouldn't let them touch it. A few weeks later, she misplaced it and was inconsolable until her father found it underneath her car seat in the van, where it had rolled after falling out of a loose pocket.

The day she showed Catherine the rock was a day Abby had been nervous about, since Grace was sticking to her story that it came from her lost cousin. They had gone to lunch at Jack and Catherine's house after church a few weeks after Ryan's visit, and while Catherine fried up bacon and eggs, Grace pulled *Rock* out of her pocket.

"Cathwin, do you like my wock?"

Catherine smiled down at the little girl. They had grown pretty close since Ryan's passing. Grace gave great hugs. "Oh, it's beautiful, honey." She reached down and ran a finger over the rock. "Neat. It's in the shape of a heart." Picking up a fork, she grabbed the handle of the frying pan to steady it while she flipped the bacon. "Step back a little, Grace, honey. Bacon grease is hot, and it spits."

"Wyan gave it to me."

Instead of flipping the bacon, Catherine's heart did a flip. A triple. The bacon lay forgotten on her fork and dripped fat into the pan. When she regained her composure, Catherine racked her brain to try to figure out when Ryan would have ever given Grace that rock. Ryan rarely went to the beach in PEI, and if he did it was to...kayak...not to lay on the beach or wander the shore looking for pretty stones.

Abby stepped in, covered her daughter's ears, and nervously whispered above Grace's head. "She misses him. She must have found the rock underneath her bed. It goes everywhere with her, just like her bunny baby. She sleeps with it."

Catherine nodded and smiled, and finally flipped the bacon over. She stood by the stove with her back to Abby and Grace and watched the meat sssst and fry. But Grace wasn't finished. Adults were always ending her conversations before she was done talking. She pulled on her aunt's skirt to get Catherine to look down.

"I asked him to stay for bweakfast, but he said he couldn't." Lovingly, Grace fingered the rock. "I wished that he could. He said he was sick. That's why he couldn't hug me."

The bacon sizzled away, forgotten again, while Catherine looked, stunned, at her four-year-old niece, who was staring up at her, moist eyes alight with innocence and pride.

The child's mother intervened a second time. "She's been telling stories. We're trying to teach her to tell the truth. We haven't been all that successful." Abby shrugged. "She's four."

The bacon fork was handed to Abby as Catherine bent down and looked Grace in the eye. "When did Ryan give you that rock, honey?"

Grace shored up her small shoulders. "When he was at my house."

"It must have been a long time ago."

"Yes. A long time." Grace punctuated the words with a succession of brisk nods. She smiled, remembering, and cocked her head. "Aftew, I went to church school and Jessie showed me how to dwaw heawts so I could wemember him bettew. I can dwaw them good now."

Intrigued, Catherine reached out and took the rock. Slowly, she turned it over in her fingers. A shot of energy bolted up her spine. The top of her head, her Crown Chakra, buzzed with electricity. Grace had only had Jessie for a teacher at Sunday School since she had moved up to the five-year-old room. That was only a few weeks ago. Grace's birthday was coming up.

"Grace," Catherine asked, "where were you in your house when Ryan gave you this rock?"

"Ummm, I was sleeping. He was sitting on my bed. I was so happy to see him since I didn't know if you could leave heaven ow not once you got thewe."

Abby dropped the fork on the floor. Catherine stooped further over and scooped it up, handed it to her sister, and the two women's eyes met. Abby looked away first and moved the bacon into a paper-towel-lined bowl. She cracked eggs into the greasy frying pan.

Catherine shook her head in wonder but decided that Grace had been dreaming. She prodded a bit more anyway. "What else did Ryan say when he was there in your room? Sitting on your bed?"

Grace took the rock back from her aunt and held it close to her heart as she had almost all day when Ryan had first given it to her. "He said he is missing me. I told him I am missing him too."

Disappointment tugged at the edges of Catherine's own heart, which she was sure had grown small and wrinkled and tight since the loss of her son. Indeed, this was just a little girl missing her cousin, whom Grace adored in death as she had in life.

"He told me to keep Wock in a special place."

Nodding, Catherine said that was a good idea. She brushed her fingers over Grace's messy hair and turned back to the stove.

Before Grace left that day, she took her aunt's hand and walked her up to Ryan's bedroom, which Catherine hadn't often had the desire to enter, much less clean. It looked as it did the day he left, with a sweatshirt hanging on the hook behind the door and a digital clock announcing the time. They placed Rock on Ryan's bureau, next to the empty can of Asian soft drink his grandmother had brought back for him from her visit to China, just ahead of some dusty quarters and nickels he'd left behind.

"A special place," Grace determined.

"That's so sweet of you, honey," Catherine managed. She swallowed past the lump of cotton suddenly choking her airway.

Reclining on his side on the bed with one knee resting on the other and an elbow on the pillow so his hand could support his head, Ryan grinned widely. It didn't matter so much to him that the adults didn't believe Grace. He hadn't thought they would, anyway. But he knew that every time someone entered this room and looked at that rock, they would think of him. He loved that Grace had decided it should live here.

He echoed his mother's words. "That's so sweet of you, little cousin."

Grace blew him a kiss. Catherine was too overcome to notice.

Ryan hoped now his mom would come in occasionally and dust the room. He thought it was starting to look a bit like a tomb.

chapter *Thirty*

Now that he had a buddy to hang out with, Ryan enjoyed an extra burst of energy that gave him the desire to see and experience more of earth. He knew he was starting to let go—of his friends, his family, Kate, his earthly life. *I could cross over at any time,* he thought. It was interesting that Dave was still around. He seemed more evolved, way ahead of Ryan on the crossover timeline. Seemed logical that he would make the transition first.

Ryan had done some exploring beyond where he'd spent his life, as he had discovered he could do with a mere thought, but the lonelier he got, the less he travelled. Now, feeling more comfortable letting his loved ones go, he jumped back into sucking the marrow out of his vivid afterlife and recovered some of the old spirit of Ryan the Adventurer. He placed his sort-of self at the Grey Cup, the Superbowl, late summer's best NASCAR races, and he even went for a cruise aboard the Swiss yacht *Alinghi*, an America's Cup Sailing race winner. He had it all figured out—if you find yourself in an earthbound state after dying, don't sweat it. Just do everything you've always wanted to do. It's not like you're in any danger; you ain't gonna exactly die a second time.

That theory was enticing to Ryan. He had missed the Running of the Bulls in Pamplona, seeing as he was too engrossed in his new existence to remember to get himself there. But heck, he could go anytime he wanted to, now. Nobody was stopping him; nobody was gonna rain on that parade. In the meantime, well, he checked in on his dad sometimes, not that he'd seen him a lot back in the old life anyway, and he stopped in to see Kate periodically, but he had to face reality: his beautiful Island girl had company these days. His mom was cool—now that she led this mostly secret writing life, her days had a new zip to them.

Ryan felt comfortable taking his own journeys, creating adventures again. Maybe this crazy crossover quandary wasn't so bad after all. Besides, there might not be a Grey Cup once he levelled up. And a Running of the Bulls? Was there a Pamplona in heaven? Did bulls go there after they passed?

Ryan and Dave changed gears. They dedicated Mondays and Tuesdays to checking in on family and friends, which gave them a five-day week to really live. This included weekends, when most major sporting events happened. They started off slow, checking in on Dave's favourite hockey stars. The Toronto Maple Leafs enjoyed their most dedicated fans ever—the boys sat in on tons of practices. They sat up front or hung out on the ice where they could eavesdrop madly while the players were coached. Ryan joked to Dave that they ought to leave notes for some of the other NHL teams so they could outskate and outscore the Leafs. Ever the businessman, Dave thought they could've made large sums of money that way.

"Standing over a player's bed and whispering in his ear all night while he sleeps would work better," he said to Ryan. "Subliminal messages."

But since they didn't care about money anymore, the whole earning thing was more of a reflection on how things had changed than any real quest for big bucks. They got tired of hockey after a while, although they made a point of going back in time to see some famous games. They watched some of the more famous goals on slo-mo, analyzing the plays by rewinding them again and again. Soon, they got frustrated watching fans guzzle beer and stuff popcorn and hot dogs into their bellies. Dave and Ryan didn't crave food anymore from a hunger perspective, but oh how they remembered the tastes. There was nothing like a cold beer during a hockey game. Silently they watched as people ate and, just as silently, they remembered.

The thought of bagpipes and drums playing in unison turned Dave off right from the start. *All that cacophony*, he said. *Not my vibe, kid.* But as soon as he witnessed his first Simon Fraser University Pipe Band practice, he couldn't get enough. Ryan took him to watch Shotts and Dykehead in Scotland, and then the great Irish band, Field Marshall Montgomery. The steady control of the drumsticks and the way the drum corps leaned in to watch their lead tip gave Ryan goosebumps. He was so choked up watching these fabulous world-class bands play that he hardly noticed Dave marching with the Shotts pipers one day. Dave goofed up on occasion, and since he had squashed himself in behind the pipe major and the second piper, he didn't have a lot of room for error. More than once he got walked through, and the second piper got in shit for stopping to wipe what felt like cobwebs off of his face.

The guys made a mental note to attend the World Championships in Glasgow the following summer if they were still on the planet. Ryan started practicing with the Shotts corps so he would be ready. He remembered how to play; he was just having trouble holding on to sticks suddenly. On the plus side, he didn't have to worry about wearing earplugs. He would have become the world's best air drummer, except for an old guy in a kilt who gave him the evil eye every time he got close. Seemed Ryan wasn't the only dead Celtic snare drummer who had dreamed about playing for world famous Shotts.

Spending time in Scotland was bittersweet for Ryan. He had longed to go so many times in his short career, and he had really hoped his own pipe band might get to the Worlds someday. If not, there had always been that dream of getting called up to SFU or Shotts one day. Now that he was here, in his otherworldly state, he was ecstatic. But his mother couldn't see him play. And she had been his biggest fan. What a trip it would have been to have played at such a high level just for her.

Then there was Kate and her new Scots buddy, Colin. Colin, who had probably never worn a kilt in his life, and who despised the bagpipes. Ryan didn't know what Kate saw in him. To Ryan, Colin was a fake, an imposter. Heck, he worked in a café, for God's sake! He cooked french fries for a living. Some Scot he was. He ought to be serving up haggis and oatcakes.

Despite the negative vibes Colin brought up, the Highlands brought Ryan back to thinking about Kate. When he got all melancholy about her, it was all he had in him not to instantly think his way back to her. But Dave was Ryan's friend. Dave understood the magnetic pull of heart-to-heart connections with former earthbound loves, and more so, he understood the negative consequences of rebounding backwards. Like an elastic, Ryan's love for Kate would only harm him in the end. An elastic could only stretch so far, and Ryan needed to leap beyond the constraints of such a bond.

Calmly one day, with an almost poetic air, Dave talked Ryan out of going. Ryan could see Kate during their scheduled Monday and Tuesday visits. Final. "You need to start letting go," he encouraged, eyes misty and overflowing with compassion.

Ryan flinched and wiped his brow with the back of his hand. He looked away, off into the distance where the sky was such a deep, inviting indigo blue that it seemed endless. He took a step towards it. Stopped. "I miss her. I miss the crazy adventures we shared." Ryan longed for one more chat with his Island girl, and he ached to hold her in the night when she needed him, which was mostly when she missed her mom and dad. He was angry at her for hooking up with Colin so quickly. But he also felt a sad kind of gladness that she wasn't alone.

In Scotland it was Dave, the pipe band convert, who finally had to recognize that the irrepressible ennui Ryan was feeling was paralyzing, and suggest they go elsewhere.

The second piper for Shotts was glad.

chapter *Thirty-one*

While Ryan and his ghostly buddy Dave reflected on their lives as they rode all the high-speed quad chairlifts at the world's biggest ski resorts, Kate continued to sink deeper and deeper inside herself. She missed Ryan—her boyfriend, her best friend—like a puppy misses its boy when the school bus swifts him away. Kate would wait in Gozo forever in the hopes that one day she would wake up from this nightmare and find Ryan at her side in bed, tickling her to get up and start the day.

Colin couldn't reason with her. If he tried to get her to talk about Ryan, which he felt would be cathartic for her, she would simply shutter up like a Prince Edward Island clamshell at sunset. She absolutely would not talk about Ryan, although he occupied her thoughts almost one hundred per cent of the time. She did move some of his things, but that wasn't because she was starting to let go. Instead, she did not want Colin interfering in any way with Ryan's belongings. Or with Ryan himself.

Colin tried to get Kate to go to grief counselling. Jack had written that he finally convinced Catherine to go. Something about little Grace and a rock. Jack said that it was too early to tell whether or not it was helping, but Kate pictured

Catherine sitting in some half-empty room with fluorescent lighting, hard wooden chairs and, worst of all, poor coffee, and she pitied her. No way was grief counselling going to help Catherine, Kate was quite certain of that. She knew the older woman too well. Catherine was one to keep her feelings on the inside. Opening up would be a travesty to herself. As for Kate, well she could manage quite well without such a service. She had survived her parents' deaths and she would survive Ryan's. The thing she was having a hard time with was the nagging truth that loving someone, holding them close to her, was probably never going to work for her.

Ever.

Everyone she loved *died*.

One day at the café, the nice young Gozo lieutenant wandered over to Kate when she was working. There she was, in the short little skirt and low-cut blouse the owner made the girls wear, pouring some guy's coffee. The lieutenant rarely made an appearance at Kate's workplace, but he had helped her obtain a temporary working visa, and he knew it would soon expire. He also had news for her. The look on his face was grim, and he didn't take a seat. Colin noticed him first, and he signalled to Kate from the open serving window behind the counter. She turned, and her good nature wanted her to smile and say *hey there, old buddy, take a seat, coffee?* But reality quickly hit, and she forced her suddenly jelly legs to go over to the coffee machine and deposit her hot glass pot before she followed the policeman outside.

The lieutenant waded in slowly. His staggered account was softened by the gentle compassion that swam across his solemn eyes. "There was a boat...fisherman...someone pulled up bones...clothing fragments...they retrieved what they could...it could be Ryan...we're running forensic tests just to be sure."

Kate only heard parts of his ragged discourse. As the lieutenant spoke, she just kept wiping her hands on her greasy apron while she stared at the dimple in his freshly shaved cheek. She heard herself saying, "What? What?" two or three times, but even though the lieutenant took pent-up breaths and repeated himself patiently, she still only caught parts of what he was trying to tell her. Her mind wasn't grasping everything—like, what did he mean by saying that they *retrieved what they could?* And why were forensic tests necessary?

Colin dropped his potato scoop on the counter and started towards the door, leaving a few hungry customers pissed and the other servers confused. But judging from Kate's scared eyes and the way she was wiping her hands again and again, it looked like she needed support. Colin figured rightly that there had been a development in the case of the loss of the boyfriend. He guessed correctly that a body—or parts of it—had been found.

Like an empty bag whipped about by the wind, blustering around Kate's head was overwhelming disappointment that she could not identify Ryan's body by sight. Kate had reflected for ages on what a body ravaged by seawater would look like. She'd told herself she was prepared to deal with it. She was tough, a survivor. She did not allow herself to consider what sea creatures might have done with her fella. She didn't care. Her mind and heart just wanted to see him again. He was her Ryan; he was bouncy and fun, talented and kind. Loved by everyone who knew him.

Especially loved by Kate. And by Catherine. They were the two women who loved Ryan the most. Kate owed it to Catherine to someday disclose what had happened. But how could she talk about Ryan as if he were dead when she had never seen his body? The answer was plain and simple—she couldn't. No way was she taking some forensic scientist's word for it. Scientists made mistakes all the time. The disconnect was self-preservation. Kate saw Ryan go under the waves that awful day. Her brain just didn't want to accept the tragic outcome until her eyes told her brain it was so.

Just as Colin reached Kate, the lieutenant pulled a plastic bag out of his pocket. Inside was a gold chain. The police officer pulled it out and let it dangle between his fingers. Its medallion was a Celtic knot. His careful fingers turned it over. The medallion's underside was engraved. Kate peered closely even though she didn't need to. She knew what she would find: *KLR*.

Kate Loves Ryan.

"I gave it to him ... for his birthday ... a few years ago. He never took it off." Kate reached for the medallion with trembling fingers, sucked in deep, gasping breaths as the world started to spin around her.

"Uh, miss"—it sounded like a distant echo— "we also retrieved a body part from the ocean this morning. Likely it was an ankle."

Colin got there just on time. He shot the lieutenant a warning look just before Kate passed out. Thanks to quick reflexes, he and the police officer caught her on her way down.

Kate was only out for a few seconds before her merciful sleep was over and she had to face heartbreak once again.

chapter *Thirty-two*

This time, Colin emailed Jack. Kate gave him the address. Jack already knew about the latest developments—the discoveries—because the young lieutenant had been in touch with him. He hadn't had the nerve to tell Catherine yet, and hadn't known what to communicate to Kate, even though he'd stopped and started ten emails and five phone calls.

Colin had wanted to call Jack, but he wasn't sure whether that would be a good idea. The loss of Ryan was still fresh in everyone's memory, and a call from Kate's new guy so soon was probably not gonna be super welcome just yet. Not that Colin was *really* Kate's new guy—they slept together and ran together and hiked together, but they rarely talked. They certainly hadn't had *the* conversation about where their relationship stood just yet. And now that Colin was aware of physical evidence that made Ryan super real, and he'd witnessed Kate's heartbreaking reaction, he doubted whether they would ever be an official couple. That was okay with him. Colin cared about her, but he was a laid-back kinda guy. He could take it one day at a time, one moment at a time.

The email to Jack was like the ones Kate had sent Jack, short and sweet. *What do I say to someone I don't know, when there is a dead body involved?* Without knowing that Jack was already aware of this latest somewhat morbid development, Colin laid out the facts:

Evidence of Ryan (how the heck else could that be tactfully and reverently said?) *was found in a fisherman's net. Kate is functional. I'm keeping an eye on her, but as can be expected this has been very difficult for her to process.*

I'm Colin, by the way, in case she hasn't told you about me. I work with Kate at the café. We run together. Cycle together.

Nervous, Colin added, *Nothing to worry about.*

It took Colin a good hour to write the email, despite its brevity. He kept changing it, erasing and then re-adding the last line about a dozen times. He felt the need to explain somehow that Ryan hadn't been replaced. He was sincere about that. Colin knew that Ryan could never be replaced.

When he finally got up the guts to hit *send*, Colin walked to the grungy one-room apartment where Kate was staying.

Except for dragging herself to the bathroom, Kate hadn't moved from the bed since Colin took her there after the lieutenant's visit to the cafe. Puffy, pink-tinged, bloodshot eyes were testament to the fact that she had cried herself into a state of oblivion. Kate's body was on the bed but, eerily enough, almost like Ryan, her mind was floating somewhere else. She lived in her head as much as she could, remembering their time together, pressing to her nose the old black Led Zeppelin T-shirt Ryan left lying on the floor the night before the accident, willing it to reveal Ryan's musky scent. She'd yanked it out from under the bed. Colin couldn't pull her from her reverie. He nudged and prodded and tried talking to her, but she wouldn't be touched. Kate lay there, immobile, small on the big bed, with Ryan's things around her—the faded T-shirt, the sunglasses, the Celtic knot necklace.

Kate, in her semi-catatonic state, went through a hundred thousand perfect memories of her time with Ryan. They came in bits and pieces, and she did nothing to try to alter them or encourage their existence in any way. Her mind was simply trying to get them all in—they were what they were, nothing more, nothing less. Later she would think of them as a stained-glass window, fragments of colour and light, that together made the most beautiful memory of all—their life together, the short time they'd had to just *be*. Her subconscious gave it all back to her, and it would be a while before she'd truly remember things the way they'd been, which was good, but marred and marked as every relationship is, so it can grow and be real. For now, her whole soul just ached for the boy she loved. She'd cried herself into a deeper place so she could be with him, fragmented bits of light and all, and as she rocked back and forth on the bed, her Scots friend gave up trying to truly reach her.

Colin lay down on the bed behind Kate and held her, and let her be. She would come back when her mind could handle this new-old loss.

Ryan sat in an overstuffed armchair in the corner of the room and watched them. As grand a time as he'd been having exploring with his soulful buddy, it was agony to be here, watching Kate suffer through her pain. He longed to be held by his girl again; he ached for the simple joy in her touch.

Ryan was rendered motionless with grief. He sat upright in the corner, silent, his fingers trying to dig holes in the frayed upholstery on the chair's arm. This would set his transition back. Clinging to Kate's pain and immersing himself once again in his own would mar his hoped-for crossing exponentially.

Occasionally Dave dropped by to see how he was doing. They didn't talk, but the older guy sensed Ryan was thankful for his company. Dave just stood there, leaning against the cracked wall of the tiny room, watching Colin hold Kate and knowing that on this day the sight of them together probably wasn't what was bothering Ryan the most. Dave could see in Ryan's shadowed eyes that he, like Kate, had gone to a deep, unreachable place in the darkened hollow of his soul. Like her, he was lost in the cherished memories of a much-missed past, in the exquisite too-human dagger of forever-loss.

As Dave stood sentinel against the damaged wall, observing the trio of lovers entangled in an ache that rendered them impotent, Dave hoped that somewhere in the ethereal abyss Kate and Ryan would find each other again, if only to have the chance to say goodbye.

Somehow, they stayed that way for hours. Even Colin held on for a while, for which Ryan was, later, glad. Such a gentle reprieve from the agony, hiding in those deep recesses of the soul. Such a beautiful escape, cradled in the clear, crystalline memories.

This was essential time spent in a far distant place where healing expanded via the powers of imagination and thought, and flourished with the simple grace of love.

IN HER FRAGMENTED, disjointed dreams, Kate did the hot-air balloon ride again. This time, her period pain was nonexistent. There were no hormone surges, nor was there bloating to contend with. She wasn't groaning with the desperate need to pee. It didn't matter that there was no port-a-potty around. She had what she needed, and that was her sexy guy, glowing and exuberant in his quest to float above the bonds of earth.

This time, she climbed into the basket with no reservations.

This time, she experienced the grandeur of flight, on the mercy of the wind.

This time, she held Ryan's hand, and nuzzled his fingers against her cheek while they drank champagne and toasted their daring, dashing adventure over the little island of Gozo.

This time, she was gloriously happy just to be with Ryan again.

Ryan could not possibly know what Kate was dreaming about, but he caught a glimpse of a smile tickling his girl's lovely, pale face. And he knew that he was safe with her, somewhere in her dreams, and he knew all sacred joys were theirs.

chapter *Thirty-three*

Two days later, a niggling hunger forced Kate out of her sacrosanct time with Ryan. Colin had come and gone over the last forty-eight hours. Ryan still sat, leaning back against the chair now, his eyes closed, his dreams of Kate yet unfinished. Dave, too, had come and gone, but now he was back, sitting cross-legged on the floor at his young friend's feet. When he saw that Kate was coming around, he touched Ryan's shoulder lightly and then thought himself someplace else. In Ryan's soul, he felt the touch, and opened his eyes.

Ryan watched Kate's sacred dreams fizzle to an end. Colin came in from the café cradling a steaming brown paper bag. The Scot went over to the bed and pulled out a white cardboard container and a brown paper bag bulging with condiments and compostable utensils. He opened the container and, with a worried look, held his breath while he showed Kate the contents. Ryan was saddened to see Kate let go of his old black T-shirt when she sat up. His heart cracked just a little when she moved his sunglasses aside so she could eat.

He knew it was time to leave when Colin reached out a hand to brush a damp, stray hair off Kate's pretty cheek, and she didn't pull away.

227

But first, a voice—Kate's. Whispered aloud. Ryan cocked his head, stared hard at a dust ball on the floor, blinked once, and listened.

"I have to let him go, don't I?"

Kate pushed a soggy french fry between her lips, chewed and swallowed it, then looked sadly up at Colin.

Quietly, Colin handed her five more fries and got her to eat almost a quarter of the club sandwich he'd made himself. He didn't answer. What would be the point? It was a rhetorical question.

"Colin?"

Colin looked at her. Fixed his sorrowful gaze firmly on Kate. He couldn't speak. Kate hardly ever called Colin by name. This was big. He put the fry he was holding in his right hand back into the bag. Watched as Kate's eyes filled with tears, and wondered *if this flood starts, will she drown too?*

"Colin ... I think I am ready to go home. I think I ... need ... to go home."

Colin's breath came in short gasps—now it was him sinking under an interminable sea. All he could do was nod and reach for her.

In the corner, Ryan slowly turned his head back to the bed and gazed sorrowfully at Kate. It seemed to him that, from the bed, she was looking right at him. He shivered as a burst of energy shot through the ghost of his soul.

Kate lifted her arms and hugged herself. Bit her lip in consternation while Colin loosely held on to her.

Ryan stood and circled slowly around like a dog looking for a place to lie down. He stopped when he was fully facing the bed. He took a step forward, half-reached for Kate. Ached to step into Colin's body if that's what it would take; if that's what he would need to do to be Kate's *real* again.

He whispered her name.

Kate closed her eyes for a moment, swallowed, and allowed herself one last, deep ache.

Then it was over. The self-indulgent memories got buried inside herself again, and Kate mustered up the courage to face the earthly demons that held her so firmly in their grasp. She raised her chin and removed Colin's arms from her body, took his hands in hers instead.

Ryan knuckled his fists until they were white, and let Colin have a bit of his girl—the outside, exterior bit—but in his heart he knew Kate would, one day, once again be his. He was sure of it. Still, a nugget of anger took hold in his belly and started to build. That mysterious "one day" could very well be a long, long time away.

He thought himself in another place, and in the moment of his leaving, both Colin and Kate felt the still air move.

RYAN WAS PISSED. Well, more frustrated than pissed. He was intensely, acutely, *emotional*. He found Dave waiting for him at Cavendish Beach. That was their arrangement: get to the beach if they needed to find each other. There was something about the beach that invited peace; it was imbued with dreamy memories that people left behind.

Ryan's gut was so topsy-turvy when he got to the beach that all he could do for the first forty minutes was stomp back and forth and mutter and curse and occasionally punctuate his ramblings with a scream. Someone besides the quiet, trusted Dave was paying attention—the seagulls took off in droves when Ryan roared out his frustration at the wide blue sky.

As angry as he was—Ryan's stomping feet did not leave footprints in the sand.

chapter *Thirty-four*

It was the hardest thing, getting off that airplane in Prince Edward Island. It had been indescribably torturous leaving the sweet Maltese island of Gozo where people lived so close to the earth. Gozo was the last physical place on the planet where Kate had been with Ryan. But then, roller-coaster memories were embedded in the Maltese Islands, and the last while had been excruciatingly painful. It was time to walk away.

After taking the car ferry to Malta, Kate had boarded a flight to London on an airline called *Ryanair*. It had made her laugh, booking that ticket. She and Ryan had flown in on Ryanair, even though they'd had to wait for a very late flight. It had seemed the right thing to do, flying on what Kate called "Ryan's airline." Leaving Malta, she'd felt as if Ryan himself was carrying her home.

Landing in PEI, Kate found that her little east coast Canadian island was absorbed with the essence of Ryan. Kate and he had been so full of hope when they last left here, although it had been deceitful and painful to leave Catherine the way they had, by going against her wishes and pretty much running away. Now Kate was consumed with fear—the anxiety of facing Catherine, the dread of seeing familiar places that reminded Kate of Ryan, the horror of facing herself. It all combined in a stew of fear in her gut. She swallowed nervously when she descended the steps of the small turbo prop plane that carried her on the last leg of her journey over the Northumberland Strait from Halifax.

Flying this time over that narrow body of water had been so vastly different from before; she simply stared at the cozy island taking shape below her, dug her nails into the fleshy parts of her hands, and tried not to feel. Last time, Kate and Ryan had laughed and giggled like schoolchildren as they tried to pick out recognizable landmarks. They had gotten such a huge kick out of the fact that, from the air, Prince Edward Island was truly alone—a mass of patchwork land surrounded by sea. They never felt that way when they were living on it. The Island had always seemed somehow connected.

Kate spotted Jack standing near the arrivals luggage carousel. There he was, shoulders slightly curved over, tall and lean in old brown work boots, droopy faded jeans, and an unzipped brown leather jacket with a red plaid shirt collar poking out. Hands in his pockets. Hair mussed as if he'd run his fingers through it a thousand times.

Catherine was nowhere in sight. Kate imagined Ryan's mom was home pacing her kitchen, trying to figure out what to say. In the meantime, seeing Jack was like connecting with an old friend. He'd always been quiet when Kate was around, although occasionally he'd come out with the oddest jokes, which seemed completely out of character for him. He'd get this little grin, and Kate could almost see the quips coming. It was like the thing he did with the cat-kens. *Alien kitty.* For such a quiet guy, he had a knack for putting Ryan's friends over the edge with hysterics. It wasn't so much what Jack said or did. It was the silly look on his face of pure joy, the lopsided grin. That was the cool thing about Jack. There was never anything pretentious about him. He never raised his voice unless he got a finger caught in a hammer or something equally horrid and sudden. Jack was simply just Jack. Thankfully.

Kate was so relieved and glad to see Jack, more than she ever dreamed she would be, that she just stood there and smiled for a few moments when she spotted him.

Most of Kate's thoughts about coming home were about Catherine and the pain Kate and Ryan caused her and what Ryan's mom was going to do—say—when Kate got there. Seeing Jack alone was such a relief. Kate probably wouldn't be expected to speak during the forty-five-minute drive home, and then perhaps Catherine would already be in bed by the time they arrived in Summerside.

Ahh, more time to think. To make up stories about what might be going through Catherine's mind. Kate would hopefully not have to face Ryan's mom until morning, which seemed like a long time away.

It took Jack a minute to place Kate. She was thinner and her hair was longer than Jack remembered. She walked almost on tiptoes, as if each footstep hurt, and eyed the floor rather than meeting the gaze of fellow passengers.

Jack wrapped his strong arms around Kate. Tears overwhelmed Kate, but she pushed them away with the back of a hand. Neither of them could speak at first, but Jack's worried grin revealed that he was intensely relieved that he had her here in his care, finally. Colin's recent short emails had worried him.

Jack put a hand on Kate's elbow and guided her closer to the baggage carousel. It was a good few minutes before he realized that he could actually let go and Kate would not run.

While they were waiting, Kate broke the silence and offered nervous piecemeal tidbits about her trip. "It was hot," she offered quietly, her voice thin. "Not much leg room on the planes."

Jack smiled and cracked a few fidgety jokes about how some of the other passengers probably didn't enjoy the flight much on the last small plane, like the big guy with the feed bag for a stomach. That was Jack, always observing, sometimes in an irreverent, judgy kind of way. He had Kate laughing in no time, despite herself, picturing the hefty passenger as he tried to squeeze himself into a seat, and for the fortieth time since she'd spotted Jack there alone, Kate reminded herself of just how relieved and glad she was to see him.

She was right about the drive. Jack didn't say too much. Kate remembered Catherine's observation about this practice. It drove Ryan's mom crazy, not being able to speak while Jack drove. She would get mad at him for no apparent reason, and poor Jack would quietly defend himself, saying he just needed to concentrate on the driving. Catherine had always loved having happy-go-lucky Ryan and friendly Kate around. Especially Ryan. One of his friends had once remarked that she wished he had a button so she could turn him off—he was chatty and animated and could tell stories for hours. Ryan always had a group of people around him, he was so engaging and quick-humoured.

Kate wondered who Catherine spoke to these days.

Maybe no one, Kate thought. And a little pang of sadness zinged through her.

As they approached the lights of Summerside, Kate was overwhelmed with loss. She hardly even realized that Jack was in the car with her. Leaning against the door, she chewed on her knuckles, already raw from the flights. The small city didn't look much different than when they'd left. It seemed to Kate that somehow it should be physically marked with Ryan's passing. As they passed the Celtic College, she would have seen a sign with black letters welcoming her home if she had looked. But she had squeezed her eyes shut long before they were due to pass it. The Celtic College was Ryan's second true love. She couldn't bear to picture it without him.

They were in the driveway when Jack spoke for the first time since the airport. He turned off the ignition of his blue SUV and pulled out the keys, but he didn't move. He let out a huge sigh. Looked up at the house.

Kate followed his thoughtful gaze. There were a few lights on in the back, *probably in the kitchen*, Kate thought. She noticed Jack looking at her sideways. Her wide eyes and clenched knuckles surely gave her fear away to him. Her heart was pounding, threatening to escape her chest at any moment. She hadn't made a motion towards taking off her seatbelt; instead, she just sat there, her breath coming in short gasps.

"She needs you here," Jack informed her, gently. "Everything will be fine."

Kate looked over at him and forced a smile. "Thanks for coming to get me, Jack."

Kate remembered another of Catherine's "Jack fault list." He overused the word *fine*. The world could be ending, and if you asked him, he would say it was fine. Kate thought at least it simplified things, and maybe wasn't such a bad idea to use one word for so many purposes. You could cover a tremendous spectrum of emotions with just the word *fine*. Cookies you bake come out black? No point in getting angry—*they're fine*. Cat pee on the floor? *It's fine*. Bad day at work? *Fine*. Just think of the battles one could avoid by taking emotion out of one's vocabulary.

Jack slid out from behind the wheel and went to get Kate's things out of the back of the SUV while Kate forced her feet up the back steps to the deck. It was one of the longest journeys she would ever take. The exhausting trip home from the Maltese Islands via London, Toronto, Halifax, and Charlottetown didn't come close to comparing to this short walk. Her legs were weak and wobbly, her brain spinning. Someone else's hand reached out and opened the door to the house. Jack. Kate hadn't heard him approach behind her. He had to nudge her with her overloaded knapsack to get her to go inside.

When the door closed behind them, Kate turned frantically back towards it. She had avoided coming here for so long that she had willed herself into believing Ryan's home was on some distant planet. There had been a time when she was pretty certain she would never come here again.

Like, ever. But now it was real, spread out before her like a distant field a hungry eagle was circling in its search for prey. All Kate had to do was take off her shoes and coat and step out of the mud room and into the kitchen. But she was deathly afraid. Her parents were dead, and now Ryan was gone. All the time she spent at Jack and Catherine's home after her father's death meant that Ryan's family and house had become a sanctuary. Kate's *only* sanctuary in her home province. By going deeper into the house, Kate would have to face more than just Ryan's passing. She would have to face her entire past.

Stepping into the kitchen—well, that would mean that Kate had truly come home.

WHEN CATHERINE HAD gotten the news that Kate was ready to see her, she responded at first with hesitation, and then with a simple nod.

"It's time," she said.

Jack had read the email and then acted as messenger. He broke it to Catherine the way he delivered most of his news to her, which was usually in the middle of doing something else. This time they'd been cooking dinner together, one ear tuned to the late afternoon radio show out of Charlottetown, *Mainstreet*. He peeled some garlic and, without looking up, said out of the blue that Kate was coming home. That was it. No more.

They didn't talk about it again until they went to bed. And then it was short and sweet.

"When?" asked Catherine.

"Few days," replied Jack.

Which in the end left Catherine five days to sweat.

chapter *Thirty-five*

Kate.

It was the thought that Ryan was not alone in the water when he died that gave Catherine strength when she finally faced Kate, the girl who had stolen her son away from her forever. The girl was Ryan's angel the day he left his earthly bonds behind. At the very least, Kate's face was the last human face Ryan saw. Hers was a face he loved. A face he trusted. A face he would die for.

Ryan hadn't been alone, not really. Angel or no angel, God or no God, Kate had been with Ryan when he died. Kate was the girl whom Ryan loved most (*next to me of course*, Catherine told herself with a smile), and Kate earnestly loved him back.

Somehow Catherine would find it in herself to remember that the kids had done what they felt they needed to do. Even the leaving part, as painful as that had been. She could do this. Maybe seeing Kate again face to face was a true definition of courage.

Very short distances can sometimes be the longest to bear. It was that way when Catherine heard Kate come up the outside steps and cross the deck. Catherine forced herself to go down the stairs from the bedrooms. She rested her hand on the corner of the wall for balance and stability, left her womb of safety, and forced herself out into the open kitchen where Kate waited, trembling. The two women took each other in, unaware that time was passing without benefit of the spoken word. Then, suddenly, Kate's hand plunged into her pocket. She pulled out a small clear bag and, slowly, held it out to Catherine like a peace offering. Catherine stepped forward and, with a quick inhale, accepted the gift. It was Ryan's Celtic charm necklace. It had been a part of him for a very long time and was with him when he died. It was an offering from the sea.

Catherine had shed enough tears, so she fought the threat of new ones. She went the rest of the way forward, the necklace gripped tightly in her hand, reached out to Kate, and took her in her arms.

"Welcome home," she breathed.

Kate had not shed enough tears. While she cried and raised her arms to hug Ryan's mother back, Jack quietly took her things upstairs. The two women whispered softly through their pain in the kitchen by the island, divided by time but united by their shared love for Ryan.

When Jack tiptoed back down to the kitchen, he had to clear his throat a few times but after a while he felt in control again. He did what he always did—he plugged in the kettle and made tea. It wasn't as good as sex for making things seem better than they really were, but in Jack's books, a hot cuppa would do just fine.

IT WAS LATE, but the women stayed up until the wee hours of the morning anyway. Jack was off to bed the first second he could get there, and when he left them, Kate and Catherine swapped out the tea in favour of a bottle of Malbec, slid onto the hard wooden stools by the kitchen island, and talked. Sitting there in such a familiar place made it seem, to Kate, that Ryan would come bouncing down the stairs at any second. He would tell animated stories about crazy things that happened at the music store or in the pipe band, and they'd all be in stitches. That was Ryan, able to ease the tension with a quick tale and a grin.

The uncomfortable stools kept the women awake; they wrapped their hands around their glasses and used the inky red wine as a soothing focal point. Kate read and reread the few magnets on the fridge a hundred times—most were cheap tourist magnets from places like Mexico, or Spain, where Kate knew Jack and Catherine had never travelled. The couple never went anywhere off Island. She wondered how the colourful magnets came to be there, in Ryan's house.

Catherine stared at Kate's worn fingernails and at the mug Jack had set on the island just beyond Kate's glass, and a dizzying sickness enveloped her. So many memories. The mug was distorted through the glass. Catherine remembered a youthful time of hope. She had purchased the white mug with the red heart and the emblazoned *Toronto* logo on it when she was sixteen, during a pit stop at the Metro Toronto airport after a school trip to Calgary. That cheap mug was one of the oldest things in the house now, apart from her and Jack. If it could talk, oh the stories it could tell. It was witness to her life from sixteen on—University at St. F. X. in Nova Scotia, marriage (and then divorce) to Ryan's dad, life in Alberta, Ontario, Nova Scotia, and then back to PEI.

The mug was around during the time of Ryan's birth, was still in the cupboard while Catherine struggled as a single parent, was used by Jack for his tea, and now—this. Tonight. Absently Catherine wondered if a mug would be her undoing. It held too many memories. For a moment Catherine wanted to throw it against the wall and watch it explode into a hundred pieces. Yet, it was a reminder of Ryan. How many times had Catherine served him hot chocolate in that mug? She wished, for the umpteenth time, that she'd paid more attention to the little things when her son was alive.

Maybe she was overdoing things. Being dramatic. Melancholic. Maybe Ryan never had a drink out of this mug at all.

Catherine had a lot of hard questions for Kate, but those could wait. Mostly what they talked about now was Ryan's everyday life during his and Kate's travels. Simple things, like, "Was he practicing his drumming? Did he eat well?"

Mother things.

As if he were still alive. As if he would be on the next flight home.

Kate understood, so she answered honestly and sincerely. She knew that Catherine was just filling in the gaps. Mothers needed to know what their sons were doing, to a point. Losing a son meant that the gaps were oh-so-much-more-important.

The conversation was stiff at first, but after Catherine drained the bottle, holding it upright for a few extra seconds and making a joke out of squeezing it to drain it (it was the only bottle of alcohol in the house), both women relaxed a bit. The awkwardness was manageable until all that wine made Kate want to pee. She excused herself and went upstairs, but halted when she reached the washroom, which was directly across from Ryan's room. His bedroom door was closed, so Kate forced herself to look the other way and go into the bathroom instead. She leaned against the wall when she got inside. Gripped the edge of the cupboard and took a deep, jagged breath. Swung out a foot and shoved the bathroom door closed so she couldn't see Ryan's closed-off bedroom.

Kate took her time in the washroom. She sat on the toilet and peed, holding her head in her hands, her breathing quickening and her hands trembling. There was a certain amount of relief in the fact that she'd arrived in Summerside, finally, but now that she was here, in Ryan's home, she knew she'd have to face the loss of him once and for all. She was relieved that Catherine was holding herself together. She seemed okay, saner than Kate imagined she would be. One potential nightmare had, so far at least, been averted. Kate didn't know if she could stand up under the pressure of Catherine breaking down.

When she finally got her breath under control, Kate slowly stood, ran her hands under cold water, and tempted fate by choosing not to use hand soap. She did crazy silly stuff like that all the time these days. It was as if she was saying *screw you, universe, the worst has already happened. You left me here alone, so no matter what I do, you can't hurt me anymore.* Once she had even closed her eyes and walked out in front of a moving car. But apart from a really pissed-off driver, who threw open his door and ranted and raved at her, she was fine. She chose to believe that Ryan was looking out for her, and that he had somehow stopped the car. She couldn't wait to have a conversation with him about that particular incident; they'd have that chat some day in heaven, *maybe sitting on a cloud,* Kate joked, *eating yogurt.* These were the times she smiled these days—when she imagined her future chats with Ryan. She could picture him yelling at her, shouting, "What the hell were you thinking, walking in front of a car like that?!" And "Wash your damn hands, girl!" But she didn't care. She would be so happy to be with him again that she would throw her arms around his neck and kiss him and, like always, her sweet, lovable Ryan would forgive her.

A few minutes later, Kate found Catherine standing by the kitchen sink, peering out into the darkness. Catherine turned and told Kate that she had started going to a grief counselling group session. One of the women in the group had lost her four-year-old in an accident. The little boy had been sliding with his brother and sister and had ended up on the road underneath the wheels of a van. He died in his mother's arms, reaching for her, begging her to help him. Catherine said that in her grief, the woman had gone to see a psychic, who told her that every time she washed the dishes her son was there, outside the window, watching her cry. This gave the woman hope. She still cried when she washed the dishes, but she also talked to her boy, told him about her day, talked about the adventures his brother and sister were having.

Without him? Kate thought. She bit her lip and didn't say it out loud.

Catherine allowed herself a tiny half-smile and said that the other grieving parents in the group would have thrown the woman out for being nuts if she had shared this before they lost their own children. But after losing a child— "Well," Catherine considered, "you just hang onto any little thing you can if it helps you believe your loved one is still out there somewhere." She talked about websites by or about psychics, mediums, spiritual consultants—some were legit but others hauled in the vulnerable. Such sites preyed on the despondency and sorrow of the most weak and desperate parents of lost children, asking for money before making up false stories.

Kate didn't quite know how to respond to this. What was Catherine telling her? That something had happened to make her believe that Ryan still existed somewhere? That he watched them, wanted to make contact with them? Kate knew that Catherine believed in such things. Or maybe she didn't, anymore. Maybe her faithful, guileless belief had been ripped away with her son.

Kate picked up their wine glasses and Jack's abandoned mug and placed them carefully in the dishwasher. "Are you asking me if I feel him," she whispered with her back to Catherine, "or just whether I believe that I can?" She looked sideways, picked Ryan's mother out of the dim lighting in the small kitchen.

Ghostlike, hazy to Kate's tired eyes, Catherine paused and considered the question. "I never stop hoping," she answered truthfully. "Maybe someday he'll find a way to break through."

So, Kate thought. *She still believes.* She shrugged in the most non-committal way she could muster, but her heart picked up with hope. Catherine was an ally, a comrade in the need to believe in something, anything, that meant Ryan still existed. Any little thing would be good, some sign that life did not end at death. She made a mental note to ask Ryan to make himself known to his mother. Kate didn't feel she herself really needed proof, or an actual sign. She was strong, and she knew Ryan was still with her somehow. Her faith meant that she didn't require proof. She spoke to Ryan, still, always out loud. She wasn't sure whether he would hear her if she only *thought* what she wanted to say to him.

"You're the one who is closest to him," Catherine was saying. Kate tuned back in and interpreted this as *you might get through.*

"What?" Kate turned and fully faced Catherine.

Catherine shored up her shoulders and continued. "Mothers give birth to their children, but we get replaced, Kate. At least on some level, we do. I know Ryan loved me, but before he passed, it was you whose presence he craved. I think it's you that he would try to reach. If he could," she added carefully, watching Kate to see how she would react. "Come," she said, and smiled.

Catherine led the way up the stairs to Ryan's room, where the little grey heart-shaped rock from Gozo sat unnoticed in quiet repose on his bureau. Catherine watched as her son's girlfriend slowly made her way inside, placing one hand on the wall for support.

"His room looks the same," Kate whispered.

She felt that if she spoke louder she would be disturbing something sacred. Ryan's home was like a chapel to Kate, a place of sacred space and peace. The air should not be disturbed here. Kate's legs would not support her any longer. She let herself down onto Ryan's bed, which still bore the grey-green duvet and the stuffed elephant his father had sent him for Christmas when he was ten. She gathered the squishy elephant into her arms and pulled her knees up to her chest. They'd had many discussions about that elephant—its trunk was pointing down, and Kate had always insisted that if you had any kind of a stuffed or decorative elephant in your home, the trunk ought to be pointing up. *It has to do with the luck not running out*, she remembered saying at the time.

Kate didn't cry in front of Catherine, although she barely registered the older woman's presence in the room. Instead, she waited until Catherine backed up and closed the bedroom door behind her, then she lay fully down on Ryan's bed and rubbed her cheek on his duvet. She imagined Ryan lying next to her, and by doing so she could almost feel his arms encircling her. The elephant felt warm to her, as if he had just been holding it, and it smelled like he always did when she spent time with him here. *Faintly of pizza*, she thought with a little gulping laugh. Ryan would have eaten pizza every day of the week if he could. Pizza and cheeseburgers.

Lying there, curled up in a tight ball, Kate noticed odd things about the room, like the fact that the computer keyboard was dust-free. When Ryan lived there, the computer was always dusty. Also, the room was clean and tidy—there were no clothes on the floor and no half-full glasses of water staining his desk, luring one of the cats into knocking it over. Kate stifled a chuckle as she remembered how Ryan had always left his pants on the floor as if he had just climbed out of them. The socks were usually crumpled up inside the legs. They looked as if some silly sculptor had molded them into place.

Kate climbed into Ryan's bed and pulled the covers up over her and the elephant with the bad-luck trunk, so that only the top of her head showed. She needed to be completely wrapped up in her beautiful Ryan; only then did she let the tears fall, slowly at first, and then heart-achingly in a flood until she was as dry as a PEI dirt road on a blistering hot August day.

chapter *Thirty-six*

With Kate secure in Ryan's bed for what remained of her first night back in Prince Edward Island, Catherine stood in the hallway and stared at the closed bedroom door. Kate's sobs derailed her. Catherine ached to go back inside to offer comfort but instead forced her legs to take her to her own bedroom. She found Jack already asleep, and tried to undress in her unbalanced state, but had to grab the arm of the rocking chair in the corner to keep from falling over. A clumsy elbow knocked a ceramic cat and a couple of bracelets off the dresser. They hit the hardwood floor with a crash. Jack groaned and rubbed his eyes, and when Catherine dropped slowly down to sit on the edge of the bed, he rolled onto his side facing her and blinked himself more fully awake.

Catherine's shoulders drooped. She whispered to him in the darkness. "She's in Ryan's room for the night."

Jack murmured something unintelligible. The blind was up partway to allow clear air flow from the open window into the room. Jack believed in open windows every night of the year, even when it was minus twenty outdoors.

With a shiver, Catherine pulled the duvet haphazardly up over a leg. "She looked so small on Ryan's big bed." Jack leaned up on one elbow and tucked the duvet tightly around Catherine's lower back. "She was curled up into herself when I left her, her arms around her knees on the bed, hugging Ryan's old elephant stuffy from when he was little." Catherine twisted around to face Jack. "Do you think she'll be okay?"

"She's safe here with us." Jack's sleepy, husky voice was a beacon in the night. A lighthouse in a storm. "We'll all take care of each other."

"It's all so tenuous," Catherine breathed, and blinked. Her eyelashes were damp, her vision misty.

"What is?"

"This. Life. Us."

"I won't let anything happen to my girls," Jack said, and Catherine was amazed that he had *so much to say all of a sudden*. She was afraid of everything these days, and now that Kate was a part of their household, Ryan's girl was a physical reminder of all that had been lost. But Jack's words calmed Catherine. He rarely spoke, so when he did, she had learned to listen. For it was times like this that a thousand words could not be more eloquent.

A slow exhale. Catherine lifted the duvet and slid slowly underneath. She lay on her back, drew the duvet down to her belly button, took Jack's finger, and drew a small circle around a nipple. Sleepily, Jack opened one eye, and then the second eye, when he saw how pretty the bleached moonlight was on his lady's pale breasts.

Catherine let go of his finger, and cupped her palm over Jack's rough hand when he laid it on her hip. She caressed him for a moment and didn't turn her head away or remove her hand when he moved his palm upwards, and instead smiled softly while he navigated her breasts and belly. With her left hand, Catherine cupped a breast. She let the tips of her fingers and her thumb move rhythmically from the crease where her breast met her chest, up to her nipple and back, as Jack repositioned himself so one hand could explore Catherine's breasts while the other moved between her legs. She parted at his touch, and moved a hand down Jack's belly to feel for herself just how awake he was. He was less muzzy after a few firm strokes.

Jack leaned over and kissed her softly on the mouth. He didn't kiss her on the mouth very often.

With his thumb, Jack wiped away a tear that slipped its bond and slid silently down Catherine's cheek. She turned her head more fully towards him and closed her eyes and, with her left hand, pulled his head closer. She stole another tender kiss.

She parted her legs a little wider, allowing him to find that deepest part of her. Soon, Catherine heard herself moaning quietly, mournfully, painfully, as the man she had come to know she loved beyond words carried her to a place where it didn't hurt as much anymore. Catherine felt the life in her begin to pulse while Jack held her as tightly as he dared, and when he came they were as close as they could ever hope to be, their bodies wrapped around each other in an embrace so tight that when he rocked from side to side in pleasure he absorbed her inside of him.

The moonlight let itself more fully into the room so that it could dance with the sweaty droplets on Jack's back, and as they were drawn back to earth and he quietly moved aside, Catherine traced swaths of white light on her lover's right hip. She found her favourite crease on his body, where his leg met his belly, and she bent forward and kissed him there. He rubbed her back when she climbed on top of him and lay there listening to his heart as it returned to its regular rhythm.

Catherine looked at her man's closed eyes and traced his lips with a fingertip.

"I love you, Jack," she murmured so quietly the words were barely uttered at all.

He smiled but didn't open his eyes until after he spoke. "I love you back."

Catherine laid her head on his chest and sighed. Maybe the world could be a safe place after all.

chapter *Thirty-seven*

Kate watched from her perch on Ryan's bed as Grace's tiny hand reached up for the heart-shaped rock, which was resting comfortably on the dresser. Standing on tiptoe, the little girl had to stretch to scoop it up, and Kate was prepared to help her, but a child's independence is sometimes a delicate thing. This treasure retrieval seemed important, so Kate chose not to interfere with the process. Grace's small fingers groped for and then located the rock and scooped it forward. It fell into her free hand, and she stared at it reverently for a few moments before blowing off the filmy coating that enshrouded it like fairy dust. For extra safety, Grace cupped the precious rock tightly.

Kate, obediently sitting on the edge of the bed as Grace had asked, couldn't help peering over the small shoulders to see what was so important. The youngster had said she had to show Kate a gift from Ryan, "A tweasure."

"Wyan asked me to keep it in a special place," Grace had said.

Kate had smiled sadly with the respect such a sacred request from a child deserved.

This twelve-by-twelve room would always be Ryan's space. It was indeed a place filled with treasures, the kinds of treasures a boy accumulated over years. Whatever Grace had in her cupped hands belonged here, amongst Ryan's old T-shirts and dusty CDs and ne'er-to-be-watched-again classic DVDs.

Grace turned to Kate and reverently held out the object cradled in her hands. Kate took a second to promise herself she would act surprised and appropriately respectful when she saw whatever Grace was holding so carefully, and then she would give Grace a hug and say thank you. It was obvious from Grace's demeanour that, in her little girl world, this object that her favourite lost cousin had once touched was of supreme importance. It wouldn't do for Kate to laugh or giggle or turn her attention elsewhere.

The little fingers opened, graceful and delicate, and there it was—the earthly object Grace called Wock. Kate smiled at first, and spying the gentle curves where the Maltese island sand and seawater had defined the rock's form, she became attuned to its unmistakable heart shape. A gasp, and then— "Grace!"

Kate wanted to ask Grace, truthfully, where she had gotten the rock. But words wouldn't come. Only tears.

Grace was wearing a milky-white linen dress she'd picked out herself this morning. Since it was chilly outside, Abby had convinced her daughter to button a thick cotton cardigan over top. It was also a luminous white. A golden light (or was it Kate's imagination, when in later years she recalled the moment?) enveloped Grace the moment she opened her hands. Kate would always remember that the beautiful, rare gift she was handed that day came from a little girl who looked like an angel.

The rock, the moment Kate first saw it, was aglow.

Kate, the love of Ryan's too-brief life, gently reached out and touched the lovely curves that defined Rock. The beautiful, heart-shaped silhouette whispered softly to Kate, *I am here.*

Later Kate would think that perhaps Grace, with her luminous eyes and serene state of *knowing*, was a Crystal child, come to help change the world's vibration. Over tacos at dinner one snow-stormy day a few years ago, Catherine had told Kate about such children. Grace truly seemed to believe this occasion was important, that its meaning went far deeper than she could ever truly understand. Grace knew Kate had to see the rock. She knew it was a gift from Ryan. Kate had read about Crystal children online. They were supposedly the new generation, highly sensitive to the realm of angels and the afterlife. Their veil between this world and the next was presumably thinner than that of their parents.

Kate had sometimes secretly believed Ryan was an Indigo child, the generation of children who came before the Crystal children. Named for a gentle dark blue aura, Indigo children seem wise beyond their years. It was a fitting descriptor for Ryan, plus he had no use for the current education system. Supposedly this was also a trait of Indigo children. Later Kate would tell herself that was why Ryan and Grace could communicate. They shared an incredible otherworldly connection that had allowed Ryan to give Grace the heart-shaped Gozo rock. There could be no other explanation.

Now, on the morning Grace gave Kate the gift of Rock, Kate smiled reverently at Grace through shy, hopeful tears.

She reached out shaking fingers and took the little girl's face in hers. She leaned forward so that their noses touched, the old and the new, the lost and the found, and she held Ryan's cousin so tight and for so long that Grace thought about asking her to let go.

But she didn't. Grace was happy. She could feel Kate's love; it created every bit as much a warm glow around her and inside her as the radiant sunbeams gently filtering in from the window. She opened her eyes for a moment and smiled beyond Kate at Ryan, who was reclining against his old pillow like he always used to when he helped Grace explore learning sites for little kids on his iPad. He winked at her, then put a finger to his lips as if to say *this is our secret*.

Grace, perhaps one of the blessed Crystal children, was smart for her age, and so she understood. She was afraid to close her eyes in case her cousin would be gone when she opened them again, but when you're being hugged that tight it's awful hard not to.

chapter *Thirty-eight*

It took Kate three days to tell Jack and Catherine about the rock. When she finally mustered up the courage (she didn't want them to think she was bonkers—she had to live here for the time being, after all), even ornery old unbeliever Jack had to admit that it seemed like a tremendous coincidence that Grace had come upon a rock in the same shape as Kate and Ryan's Maltese island treasure. For her part, Kate never doubted the truth of Grace's story, that the rock had been held in Ryan's strong hand and delivered to the child in a midnight meeting, illuminated by a milky moon and a child's immeasurable love and faith.

Catherine's initial shock at Kate's story went two ways. First, clearly Kate needed something to believe in. Fear, loss, loneliness, and despair were powerful motivators to stretch the imagination. Kate had a need to hang on a little longer, to hope, to believe in the enduring existence of the boy they all so desperately loved and missed.

On the other hand, Catherine the dreamer, the writer, the mother, the friend, nodded in certainty as she passed a delicate finger over Ryan's rock. It wasn't about whether this was the *actual* Maltese island rock Kate had handed Ryan on that fateful day; what mattered was that suddenly, undoubtedly, this was a sign. That alone was something tangible to hold on to, in more ways than one.

The rock's wind and sand-smoothed surface was almost certainly the last link to a life lived with hope and passion, to a soul that shunned the bonds and fetters of earth even while the body it lived in was embedded on the planet. To a life that toasted the gods of music and art and adventure; a free spirit who showed a woman how it is a mother should love—unconditionally and certainly despite disagreements, outbursts of independence, and sometimes polarized views.

Like the blossoming of a rose, Catherine let the realization unfold. Another truth alighted. It seemed her child was imparting an even greater lesson. That Catherine—despite all the years working as a museum curator and then writer in her own solitary company or with fabricated ghosts (or maybe real ones, souls that had shuttled off the earth and come back to say hello), alone and thinking she could ONLY be alone—was wrong. Catherine didn't need to, but if she chose to, she could function in the company of a partner. She could thrive.

Even with a quiet guy like Jack.

Catherine had had Ryan's love and exuberance for a time, just long enough for Catherine's bruised inward spirit to let down its walls. Long enough for Catherine to learn how to share her life with another. Now it was time to share herself fully with a friend and lover. Jack, antagonizer of cats, giver of ecstasy. It wasn't always easy, but Catherine had learned that she did go off the rails a little at times, that Jack could help her learn and grow by encouraging her to face her own truths (as Ryan had on occasion), and that these harder elements of her essential being were okay.

Loving Jack was not easy for Catherine. Letting him love her back was even harder.

Love was like the water that flowed easily beneath the keel of Catherine and Jack's C&C sailboat; it helped shed the depths of fear when they glided through it, safe in their fibreglass sanctuary over a healing greeny-blue ocean. Like the ocean, love was fluid; it was organic, constantly moving, and sometimes demanding.

Loving a man, a child, a partner, or a parent, would one day end here on the physical plane. Loss was the greatest price for risking love, but sharing lives together, however finite, was worth that risk.

Catherine and Jack would see the sun set in the west, see it rise again another day.

The Gozo rock and Kate's trusting eyes were a revelation. Catherine knew with certainty that her son Ryan lived. If not too on some other plane or dimension—call it heaven or call it home—he lived in her heart, in her mind, in her body. He was, and always would be, a child of Catherine, a lover of Kate, a nephew to Abby, a cousin to Grace, a drummer and friend to Chelsea, a human to Old Uncle DC and the cat-kens, and a friend to Jack.

At breakfast one morning, Catherine picked the rock up from where Kate had set it next to her juice glass on a sunny yellow placemat. She rubbed it, enclosed her fingers over it, gently laid it back down. She let her hand fall away from its smooth surface, and a small smile tickled the corners of her lips. Looking up at Kate across from her, Catherine lost herself in the deep brown eyes her son loved.

Imploring, in return Kate searched the older woman's wise, ice-blue eyes. She could almost see Ryan reflected there, so deeply embedded was he in Catherine's consciousness at that moment. A knowing look passed between the women, and it didn't matter about the truth of the rock's origins or what anyone in the room truly believed. The only thing that really mattered was that Ryan did exist and would continue to exist, and that because of him and people like him, there was love and hope and beauty and adventure and freedom in the world.

Kate nodded, picked up the rock, and for a moment she was quite certain she saw the Ryan in Catherine's eyes move, almost imperceptibly. As she cradled the rock in her long, graceful fingers, she glanced down at the floor with a sigh at her willingness to bring him forward, and her subsequent need to let him go.

Ryan, standing near the two women he loved most in the world, reached out and, with his heart, touched his rock. A shiver passed through Kate as Ryan begged her to look up and see him, the real him, as Grace had—just this once. He prayed that the rock had magic power, that it was a conduit between the two worlds, the one of floating and dreams and earthbound spirits unable to fully let go, and the one of rocks and earth and trees and ocean, where people were too busy or distracted to truly appreciate their freedoms, lovers, families, friends.

Full of longing and hope, Ryan turned to his mother and saw himself as Kate did, reflected in wise, compassionate eyes. He spied peace pass between the two women, and because Ryan was full of a seemingly endless longing, he sorrowfully turned to think himself away. These women had earned their difficult, quiet hearts, and Ryan was afraid that, like a bolt of lightning, he would disrupt them. He caught a reflection of himself in the window in the seconds before he left, slightly distorted in a tiny crack Jack had not gotten around to repair or replace, and he straightened his shoulders with a bellyful of aching pride in the knowing that at least if his beloved Mama Bear and gal could forever see his soul embedded in a sand-blown rock, that his foundation in their hearts and bodies was secure.

He needed to find a way to let them go.

He needed to find a way to go.

chapter *Thirty-nine*

One day, Catherine and Jack were sitting on the deck enjoying the warm evening. They were getting a kick out of watching a hummingbird feast on the sugar water in Catherine's new feeder. Its diminutive wings flitted so fast that the cats seemed puzzled. The tiny, tenacious bird hovered far above them, out of danger, while Oscar and Oliver snaked around below, low throaty growls threatening. Old Uncle DC sat on the deck with his people, his only interest in the drama in the yard below the deck revealed by his tense posture. He had simply gotten too fat to drum up any interest in a bird that small. It wouldn't make much of a meal to a nineteen-pound furball.

Jack teased DC mercilessly with the toe of his leather sandal. "Come on, lazy butt. Don't let those little guys show you up!"

Catherine chastised him reproachfully. But Jack had some way about him that animals understood. He loved to grab Oliver with both of his big hands and hold him upside down, or annoy Oscar by moving him around when he was sleeping. Catherine wouldn't go pee if a cat was sleeping on her lap. It didn't seem to matter how much Jack bugged the cats though, they still loved him, maybe because he could put them in ecstasy when he chose, with his deep scratching utilizing all four fingers and a thumb.

That's the thing about loving somebody, Catherine realized, as she watched DC give Jack the hairy eyeball and then roll over relatively undisturbed. *They drive you nuts part of the time, but you forgive them because you know in your heart and soul that they'll never really hurt you. And, at times,* she blushed, *being loved by that person results in great ecstasy.* She wasn't just thinking about bedtime.

She smiled at Jack, reached out her flip-flopped foot, and nuzzled her man's calf. The look they shared was genuine and filled with understanding. Jack quickly abandoned his friendly pestering of DC and pulled his low Adirondack chair closer to Catherine's so he could take her hand in his.

Smiling silently, they sat together and watched the little hummingbird enjoy its nectar.

Catherine and Jack had found an ease and level of excitement in their lovemaking that was nonexistent a few years ago. To Catherine, the most incredibly magical part of discovering each other during their intimate moments was what it did for their overall relationship. Their sensual explorations in the wee hours of the morning were cathartic on many levels of consciousness. They carried over to daytime. Like now, when it was nice to just sit and hold hands and feel a true connection.

From inside the house, Kate watched the scene on the deck with a sense of long-awaited relief. Her breath was even and relaxed as she absently finished towelling off the stoneware pan from earlier homemade pizza. Dialogue at supper had been lighthearted banter about Kate's inaugural sailing trip on *Hope Floats*. The girls teased Jack about his desire to always heel the boat over as far as possible. For such a gentle, quiet man, he had a love of adventure that rivalled the outspoken, gregarious Ryan. He had simply been allowed to live longer—that was all. Most of his adventurous escapades, like rodeo, had come decades before.

When the teasing abated, Kate told the older couple that she'd been in touch with St. F. X. The university was happy to receive her back into its comforting fold. Kate would return to school to complete her degree. In the meantime, she'd started work at the Deckhouse again, where it turned out Ryan's friend Chelsea also worked. Chelsea's presence was a comfort to Kate, who loved to hear stories about Ryan from people who loved him. Chelsea was a chatty extrovert, and once she clued in that Kate wouldn't collapse in a mess of tears at the mention of Ryan's name, she had the entire staff in stitches with tales of Ryan at band practice, like the one where Ryan, who'd lost countless sticks and drum pads over the years, lost the set owned by his instructor. Ryan had a lot of friends. And they all missed him. So, the Deckhouse was good for Kate. It promised sanctuary and new friendships for a girl who had come home pretty darn lost.

Now, looking out the kitchen window, watching Jack and Catherine hold hands, Kate realized she had another refuge, one that would last far past this summer of regrowth and new beginnings. It had been starting to slip into her vocabulary via a word that so many people took for granted, but whose essence she'd craved since she'd lost first her mother, then her father, and then Ryan.

She'd said it to Chelsea when she left work at four that day: "I'm going home." Kate had recoiled after it was spoken, as if her mind suddenly said *what the heck? You don't have a home. You're just freeloading for a bit, so you can be close to Ryan.* But looking at Jack and Catherine and lazy Old Uncle DC now, and the brilliant, tough little hummingbird, and the youngster cats, Oscar and Oliver, as they circled the tree, Kate realized her initial, spontaneous use of the word "home" was really her soul telling her something, and that she ought to listen to it. The people and the cats and the homemade pizza and the teasing and the laughter and even sometimes the reminders to pick up wet towels in the bathroom or to help fold some clothes were just that—they were *home.*

chapter *Forty*

Ryan sat next to Dave on the bow of *Hope Floats* with his long legs dangling over the sun-kissed water of Bedeque Bay. He wistfully turned his head away from the contented sailors sprawling about the cockpit with their Corona and barbeque chips in hand, and glanced down at the seawater slipping almost silently underneath the hull. Ahead he spied a pretty mirage of triangular sails and carefully polished hulls with names like *White Tigers*, *Cajun Spirit*, *Sea Renity*, *Seas the Day*, *Stormy Nights*. His favourite was the crimson-hulled *Sunrise*—its name alone filled with the hope and promise of many a carefree pink-hued summer morning.

The boats carelessly cut through the water, propelled by a gentle wind almost too light to buffet the crafts forward. A tourist peering through binoculars from nearby red-cliffed MacAllum's Point could not see Ryan, nor could he make out the relaxed urgency in the sailors' faces. He didn't know that this small fleet was taking part in a friendly Wednesday night race. Not long after the sailboats rounded the lighthouse towards a marked buoy at nearby serene Salutation Cove, the seer watched a few crew haul down their mains and furl their jibs. The winds were too light for racing. The sailors tossed in anchors and cranked up their stereos.

Some cast themselves into the water for an evening swim. These coastal dwellers loved the thrill of the race, but they could also appreciate when to call it a day. A lack of wind breeds frustration. Better to toss that useless emotion aside and give in to nature. Have some laughs, a few beers, and maybe a carefree paddle around the safety of an anchored boat.

On *Hope Floats*, Catherine warily kept an eye on the tiller while Jack and Kate—and Jack's sons, who were starting to come around more these days—also eased into the water and splashed around. Kate kept herself moored to the sailboat by hanging onto the boat's round white life ring while Jack nipped under the water to check out the barnacle situation on the keel. An abundance of barnacles would mean a slower speed. Any barnacles Jack found would need a lot of prodding to force them to let go.

Eventually Kate rolled over and pulled her backside onto the life ring so she could settle her bum in the water, legs over one end, and lean back against the safety of the circular float. She closed her eyes and drifted, while the orange trails of the evening sun lowering in the west settled over her face like the hue of a campfire at dusk. Peace wafted through her, and she sighed with contentment.

Ryan could see, on a far-off point, the sharp outline of the Mont Carmel Catholic Church, silhouetted against the sinking sun. It cut a distinguished figure in the fading light, a marker by which sailors often set their sights. To the right of the church, visible on the Summerside shoreline, were two small lighthouses, designed to guide approaching ships into the channel for safe passage to the wharves and marina in Summerside's relaxed harbour. Ryan turned his head to the left; ahead of him across the Northumberland Strait he could see New Brunswick, a lump of fuzzy land barely visible on the horizon.

Open water, safe passage, markers to guide the way—these are the things that inform the daily lives of sailors on the water. Some of the Summerside Yacht Club group liked to take pleasurable cruises to the Bras D'Or Lakes in Cape Breton, or across to Shediac, New Brunswick, for the annual Shediac to Summerside race (and the socializing at night). On regular brisk afternoons they sailed their boats to the waves just outside the harbour. They outfitted their boats at the beginning of the season with required safety equipment, shoved the thought of danger aside, and rarely entertained the possibility of nature's fury sweeping up and ending a life. These Island folks enjoyed their ocean and had a healthy respect for its power, but sailing to them was a celebration of *life*. They revelled in the sheer freedom of harnessing the wind and sea. They were alive, and the happy sounds Ryan heard travelling across the salty, orange-hued wavelets on this gorgeous summer evening were testament to their simple joy.

Ryan's people were no exception. Catherine had not yet found the courage to swim, for she would always maintain a fear of not being able to spy what lay underneath the brackish water. But she smiled as she sipped her Corona and occasionally nudged the tiller to keep the boat facing the grand Confederation Bridge way off yonder, its arched navigation span hazy in the diminishing sunlight. She helped a dripping Kate and sodden Jack back on board, and Dave and

Ryan silently marvelled at Kate's tanned, youthful runner's body, and droplets of seawater that glowed amber as they dripped from her to the deck.

Jack dried himself off, pulled on his shorts and T-shirt, and accepted Catherine's Corona from her outstretched hand. He took a long swig from the bottle and handed it back, exchanging it for the bag of barbecue chips, which he held out to his boys before grabbing a handful for himself. He popped a few salty chips between his lips and contemplated starting the motor. With a shrug, he settled back on a cushion instead and watched while Kate and Catherine danced to the funky rhythm of the Chili Peppers, a band whose tunes Ryan and his buddies had so often played. When the happy, heartbreaking song ended, Kate disappeared below to dress and maybe to remember. Catherine took a seat on the starboard deck and let her toes hang delicately over the water. She leaned as far forward as she could, hoping to dip a polished peach-pink toe in the water, but couldn't quite reach. Instead, she settled her gaze on the calm water below, sipped her Corona, and pondered.

A greeting from a passing boat under motor—*White Tigers*—raised Catherine out of her reverie but not quite out of the tranquil moment. Ahead, heading back to safe harbour, *Tigers'* burnished, deep-blue hull was dark in the lee of the setting sun.

"Heading home," called its skipper, a family man with his wife and their two young children, wrapped in towels, snuggled together in the cockpit.

Home, thought Catherine, straightening. She lifted her hand and held it visor-like against her forehead so she could make out the backlit, sun-kissed silhouette of *White Tigers*.

Home, mused Jack, greeting the skipper with a casual wave.

Home, breathed Kate, peeking her head out from the cabin, rubbing a brightly-coloured towel through her long, dark hair.

Home, whispered Ryan, watching *White Tigers* glide its family towards the biggest of the lighthouses. Seagulls and cormorants, pleasantly standing sentinel beneath the lighthouse on the rocks of the breakwater, were lined up to greet the incoming boat.

Ryan looked up at Dave, and the big guy nodded.

"You gonna be okay?" Dave asked, standing by the furled jib.

"Sure," Ryan answered, with a lingering shadow of doubt. He looked back at his family—Jack's butt stuck up in the air as he picked up a dropped potato chip, Catherine behind him, playfully sliding a finger down the top of his droopy shorts, Kate giggling and turning away.

Kate had turned towards Ryan. Their eyes momentarily met.

Ryan sat up straight and sucked in a breath. But then he noticed that Kate's glance went further, through him to the open ocean, and he wondered what her mind's eye was seeing.

He felt a hand on his shoulder—Dave. Intention bred feeling, he supposed. Dave's eyes were as intent as Ryan had ever seen them.

"Enjoy this, my young friend. This is a freedom you've earned."

Ryan smiled sorrowfully up at him. "Why did I ever think I had to go away to be free?" The words came out in a whisper.

The heavy thought was felt throughout the boat as Jack finally started the engine and the small found-each-other family snuggled together in the stern for the slow ride home, past the wise, watchful seagulls, and the black pea-eyed cormorants, and the historic lighthouse, and the bare cusp of a sun descending with a deep, drowsy exhale towards rest.

Dave reached out as if to tousle his young friend's hair and watched Ryan turn back for one last look at Catherine, Kate, and Jack, now silhouetted in delicate deep shadow, almost obscure in the dusky pre-twilight.

Jack, with a slight twist of the wrist, powered up *Hope Floats* just a little more and Ryan watched the glowing, sandy red cliffs meld into shadow as the sun dipped and slid to a place he couldn't see. He couldn't hear the water anymore, gently lapping against the sailboat's eggshell hull, and it made him think of the transitory nature of all things *life*.

"They are happy, aren't they?" He looked up as he asked Dave, but his companion was nowhere to be seen. Dave was imbued somewhere in the whisper of the wind.

Kate's heartfelt laughter rang with gusto over the sound of the motor, and a seagull responded in pleasure as it flew away.

Ryan bowed his head towards the salty sea; towards the great expanse that had finally taught him about life and about how to be free, and then, with a reverent bow towards the enigmatic, resplendent sun, closed his eyes, and was gone.

Thanks for reading!